THE HOSTAGE GAME

LYLE NICHOLSON

Editing by Peg Billingsley: peg@writeandright.org

Book Design by Brandi McCann Design

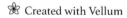 Created with Vellum

1

Anse Cochon Bay, Saint Lucia
August 20th, 2000,

MELINDA COOPER SLIPPED OFF the sailboat into the warm water. She adjusted her mask and snorkel, and with long lazy strokes swam toward the lagoon. The conversations on the boat between her father and uncle had become tiring. She needed space.

She arched her back and dove. The water was crystal clear with the bright sun overhead. A small ray glided beneath her. She followed it with a slow kick of her fins.

This was the last week of her vacation in Saint Lucia with her parents and Uncle Max. After four years of pre-med studies at Canada's University of Alberta, she was enjoying the island's laid-back life. Their forty-four-foot sailboat rocked slowly at anchor in the secluded bay.

Javier, the boat's chef, was cooking a lunch of fresh crab and lobster with what the locals called "ground provisions," which meant something like potatoes or yams. He'd mix it with the fiery local spices, and they'd sip on local Piton beer.

They'd done very little on the boat in the past few weeks. Her father, Luke Cooper, had become involved in a real estate deal with his brother-in-law Max. Uncle Max was hefty and round, with a great shock of curly black hair and bushy eyebrows. He had a slight accent from his homeland of Latvia, and his hands moved continually when he spoke.

Everyone loved Uncle Max. He was funny, the life of any conversation, and full of ideas. His new plan was a real estate deal Luke Cooper couldn't pass up.

Melinda surfaced and looked over at the sailboat to see a large motorboat approach. The sailboat's captain waved at it, taking the bowline the motorboat threw to pull them alongside.

She thought little of the boat. Max had probably run out of beer again. They often called to the resort a kilometer down the beach for provisions to keep their vacation going without having to dock. So far, this had been idyllic. Melinda snorkeled the small lagoons and lounged on the beaches, sometimes with her mother, Frida, but frequently on her own.

In September Melinda would enter medical school. This would be the real test. She'd passed her four-year science degree with ease to meet the requirements. Now, she had four years of medical school, followed by a six-year integrated cardiothoracic surgical residency. The next ten years seemed daunting, but she wanted to follow in her father's footsteps. Her father was the best cardiothoracic surgeon in their city of Edmonton, in northern Canada. Would she make the grade?

She sighed with that last thought, took a deep breath, and dove to the bottom of the lagoon. A baby reef shark swam by her. She followed it and almost caught its tail.

She broke the surface as a gunshot sounded. The noise rocketed around the bay. There was a scream followed by a splash. It was her mother's voice.

Melinda swam hard towards the boat, putting her head in the water and doing the overhead stroke. One hundred meters from the craft, she looked up. A man stood there. He had a gun pointed at her —she dove.

Three shots rang out. A stream of bullets traced in front of her. She turned quickly, kicking her fins to reach a coral reef outcrop one hundred meters behind her. She popped up behind the reef to see the man scanning the water for her.

She looked towards the beach—it was empty. There wasn't a soul she could call for help. There was no way forward—no way back. Her breath came in gasps as she watched the motorboat get underway and leave.

The motorboat was crowded with people. She couldn't make out if her father, mother, or uncle were passengers. She waited until the boat had disappeared into the distance before she swam back.

She climbed the ladder and jumped onto the deck. The boat was still. Gone were the conversations, the music, the constant bantering of Uncle Max and her father with the cook and the captain.

Her bare feet made a splashing sound on the wooden deck. She surveyed the entire boat. Not a soul on board. Venturing below, not a person there.

She walked to the radio. Her father used it to contact shore or speak to the coast guard for weather updates. She'd never asked to learn how to use it. Why would she? Relaxation before med school was her focus. Her father had taken care of all the details.

Now she wished she'd learned how to use the radio. She heard a boat coming towards her. She ran up the stairs to see the same motorboat coming back. "They're coming back!" Melinda yelled to herself. She froze for a moment, then launched into action.

Running towards the sailboat's stern, she leaped back into the water. She put her head down and with quick strokes she made her way to shore by the time the motorboat reached the sailboat.

She pulled herself out of the water near a large rock that gave her cover. She watched as the men from the boat went on board and searched it. They must have seen her come on board. Shivering from fright, she waited until they left.

A wave of despair swept over her. Were her parents alive? What had they done to her uncle Max? There was no blood on the boat. Who were these men?

Her world caved in as she watched the motorboat speed away. She drew in a deep breath, "Okay, Melinda, you need to do something." She pulled herself away from the rock and stumbled along the beach towards the resort.

2

BANFF NATIONAL PARK, CANADA
AUGUST 25TH, 2000.

BERNADETTE CALLAHAN RODE a chestnut mare at the tail end of the group of tourists. There'd be one more week of horse-riding expeditions with groups of ten tourists, and then she was off to train with the Royal Canadian Mounted Police in Regina, Saskatchewan.

She turned to look at the pack horses trailing behind them. There were four, all loaded with tents, food, and fishing rods. Her summer job had been to mind the horses, teach the tourists how to fish and how to stay upright on the horses.

Mary-Anne Hodges, on the lead horse, was their cook and naturalist. That left Bernadette to do what she did best, enjoy the Rocky Mountains and breathe in the beauty. Occasionally she jumped in to take pictures, keep a grizzly bear away, and chase the squirrels out of the food.

She turned her tanned face towards the afternoon sun and let herself take in the surroundings. She'd completed the four-year degree in police studies at Edmonton's McEwan University. This job had come to her through an ex-RCMP officer who knew of someone who needed a "wrangler," a good old-fashioned horse handler and guide in Banff National Park. Bernadette couldn't say yes fast enough.

She'd grown up around horses on a Native Cree reservation with her grandparents.

Bernadette Callahan was a mixture of Cree from her mother and Irish from her father. Her hair was a flaming red and her skin a light bronze with freckles that set off her green eyes. She was five-foot-eight, muscled, toned, and hardened from handling horses and setting up camps for the past three months.

She longed for a hot shower, a cold beer, and no tourists' questions for at least the next twenty-four hours. The line of riders snaked down the trail towards the stables. Two stable hands stood ready to help the tourists and get them to their lodging and dinner.

Sam Johnson, the owner of the outfitting company, came out of his office walking towards her. His head was down, a piece of paper folded in his weathered hand. He'd retired from the RCMP in his fifties after twenty-five years of service and bought the outfitting company. At sixty-five, he carried his tall frame well and looked like the quintessential cowboy with long gray hair, handlebar mustache, and bushy eyebrows over soft gray eyes.

"You best let the boys take care of your horse, Bernadette. I got some stuff to talk over with you in my office."

Bernadette kicked a leg over the saddle and slid off her horse. "Is everything okay with my family?" Her family was her grandmother back on the reservation and her aunt and cousins back in Edmonton.

Sam put his hand up, "No, hold on, I didn't mean to get you all riled up. Your family is fine. Just follow me."

Bernadette followed Sam into his office. It had a large wooden desk and an old wooden swivel chair that announced its age with loud creaks when he sat in it. Pictures of his days as an RCMP officer covered the walls.

Bernadette sat in front of him, her hands clenched in anticipation. "What's up, did I screw up a report of something?" After every guide trip she reported the wildlife, especially if they'd spotted grizzlies on the trail the other guides needed to look out for.

"No, it's nothing like that," Sam said as he pushed the piece of paper towards her. "We got this message for you two days ago. Sorry, I didn't know how urgent it was."

Bernadette unfolded the paper. "I need your help, please call me —Melinda Cooper." The phone number had a hotel name in St. Lucia.

"I'll call her in the morning. It's probably too late there now," Bernadette said, looking at her watch.

Sam shook his head. "No, you need to call her now. I was in Banff today and saw the news. They kidnapped three Canadians in Saint Lucia. They named two of them as Cooper. I'm not in the police force anymore, but I can put facts together."

Sam picked up his phone and handed it to her. "I'll be outside."

Bernadette grabbed the phone and dialed the number. A strange ring tone sounded thousands of miles away and a voice answered, "Hotel Macambo."

A few moments later, Melinda answered.

"Melinda, I just heard your parents got kidnapped. What's going on down there? When did it happen?" Bernadette blurted over the phone. She gasped for air. Melinda and she had been friends back in high school. They'd gone through some crazy shit together. When Bernadette had gotten into trouble with the police, both Melinda and her parents stood up for her.

"Oh, Bernie, I'm so glad you called. They told me you were out on the trails and couldn't reach you unless it was an emergency. I should have told them, but I didn't know how," Melinda said with sobs.

"Oh my God, Melinda. I would have rushed right back. What are the police doing there? Do they have any leads?"

"Not a thing. My parents and my uncle have vanished. So have the crew. They put them in a motorboat and left the sailboat in the lagoon. There's been no word, no demands for ransom—nothing."

"How long ago did it happen?"

"Five days ago. I should have called you sooner, but I've been in meetings with the police, and Travis will be here in two days. He's trying to work the phones with the Canadian Embassy from his home in Vancouver."

"Has he had any luck?"

Melinda sighed. "Did you know our embassy is in Bridgetown, Barbados? It's the same place all our banks are. They've put us in touch with the Caribbean Task Force. They claim they're working on it, but they've come up with nothing."

"I'm coming down there, Melinda," Bernadette said.

"Oh God, Bernadette, I was hoping you'd say that. I'm calling my travel agent. I'll have a plane ticket for you at the airport in Edmonton."

"You don't have to do that; I can fly on my dime."

"Bernie, yes I do, besides I'm using my father's credit card. He'd want you here with me and you know how he is about taking care of everyone," Melinda said.

"Yes, Dr. Luke Cooper, the best heart surgeon in the city with a heart of gold himself. I'll call your travel agent right now. There's probably a red-eye I can grab. If I leave now, there's a chance I'll be there tomorrow."

"I'll have a car service pick you up at the airport. I'm in meetings with the police again tomorrow."

They hung up after some heartfelt goodbyes and the exchange of information. Bernadette made a quick call to the travel agent and wrote the information down. She walked out of the office and looked at Sam. "I've got to go. Sorry, can't finish my contract."

Sam nodded. "I understand. I'll fill in for your last week. Helping a friend in trouble is what life's about. Just remember, you're supposed to be at the RCMP Depot on September 4th. If you screw it up, you probably won't get another chance."

3

BERNADETTE RAN TO THE BUNKHOUSE, stripped off her chaps, threw off her clothes, and hit the shower. The travel agent she called told her she could get her on a red-eye flight from Edmonton to Toronto, then a morning flight to Saint Lucia.

She had six hours to get to the Edmonton Airport. But her clothes and passport were at her Aunt Mary's place in the city's center. With a towel wrapped around her and her hair soaking wet, she grabbed the bunkhouse phone and called her aunt.

It rang three times before Mary picked up. "Aunt Mary, I have to catch a flight to help Melinda in Saint Lucia. Can you bring me some clothes and my passport to the Edmonton International Airport?"

"I was wondering when you'd call. Melinda phoned me and I gave her your number. Are you sure you can make the flight in time—I mean, without driving like a maniac?"

"No problem. By going straight to the airport, I'll cut an hour off the trip. I should be there by ten. Can you have someone pick up my truck?"

"Sure, I'll have Marty come with me."

"And he is...?"

"My new boyfriend. I wanted you to meet him when you got back from Banff."

"Will I like him?"

"He's the dentist I work for," Mary said. "Now quit the chitchat and get on the road. I hope that old truck of yours makes it."

"No problem, I put air in the tires last week and changed the oil myself," Bernadette said. She hung up the phone and threw off her towel just as the guys walked in.

"Wow, Bernie, we weren't expecting a strip show on your last day," Lincoln said. He was the lead stable hand and a rowdy nineteen-year-old. Cody, the twenty-year-old assistant cook, was beside him.

"You couldn't knock?" Bernadette asked as she grabbed her towel and headed to her closet. The bunkhouse was open with a curtain that gave Bernadette and Mary-Anne their small bit of privacy.

Lincoln's face went red. "Ah, yeah, sorry I forgot... hey if you need any help packing or anything..."

Bernadette peeked out from behind the curtain. "No, I got it. Sorry I yelled at you."

"Ah, that's all right, I deserved it—but thanks for the parting memory," Lincoln said as he grinned at Cody.

Bernadette shook her head. She grabbed her few clothes out of the stand-up closet, pulled on jeans and top while stuffing the rest into a duffel bag. For three months she'd lived in jeans, t-shirts, and denim shirts. It was the mountains. No one expected you to be fancy.

Grabbing her duffel, she headed for the door and met Mary-Anne coming in. "Hey girl, I wanted to do a long goodbye and beer, but this is a quick hug."

"I heard from Sam. I hope you can help your friend," Mary-Anne said. "And don't screw up your chances with the RCMP."

Bernadette hugged her hard. They'd been great friends on the trail and had bonded over beers in the bunkhouse. "Look, give all the others a hug for me. Tell them I'll miss them all."

"Oh, you won't get off that easy—they're outside," Mary-Anne said with a wink. "But Sam wants to talk to you first."

Sam stepped inside the cabin with an envelope. "Here's your pay.

I added your bonus for the season. You were one hell of a trail guide, the guests loved you, but I don't want to see you back here—so I am going to give you the best piece of advice I can."

Bernadette took the envelope and rested her hand on Sam's shoulder. He'd been like a father figure to her over the summer, with conversations by the campfire.

Sam took a moment, then stared directly at Bernadette. "I know you're all fired up about helping your friend, and that's the right thing to do, but you have to realize the situation you're in with the RCMP."

"What's that?"

Sam lowered his voice. "The fact of the matter is you're a woman and a minority. That's going to be like a red flag to most of the old guard in the force. And I speak from experience. You're smarter than most of them with that university degree of yours." Sam took a moment and paused.

"If you get into any trouble down there, appear on any police report, or make a statement in any investigation, some dickhead with a hate-on will push you out of the force. It's top-heavy with men that would like nothing more than to fill it up with a bunch of ticket-writing dumbasses who haven't any common sense. You can change that. Don't give them a reason to take you down—you hear me?"

"Thanks Sam, I'll be careful," Bernadette said. She hugged him and stuffed the envelope in her pocket.

She headed out the door where the staff had lined up to say their goodbyes. She had to submit to a hugging line before she could leave and a promise if she caught any of them speeding or in disorderly conduct, they'd get a verbal warning.

Bernadette hugged Lincoln at the end of the line. "Okay, you guys, you know I love you all, but if you piss me off when I'm in uniform, expect a kick in the ass! You got that?"

The crew laughed as she jumped in her 1980 Chevy half-ton. The engine fired up with a roar and a plume of smoke. She threw it into gear and spun the tires on the gravel as she headed down the winding road to the Trans-Canada Highway.

She had a four-hour drive to get to the airport and lots of time to think about what she'd agreed to. There was no way she could refuse a plea from Melinda for help. She'd been her rock when Bernadette entered police studies at McEwan University.

When her Aunt Mary finally challenged herself with Bernadette's nagging and entered the three-year dental hygienist course at the University of Alberta, it was Melinda who became her tutor to get her through.

They'd stayed in touch when Bernadette had summer jobs, planting trees, and driving a truck for the oil rigs in the summer. Their paths couldn't have been any more diverse, but their friendship had always held.

The highway spun by as Bernadette thought of the past four years since leaving high school. Her goal had always been to join the legendary Royal Canadian Mounted Police. Once she had a goal in mind, it was like a laser beam that penetrated the darkness.

The RCMP was formed in 1873 to fend off the American whiskey traders who came over the Canadian border from Montana. The original North-West Mounted Police rode into the Canadian Prairies and established order by setting up forts and outposts that they called "detachments." - a name they still use today. Something about the legendary force and their willingness to work in the wilderness appealed to Bernadette.

She'd applied to the force before she'd finished her degree. Everyone she spoke to told her no one got in on the first request, they might have their quota of women, and she'd have to wait another year. When the acceptance letter came in the mail with a command to "report to RCMP Depot Division, Regina, Saskatchewan," it had overcome her with emotion.

The warm thoughts kept her imagining what it would be like as the scenery rolled by from Banff. When Calgary appeared on the horizon, she took Highway 22 to bypass the busy city. The two-lane highway took her past the rolling foothills and cattle ranches. Turning east, she joined up with Highway 1 to head north until she reached the Edmonton International Airport.

She pulled into short-term parking, threw her duffle bag into the passenger seat as she knew her riding clothes wouldn't be useful in Saint Lucia, and headed for the airport. It was ten p.m., her flight boarded at eleven-forty-five.

Aunt Mary waved to her beside the Air Canada check-in counter. A tall, handsome black man stood beside her. He was older than Mary, had gray hair with a goatee and fashionable glasses.

Bernadette and Mary hugged, then Mary turned. "I want to introduce you to my friend, Martin Flemings."

Martin stepped forward and shook Bernadette's hand. "Call me Marty. Your aunt has told me a lot about you."

"I hope only the good things," Bernadette said. "Your accent sounds Caribbean, Marty. Any chance you've been to where I'm heading?"

Marty laughed. "Your aunt said you were direct. I'm Jamaican, and I've never been as far south as Saint Lucia. I hear they're good people, with a police force that is polite and understaffed. I hope you'll be able to help your friend down there."

Aunt Mary placed her hand on Bernadette's shoulder. "I have some notes from Melinda I need to give you." Aunt Mary was almost as tall as Bernadette. She was full Cree and looked like a softer image of Bernadette's long-dead mother.

An announcement came over the PA system. Bernadette's flight was boarding.

Bernadette stepped aside with Mary. "I guess we don't have as much time as I'd hoped."

Mary pulled an eight by eleven envelope out of her large shoulder bag, "Here's the police report from Saint Lucia that Melinda sent me, plus I photocopied the latest news about the kidnapping from our Canadian newspapers and some I took off the internet."

"Thanks, Aunt Mary. This will get me up to speed on my way down there. I'll call to let you know what's happening."

"I'll be saying a prayer for the Cooper family every night. They are a special family. They've always been there for you and me, and even for my kids. Anything you can do to bring them home safely..." Mary said as tears welled in her eyes.

"Hey, you know I will. Now I need my luggage and an idea of what's in it if security asks me."

Mary wiped her eyes with a tissue. "It's your usual, seven pairs of underwear and bras, three pairs of shorts, swimwear, five t-shirts, two pairs of slacks, and a sundress. I threw in your runners, walking shoes, two pairs of sandals, and a hat. There's sunscreen in the bag, so throw it into your baggie, and I cleared your drawer of most of your makeup just in case you're in a police line-up."

"Thanks, I'll try to avoid the line-up. Now I'd better go, get my ticket, and get my things in order. And we'll need to talk about Marty when I get back," Bernadette said with a grin.

"Not much to say, he's wonderful, thinks I'm incredible and loves my kids."

"Does he know the price he'll pay if he breaks your heart?" Bernadette said with an arch of her eyebrow.

Mary laughed. "Yes, he's heard that you achieved your second-degree black belt in karate. And don't forget, the girls aren't far behind. He knows he'd be in a mess of trouble, but he's a kind man. His wife passed away from cancer three years ago. We have a wonderful relationship—now go, get on that plane and help Melinda."

Bernadette hugged Mary, turned to Marty, and gave him a hug as well. "I'll look forward to getting to know you when I return." She grabbed her roller carry-on bag, picked up her ticket from the counter, and headed into security.

THE PLANE WAS PACKED on the flight to Toronto. They gave Bernadette a window seat where she consumed a sandwich and a soda, then put her head on her rolled-up jacket and slept all the way until landing.

In Toronto, she bought a lounge pass and changed into shorts after giving her legs a quick shave with no unnecessary bloodletting. The days in the mountains had been wonderful, but unladylike, for personal grooming.

She boarded the flight to Saint Lucia, found another window seat, and pulled out the package of files her aunt had given her. There was no more there than what Melinda had said on the phone. A motorboat had taken the Coopers and their brother-in-law off the shores of Anse Cochon bay.

They had made no ransom. Bernadette's four years of police studies had drilled in the doctrine that although there were few acts of random violence, the statistics pointed to someone you knew or who knew you well enough to make you a target.

She took out a pad and pen and wrote ideas. She had to find out how long they'd stayed in Saint Lucia, what business the Coopers were in, and everyone they'd encountered.

Pulling out the rest of the files, she perused the newspaper clippings. The reports were about Luke Cooper and his wife. They'd been the pillars of the medical community in Edmonton, Canada. Frida Cooper was on the board of the Heart and Stroke fundraising and gave up her Christmases to serve food at the homeless shelter.

Hearts were breaking across Canada as people weighed in with the good deeds these two people had done. But their brother-in-law Max—not so much. He seemed to be an entrepreneur who invested in land deals that never quite hit the mark. He had lawsuits trailing him that were mired with dueling lawyers.

There wasn't much she could do until she landed, but there was a lot to talk about with Melinda when she met her. The fasten seat belts sign came on, and the captain announced they'd be landing in twenty minutes.

BERNADETTE FOLLOWED the passengers down the steep stairway to the tarmac and was hit with a wave of heat and humidity. She was glad she'd changed into her shorts, but now even her legs were sweating.

The airport building was small, with large circulating fans overhead that pushed the hot air around to make it seem like it was doing some good. She inched her way to customs, got her passport stamped, and made her way towards the exit.

A large black man wearing a white shirt and black pants held a sign that read "Callahan." He stood just inside the entrance and smiled at Bernadette when she approached.

"I'm Bernadette Callahan."

"Welcome to Saint Lucia. My name is Steven. I am your chauffeur. Please follow me, my car is waiting."

Bernadette put on her sunglasses and followed Steven to his late-model Mercedes sedan. He opened the trunk, put her bag inside, and opened the back door for her.

Bernadette slid into the back seat. The air conditioning was running and a small cooler was on the seat console.

"We will be an hour-and-a-half on our journey. If madame would like a soft drink or cold Piton beer, please help yourself to whatever you wish in the cooler."

"How kind of you," Bernadette said. She opened the cooler, pulled out a Piton beer, and opened it. Settling back in the car, she felt relaxed and ready to take on the mission to find the Coopers.

The car motored out of the parking lot; Steven paid the parking attendant and proceeded down the road. A few minutes later he slowed the car down to stop beside a man on the road.

"This is my friend, Michael, he'll be joining us for the journey," Steven said looking into the rear-view mirror.

Michael climbed into the front seat and made a quick nod in Bernadette's direction. There was something in Steven's tone and Michael's look. Her senses went on high alert. What was happening? This seemed so simple, but everything about it seemed ominous.

She took another sip of her beer to calm her nerves. Was this a common thing—locals helping each other? Perhaps she misread the signals. There was jetlag and a new country. Maybe if she sat back and relaxed... then she saw the road sign.

The car came into a round-a-bout. Instead of following the sign to Castries, Steven kept going to the turn to the south. Bernadette leaned forward in her seat. "Why are we going to Vieux Fort?"

"This is another way, not to worry, madame," Steven said. He looked into the rear-view mirror and smiled.

"No, there is no other way. I've seen the map of Castries. You missed the turnoff. You need to turn around and go back."

"Not to worry. I have lived here all my life. I know the way. I will see you there safely," Steven said.

Michael turned around, "Not to worry, this is a pleasant way, lovely scenery, drink your beer, open another, and enjoy."

"Gentlemen, I've studied the map. This island is one big volcano with roads that only go up and over the mountains. You either turn around and head for Castries or let me out and I'll find my own way."

A loud click sounded—the car doors locked.

Michael turned around again. This time, he held a large knife. He rested it on the headrest. "Sit back and relax, my lady. We are taking you someplace safe. You will not be harmed."

4

BERNADETTE SAT BACK in her seat. Michael eyed her, the large knife waving back and forth in his hand. Steven looked at her in the rear-view mirror and smiled. They had her. How had she fallen for this? She realized they'd approached her inside the terminal, not at the meeting point with the other drivers. A classic setup and she'd missed it.

She reached for another beer in the cooler. She made as if to open the beer but kept the cap on, covering it with her hand. Any weapon was a good one.

The next moments would be the ones that mattered. One of them would make a mistake. She wanted to be ready. The large Mercedes rounded a curve and met a transport truck passing a bus.

Steven let out several curses as he braked. Michael looked forward. That was it—Bernadette struck.

The beer bottle in her hand shot forward to connect with the side of Michael's head. She lunged forward, grabbed his hand with the knife, and twisted his wrist so hard he screamed. The knife dropped into the back seat.

She threw her elbow into his head. Michael bounced off the

window and slumped onto the seat. He was out cold. Steven turned to look at her. "What are you doing?"

"I'm changing the itinerary of this ride," Bernadette said as she put the knife beside Steven's ear. "Slow down and park on the side of the road."

"No, I will not," Steven said. He was sweating, his eyebrows danced up and down as he looked at Bernadette and tried to keep the car on the road.

"There is another way, Steven," Bernadette said in a soothing voice. "I can run this blade across your neck, and you'll bleed to death —it will be very slow. You will get sleepy, and I will have to crawl in the front and take the wheel from you. Is that how you want to die?"

"You would never do that," Steven said.

Bernadette leaned forward and ran the blade along his neck, just enough to let some blood flow. "That's your blood, Steven. Want to go for more?"

"I'm stopping the car. I'm doing it now. Please stop what you're doing." Steven pulled the car to the side of the road.

"Shut off the engine and hand me the keys. Put both your hands on the wheel," Bernadette commanded. She grabbed the keys, jumped out of the back seat, and opened the driver's door. "Get out."

Steven slid out of the car, holding his neck. He looked at her as if she was the vilest woman he'd ever met. "We meant you no harm. You would have been safe with us."

"Where are your handcuffs?"

"We have none."

"My offer to slit your throat still stands. Where are they?"

"In the glove compartment."

"Get them out."

Steven leaned across Michael and brought back two pairs of handcuffs.

"Pick up Michael and follow me," Bernadette said.

"Where are you taking us?"

Bernadette smiled, "Somewhere safe."

Steven was much larger than Michael. He pulled him out of the car and carried him over his shoulder. Bernadette guided them to a stand of trees. She had Steven stand up in front of the tree and Michael's limp body on the other side. Pulling out the handcuffs, she shackled them around each other and fastened the cuffs.

"You cannot leave us here. We could die. There are snakes in this area," Steven pleaded.

Bernadette chuckled. "Well, since I've corralled two of the most dangerous snakes I've met on the island, you should be fine. I'll let the police in Castries know where to find you."

She turned and jangled the keys over her shoulder as she walked to the car. "Thanks for the lift, boys."

Bernadette got in the car and tried to stop the trembling in her hands. She'd just got away with the biggest gamble and bluff in her life. If Steven hadn't believed she'd cut his throat, there was no way she could have followed through with it.

She started the vehicle, threw it into gear, and turned it around to head back to Castries. "One day you'll get yourself into a pile of shit with the stuff you pull off, girl."

THE ROAD to Castries was pleasant. It wound past little villages and farms with coconuts, bananas, citrus, and yams. There were small shacks that served local sandwiches, Piton beer, and rum, and although Bernadette was hungry, she pushed the Mercedes until she came to the lookout above Castries.

Looking down over the tiny port town, she could see two cruise ships in the harbor and a busy road with cars and trucks in the narrow streets. With a map beside her, she navigated her way to Hotel Macambo near the harbor. She parked the car two blocks from the hotel, pulled her bag out of the trunk of the car, and walked to the hotel.

Hotel Macambo was off a small side street with a view of the bay. It looked like they had built it in the seventies as a little hideaway of the modestly rich. The fifty-room hotel had gone through a complete makeover with a style reminiscent of nineteen-twenties Miami Beach.

Bernadette entered the front lobby, filled with art déco fixtures and low-slung seats that few dared to sit in if they ever wanted to rise again, and headed for the front desk.

A slim, young lady with a plain blue dress and a red flower in her hair raised her eyes and widened her smile to greet her. "Welcome to Hotel Macambo. How may I help you?"

"YES, my name is Bernadette Callahan. I'm here to meet with Melinda Cooper. Please let her know I'm here."

"Yes, one moment please." She dialed the room number. "She'll be right with you."

Bernadette waited under a large fan, blowing enough air to cool her off. The five-minute walk had made her sweat. The lobby had a glass water dispenser filled with lemons, so she poured herself a glass and let the liquid cascade down her throat.

Melinda came running into the lobby and threw herself into Bernadette's arms. She'd grown into a beautiful lady with long blonde hair and bright blue eyes encased behind large glasses.

"Hey, Mel, good to see you too," Bernadette said as Melinda hugged her neck and rested her head on her shoulder.

Melinda raised her head, her eyes filled with tears. "I'm sorry to drag you all this way. I didn't know who else to call."

"You know, we've always had each other's backs. This is serious, and I'm glad you brought me in."

"How was your trip here?"

"Strange," Bernadette said. "Let's sit over here. I'll get you some water."

She guided Melinda to two plush rattan chairs in the lobby far from the front desk, where they could speak in private. After filling two glasses with water, she sat beside Melinda and told her the story.

Melinda sat there in shock as Bernadette told her about the two men who'd tried to take her hostage that morning. "How is that possible?" she blurted out.

The young lady at the front desk looked up from her computer.

Bernadette put her hand on Melinda's. "Let's keep this between us."

"But how did they know you were arriving? I only told Travis. He'll be here later today."

"Do you have a car picking him up?"

"Yes, I had the front desk arrange it."

"Did the young lady at the front desk make the arrangements?"

"No, it was a lady who works here in the evenings. After you called, I came out and asked her to arrange it. She said she'd do the same for Travis."

"Travis might get the same welcome I did—we need a rental car. The one I drove in might be reported as stolen," Bernadette said.

"You stole a car?"

"Borrowed," Bernadette said. "I left it up the street. If my kidnappers get free, they might report it stolen. That's if they have friends in the police force."

"What do we do? Travis's flight is due to arrive two hours from now."

"You get us a car—I'm going to make a phone call," Bernadette said.

Melinda approached the front desk while Bernadette dialed the number of the local police station. The number was on her travel map. When the police answered, she quickly gave details of where she'd seen two men tied up near the roundabout to Vieux Fort.

As the police receptionist asked for more details, Bernadette hung up the phone and joined Melinda.

"They'll have a car for us in a half-hour. It's the best I could do. We'll be cutting it close. There's no way I can reach Travis, he's still in the air."

"Phone the airport, see if you can have them contact Travis on arrival to wait for you to pick him up," Bernadette said. "I'll drop my bags in your room and we'll get ready to leave."

FORTY-FIVE MINUTES LATER, a new 2000 Peugeot GTI hatchback arrived. The rental car representative, with smiles and handshakes, wanted to show them the car's features.

"Does he have your credit card on file—did you sign the papers?" Bernadette asked.

"Yes, I gave it to him," Melinda said.

Bernadette looked at the man. "I need the keys now. Sorry to be rude—we have to go now."

"Of course, please go. I have a short walk back to the agency; I'll enjoy my time away from the office," the man said with a smile.

They jumped into the car, Bernadette threw it into gear and hit the gas. The car's tires squealed as it shot out of the hotel driveway into the street.

Melinda held onto the armrest as the car careened around a corner and passed two cars as they up picked speed. "I do not know how these people can be so nice to us, and yet someone on this island is putting my family in danger."

"It's the law of averages. There are always a certain number of people who want to make money from crime. I learned that in my police studies classes," Bernadette said as she pulled out from behind a tourist bus and shot by it.

Melinda stared ahead as they dodged a large truck to get back into their lane. "Why aren't we calling the police to tell them of your attempted kidnapping and why they shouldn't be assisting us at the airport?"

Bernadette turned to Melinda. "We don't know for certain if they'll try again on Travis. A former RCMP officer warned me I need to stay out of any involvement with the police when I'm here."

"And you came anyway?" Melinda asked.

Bernadette hit the brake to avoid ramming into a taxi. "Yeah, nothing could stop me. Don't worry, we'll figure this out. I'll keep in the background and help you find your parents—how much time do we have before Travis lands?"

Melinda looked at her watch. "He lands in an hour. I just saw a sign to the airport that says we're fifty kilometers away. You think we'll make it there in time over the mountain roads?"

Bernadette hit the gas. "Going to be close."

5

Travis Cooper's flight was coming in early. The captain put on the fasten seat belt signs and told everyone to be ready for a warm stay on arrival. The temperature on the island was thirty-five Celsius, with eighty-five percent humidity.

Travis was weary from his long flight. He'd left Vancouver the day before, stayed in Toronto overnight, and caught the afternoon flight to Saint Lucia. He'd spent his morning in a meeting with a detective agency to assist in the search for his parents, uncle, and ship's crew.

The detective agencies in Saint Lucia were proficient in fraud and blackmail and might be good for local knowledge, but Travis wanted something deeper. That would take someone from the FBI, but his parents were Canadian, not American.

He'd discovered a detective agency in Toronto with a deep resume of ex-Canadian military who'd served in Security and Intelligence. The owner of the company, a man named Thomas Davina, was taking over the investigation personally. Davina assured him he had connections in the Caribbean and would be on the ground the next day.

The cost didn't come into question at this point. Travis had liquidated numerous assets in case of a ransom call. There'd been none. Now he was building resources to find his parents, uncle, and crew.

At twenty-seven, he was the owner of a software company that had profited from the recent Y2K scare in the computer world. He couldn't hire programmers fast enough to assuage the anxieties of major Canadian and American companies that feared they would lose all their data when 1999 turned to the year 2000. Travis knew there'd be minor problems, but no one wanted to pay him for his advice. They wanted his programmers to rework their computer systems. Travis took the money and hired the programmers. He made millions.

They listed Travis Cooper as one of the top CEOs of Canadian computer companies to watch in the twentieth century. It estimated his fortune at thirty million and he'd give it all right now to have his family whole again.

The plane landed with a hard thump on the runway. A cloud of moisture fogged up the airplane's windows. Travis looked out to see rows of palm trees and clear blue skies with puffy white clouds. If he'd been in the mood for a vacation, which he rarely took, this might be a pleasant journey.

The flight attendant in his first-class cabin handed him his jacket. He proceeded down the stairway with his laptop over his shoulder. He lined up at customs and shuffled along with the rest of the passengers.

An announcement came over the intercom regarding where his luggage would arrive as he moved to the customs agent. A baby wailed behind him. He tried to block it out as the customs agent asked him questions regarding his stay. He had to lean forward to make himself heard as another announcement came over the intercom, looking for a passenger named Cooper to come to the information desk for a message.

Travis satisfied the custom agent's questions and moved on. He found his luggage and walked towards the exit. A man in a white shirt and black pants stood inside the building with a sign that said "Cooper."

6

BERNADETTE PASSED another truck as they came around the corner to see the airport in sight. She slowed down to get into the lane of traffic leading into the terminal.

"Keep your eyes open. He might wait for us if he received your message," Bernadette said.

"I don't see him. We're a bit early. Maybe his flight isn't in yet," Melinda said.

"I'll park and we'll go in. I want you to stay close to me in case any of those men who tried to take me this morning are hanging around."

Bernadette pulled out of the line of traffic and headed for the car park. She almost hit the brakes when she saw the two men in front of her.

"Is that Travis?"

"Yes, it's him!" Melinda screamed.

Bernadette gunned the engine and headed straight for them while pounding on the horn.

"What are you doing?" Melinda yelled.

"That's Steven, the bastard that tried to kidnap me this morning," Bernadette said. She aimed the car right at them.

Travis jumped to one side—Steven jumped to the other. He was on Bernadette's side. She opened her door and kept the car going—the door hit him squarely in the back. It propelled him forward—he kept running.

A vehicle came beside him. Steven jumped in and the car sped off. Bernadette wanted to chase it. She looked at Travis and knew she couldn't leave him.

Bernadette stopped the car and jumped out. "Hey Travis, welcome to Saint Lucia."

Travis got off the ground and dusted himself off. His face was red, and his eyes squinted at Bernadette. "I see your driving hasn't improved. You want to tell me what that was about?"

"Bernadette was saving you from the same man that tried to kidnap her when she arrived this morning," Melinda said, holding onto his arm.

"Oh my God, Bernadette, I'm so sorry—I should have known. I apologize, you're always saving my ass," Travis said as he engulfed her in a hug.

Bernadette folded into Travis's chest. She hadn't seen him for several years. He'd become remarkably handsome with long blonde hair, those bright blue eyes, and a nice pair of biceps that held her tight. She tried hard not to have feelings for him—again. But her resolve weakened the moment he said he was sorry.

They were attracted to each other when she was eighteen at the Cooper family's lake cottage. They'd made love in the boathouse. He'd been her first. He returned to Vancouver before she could sort out her feelings for him. Now she needed to get over him and get her head back in the game.

Bernadette pushed herself away. "Good to see you safe. I didn't mean to scare you, but that guy tried to kidnap me at knifepoint this morning. I didn't want that happening to you."

Travis tried to hug her again. Bernadette spun out of his arms. "We'd better get going. A police officer might show up and I don't want to make any statements."

"Why not?" Travis asked. "You might make a positive ID on the guy, and it could lead us to the kidnappers."

Bernadette whirled and looked at Travis. "Because I called the police to tell them where I'd handcuffed them to a tree. I did that three hours ago. Now, I see the same man trying to take you hostage."

Travis looked at the ground, then back up at Bernadette. "You think it could involve someone from the police?"

"I can't say for certain. But we might find some answers back at the hotel. We need to find out who booked the car service that was sent for both of us," Bernadette said. She turned to Melinda. "Do you have anyone inside the police force you think you can trust?"

MELINDA BLEW OUT A BREATH. "I'm not sure, they are so nice. All the people on this island seem nice. You know I'm a terrible judge of character."

Bernadette motioned for everyone to get into the car. Travis threw his bag into the car's trunk and folded his tall frame into the back seat. Melinda got back in the front passenger seat.

"You know, this is a crazy time to say this, but I'm so glad we're back together again. I've missed all of you. This is a dangerous situation, but I know we'll get through this," Melinda said.

"My God, Melinda, you were always the positive one. We will get through this and we're going to solve this." Bernadette said.

"You have a plan?" Travis asked.

"Yeah, someone in Castries is going to get an ass-kicking when we get back to the hotel," Bernadette said.

Travis leaned forward. "Bernadette, I know you've ideas on how to work on this case, but I hired a high-profile agency in Toronto yesterday. A man named Thomas Davina will be here by tomorrow. He's a specialist in hostage negotiations."

Melinda turned to Travis. "Oh, thank God you've done that. The local police have nothing so far. They're so kind, but they seem overmatched by this."

"They're a force of just over seven hundred officers that cover everything from policing on land to the coast guard. There are one hundred and fifty thousand people on this island, and they're spread thin in fourteen districts," Bernadette said.

"And it just got worse for them today," Travis said. "One of the cruise ships lost a passenger at sea. I saw it in the Canadian newspaper before I boarded my plane. The Saint Lucia police are investigating."

"That's going to throw a wrench into your family's investigation. I'm going to find out who your hotel called to pick us up at the airport. I promise I'll turn everything over to the police and your detective when he arrives," Bernadette said.

Bernadette slowed down to follow behind a tourist bus. She wondered how she'd find the information on the car service. There had to be a connection at the hotel. Her problem would be how to stay off the grid while she made inquiries.

They rounded a corner to see the bay below them. The cruise ship that should have left had several police cars on the dock.

7

THOMAS DAVINA STAYED at his desk long after his staff had left. He was forty-seven years old, tall, with dark features and a receding hairline. His big hands pounded on his keyboard as he sent one email after another to direct his people to start the investigation into the missing Cooper family and the crew of the sailboat.

Thomas was born in Holland and came to Canada when he was five years old. His father had moved them along with his business in international banking to their new country. They'd settled in Ottawa, Canada's capital, where his father cultivated rich foreign clients. Thomas disliked banking and school. He finished high school and joined the Canadian Army when he turned eighteen.

His large stature and fast reflexes in combat training got him into the military police. He excelled in his unit and moved up the ranks into the Intelligence unit. He did little more than investigate low-level crimes and breaches of army protocol until the Gulf War broke out.

They assigned Thomas to a unit to retrieve personnel captured by the Iraqis. He was good at it. From there, Thomas served in the Somali Civil War in 1992. His talents in finding and negotiating the release of prisoners became noticed. He was in high demand.

He left the force in 1995 to set up the Asset Protection Agency. It should have been called the Asset Retrieval Agency. Clients flocked to him as the business of kidnapping for ransom had grown exponentially. The agency set up a bodyguard service as well. This work alone netted millions in income per year.

But the largest revenue came from hostage negotiations. Criminals grabbed their targets off the streets for money. Thomas helped get them back, for a hefty fee. Before he agreed to the meeting with Travis Cooper, he ran an assessment of Travis's company and that of his father's wealth.

He'd smiled when he saw the numbers. They were good, but there'd be some hard work to get the liquid cash that criminals wanted. Dr. Cooper's money was tied up in real estate holdings and stocks, while Travis had over ten million in negotiable securities available.

The common practise of kidnappers was to make outlandish requests for ransom. Thomas would listen to them, nod, and then start a slow and often painful process of getting them to understand reality.

"Seriously," he would ask by phone, fax, or email, "You want one hundred million, how many people you think have that kind of liquid cash? Let's get real, I can get you two million cash—and the captives better be in good health."

Thomas affectionately called his negotiations the "Hostage Game." This game had begun in ancient Rome. Hostages from conquered lands were paraded for the Romans to see what great prizes their army had won. In Medieval times, hostages were exchanged by kings to maintain a truce. It was during the Crusades that hostages were held for ransom. The world discovered the true game—human beings could be bartered—if they had value.

Thomas sent his last email to his operatives. One would arrive from Miami, a thirty-five-year-old former US Ranger named Andres Ramirez. He'd done several personal protection assignments for him before, but he excelled at digging up information. If this operation ended up with the hostages in Venezuela or Columbia, Ramirez's fluent Spanish and his Salvadoran heritage would be useful.

Ezra Williams, a forty-seven-year-old ex-British Army officer who lived in Belize, would meet up with Ramirez, and together they'd start combing the local hangouts in Saint Lucia to check on any information that had surfaced. They'd start with the fishermen and charter boat captains. Thomas had reviewed all the reports from the disappearance.

The Saint Lucian police claimed the motorboat with the hostages had vanished. Nothing vanished in Thomas's world. The kidnappers would look for a secure place. Once they'd established it and had covered their tracks, they'd make their call for money.

Thomas would be ready for them. He closed his laptop, grabbed his suit jacket, and made for the door. He was going to see this one through himself. Normally he'd stay in his office and run a command center. He planned to take a much-needed vacation and book a room at Sandals Resorts in Rodney Bay after this. He'd sink into some large rums with all the money he made on this job.

8

BERNADETTE PULLED the rental into the driveway of the hotel. A police car was outside. There was no one in it. Which meant they must be inside.

"You'd better go for a walk," Melinda said. "If the police have questions, Travis and I will answer them."

"Good plan," Bernadette said as she stepped out of the car. "I'll walk down to the pier and get myself a drink."

Travis grabbed his luggage and followed Melinda inside. Bernadette walked towards the pier, taking her time as if she was just another tourist. The one thing she'd learned in criminal investigative studies was anyone in a hurry best be a jogger because otherwise, you've got a suspect. She didn't want to be subject to any police questions, and she wasn't about to hurry away to make an officer notice her.

She wandered towards the pier. A white cruise ship blocked the view of the rest of the harbor. A small bar with a thatched roof and a sign that said, "happy hour," got her attention.

Bernadette propped herself on a stool in the open-air bar and ordered a rum drink that looked semi-inspired. It promised to be "rum-tastic!" At this point in the day, she could use anything that played on the word fantastic.

A man who looked in his thirties sat beside her, nursing a large coconut with a straw sticking out of it. He turned to her for a moment, smiled, then looked away.

Bernadette's coconut rum-tastic appeared before her, garnished with an umbrella, and some pineapple skewers stuck into it. Bernadette took her first sip, realized it was mostly rum, and tried to catch her breath.

"If you drink three of them, the fourth one is free," the man said.

Bernadette shook her head. "How would you be conscious enough to know when you've had the third?"

The man looked over and smiled. "They lower the rum content with each one. I'm on my third—I'm hardly feeling a buzz. The name's Paul, what's yours?" he asked. He had a buzz cut, large biceps protruding out of a muscle shirt, and a gold chain around his neck. His shorts were super short, and his quads showed like he'd been doing nothing but squats with heavy weights all morning.

"I'm Ginger," Bernadette said.

"I don't think that's your real name," Paul said. "You don't look like a Ginger."

"Really," Bernadette said. "They loved me on Gilligan's Island."

"Now, that's funny. You could be on my show," Paul said.

"You a movie producer?" Bernadette asked.

Paul chuckled, "No, I'm a television producer. I do a reality TV show called Hollywood Lights. It's about up-and-coming actors trying to get into show business."

"And people watch this?" Bernadette asked, taking another sip of her drink.

"It's got high ratings. We're riding a wave of new television viewers who love to watch other people's daily struggles," Paul said.

Bernadette shook her head in disbelief. "To think that television would be about us watching other people's lives. I can't see it taking off."

"You wait, it's going to be the next big trend. So, what brings you to this dive bar on the dock? Are you hiding out from someone?"

Bernadette smiled, "You got me, I'm running from the law. How about you?"

Paul sighed, "I've been on a cruise with my boyfriend, and everything got shit-canned over some silly passenger who went missing yesterday."

"I guess that's tough for you, but a major bummer for the missing passenger. Did you know the person?" Bernadette asked.

"Not really, but my boyfriend was the last to see him, so he's getting the third degree by the police while I fill myself full of cheap rum."

"Hey, you could use this for one of your reality shows," Bernadette said. "Call it Danger In Paradise or Missing In Paradise."

Paul sipped his drink. "You know, If I could get my cameras onto cruise ships and follow the crew around—"

An older gentleman slapped Paul on the back. "What are we drinking and who's your friend?"

Bernadette looked up to see a man in his mid-sixties, wearing a cream-colored Hawaiian shirt and white pants with white shoes. He had a full head of silver-gray hair. His enormous face contained an equally large nose and ears set off by a pair of designer glasses.

"Hey Fred, this is Ginger and we're doing a coconut buzz," Paul replied.

"Too rich for me, I'll have a rum on ice with one lime," Fred said. He sat down beside Paul and leaned around him. "So Ginger, this is your real name?"

Paul smiled at Bernadette and then back at Fred. "I think she's hiding out. Maybe in witness protection—maybe on the run from Gilligan's Island," he said in a whisper. He now sounded a little drunk.

"Fine by me," Fred said with a laugh. "I was hoping to find out who the professor slept with—was it Ginger or Mary-Anne?"

Bernadette leaned forward on the bar and looked at Fred. "Maybe it was both."

"Ha, I knew it, a threesome. Damn, I miss that show."

"I understand you had to speak with the police?" Bernadette asked. She couldn't help herself.

Fred sipped his rum and put it down. "Yeah, I met this crazy-ass guy in the martini bar last night. He was making like he was some big real estate hotshot, doing deals all over the islands. So, I asked him some pointed questions."

"You're in real estate?" Bernadette asked.

"Forty years. I started with my father, building houses in Hollywood Hills. We branched out into building apartments and developments. That's why I could tell this guy was blowing smoke up everyone's ass. He didn't know the first thing about land assembly or the process that goes with it. I figured him for a scam artist—I told him so, he got all pissy and he left."

"And you never saw him again?"

Fred sipped his drink and looked at Paul. "Your friend Ginger sounds like a cop."

Bernadette smiled, "Sorry, the truth is I'm on the island regarding my friend's disappearance. His name was Dr. Luke Cooper. He was involved in some real estate on this island. I don't know if you heard about him, but they took him captive."

"I read about that before our ship left Miami. Do the police have any clues?" Fred asked.

"Not a thing. My friends are bringing in some detectives. Do you have the name of the man that went missing?"

"Sure, his name was Valdis Kalnins. I've never heard of him before. The police told me he was getting off the ship here in Castries. When he didn't get off, they checked his room. His bags were there, and they found blood on his balcony," Fred said.

"And they suspected you?" Paul asked, with his eyes going wide and his voice slurring even more.

"They suspect everyone," Bernadette said, then added, "I read a lot of detective books."

Fred sipped his drink and nodded in agreement, "Yes, Ginger is right. They gave me a lot of grief, but after they reviewed the ship's phone logs and saw I had made several phone calls back to Los Angeles from our room, they let me go."

"And they haven't found his killer?" Paul said, taking another sip of his coconut.

"If they have an idea, they wouldn't tell me," Fred said. "I checked this guy out on that new site called Google—"

"Google isn't new, Fred, it's been around a few years," Paul said.

"Well, it's new to me. Anyway, this guy Valdis turns out to have some weird website for Caribbean real estate where he claimed everyone who invested would make millions. In all the years I've been in the business, anyone who makes claims like that is bullshitting."

Bernadette took some money out of her pocket to pay her bill and pushed her coconut away. She felt the buzz of the alcohol and didn't need anymore.

"Please, your coconut is on us," Fred said. "How often is it I get to meet the amazing Ginger at a Tiki bar? And besides, I got to blow off steam about that idiot who went overboard. Maybe the fish found him tasty."

"Thanks Fred, it was a pleasure meeting you both," Bernadette said as she left the bar. She wandered back to the hotel, saw the police car had left, and decided it was time to ask some questions regarding the car service the hotel had arranged. Someone on the island was trying to put a stop to the investigation of the Cooper family's disappearance. She wanted to find out who it was. Walking to Melinda's room, she knocked on her door.

9

DR. LUKE COOPER paced the small room. The place was sparse with a bare light bulb. They had a table with two chairs, a sink, and a toilet inside a closed room. Outside the room was a long series of hallways they saw when the door opened. Overhead were industrial conduits and wiring that made them think they'd been imprisoned in a basement of a warehouse. Frida Cooper lay on the bed with her eyes closed.

Frida was fifty-five years old, her hair a decided red, as that is the color she dyed it, with a firm figure from a dedication to the gym and a careful diet. She was trying to let the events of the past few days wash over her.

Their captors transferred them to a large fishing boat and shoved them into the hold. In complete darkness, they were pulled from the hold and taken to a beach. A van brought them to a doorway. It led them down some stairs and placed in separate rooms. She hadn't seen the cook or the captain from the boat. She assumed the kidnappers had murdered them. Max was somewhere nearby; she'd heard him snoring a few nights ago. It was the same snore that kept her up nights on their boat, and the same snore that her sister, Constance, had said made her crazy.

Constance had passed away one year ago. Max had cared for her to the end. He'd loved her madly and was inconsolable for months. It had only been in the past several weeks that Max had cheered up. Frida loved him like the brother she'd never had, and Luke found his humor a welcome distraction after the hard work of his medical practice.

She did not know what would become of them. The gruff Spanish-speaking man with the wicked grin had said little to them. She assumed they were to be ransomed, but they had said nothing. Her major concern was Melinda. After the men boarded the boat, they heard gunshots. One man said in Spanish, "la chica escapa," which Frida knew meant the girl escaped.

Not knowing if they injured Melinda kept Frida awake at night. During the day, or what they assumed was day, the thought kept coming back to her. She tried to keep it to herself. Luke was agitated enough for both.

Luke stopped in the center of the room. "Did you feel that?"

Frida didn't open her eyes, "Feel what?"

"I felt a tremor."

"I didn't feel it."

"There it is again—you must have felt it that time."

"Okay, sweetheart, I felt it. Maybe a large vehicle went by. We must be in a basement next to a road."

"I smell something burnt. Like sulphur."

"Could be exhaust fumes. And speaking of exhausting, your pacing is wearing me out. Why not lay down for a while?"

Luke stopped in the middle of the room. "Why don't they tell us anything? I thought by now they'd be coming in here looking to take our pictures and send them off for ransom."

Frida sighed and sat up. "Maybe this is the first time they've done this. Maybe they have to get the channels of communication organized."

Luke sat beside her. "What would I ever do without you? You, always the positive one like our wonderful son and daughter, and me seeing only the worst of situations."

Frida put her head on Luke's shoulder. In their thirty years together, they'd faced nothing like this. Luke had always been stalwart and stoic in his dealings with the world, as he'd risen to be one of the leading cardiac surgeons in their city. Now he looked worn out.

They were still in their shorts and tops from the boat. Their abductors had grabbed them and shoved them into the motorboat. Luke had worn his favorite t-shirt with the large sailfish print on the back and the words "Relax Bahamas."

He looked anything but relaxed. His long blonde hair with touches of gray was matted and stuck to his head. Frida was glad they had no mirror. She didn't want to see the state she was in. But the one thing they did not want to talk about was the obvious. The kidnappers had let them see their faces.

They hadn't worn masks when they took them prisoner, and when they brought them food, none of them hid their faces. With each passing hour, Frida lost a little more hope. But she tried to keep a brave face for Luke and hoped that if Melinda had survived, she would have teamed up with Travis to find them.

A slight tremor came through her body. This time she felt it, but it wasn't from the outside.

10

MELINDA SMILED when she opened her door. "It's totally okay, Bernie. The police came to follow up with me on their investigation."

"And? What have they found out?" Bernadette asked as she walked into the hotel room. They tastefully furnished it with two single beds, art deco furniture, and paintings of nineteen twenties Miami. A trio of pink flamingos in endless flight adorned one wall, with the bathroom surrounded by glass brick.

"Nothing really, it's what I thought. They apologized as they have to focus on the cruise ship's missing passenger," Melinda said.

Bernadette sat in a coral-colored scallop chair with chrome legs. She tried not to notice a lamp with the figurine of a woman holding up a vase. "I doubt if they have the resources for two serious crimes."

Melinda nodded her head. "I'm so glad Travis hired someone. And that brings me to apologize for bringing you all the way here."

"Why? You know I'm here for you." Bernadette said. "I'll do whatever I can."

Melinda sat in the other chair and took her hand. "But I've brought you all the way down here, and with the detective Travis has brought in, you'll just be hanging out on the sidelines. I didn't intend that to happen."

Bernadette squeezed Melinda's hand. "I have nine days until I report to the police academy in Regina. Until then, whatever I can do to help I will, and if you need me to pack up and leave, I'm good with that too."

"My God, you're an incredible friend," Melinda said.

"I'm glad you think that because we need to find out who in this hotel booked the car service for Travis and me."

"Shouldn't we wait until the detective arrives tomorrow?"

"No, it's a hot lead. Whoever arranged it knows they're discovered. I want to find out before they try to cover it up. You get where I'm going on this?"

"That's why I love you, Bernie. You think like a cop."

"I like to think that's being an intelligent human being. But never mind. Where am I bunking while I'm here? Don't say with Travis because I'll probably put some moves on him," Bernadette said with a laugh.

"You're in here with me. I unpacked your bags and hung up your things, and your toiletries are in the bathroom. You pack really light by the way."

"I recycle and I wash my underwear. Now let's go ask some questions at the front desk."

"Don't you want to shower—maybe change your clothes first?" Melinda asked.

"Do I smell bad?"

"Ah... no."

"Do I look like they have rolled me in the ditch?"

"No, no, you look fine."

"Let's get after this. I had a shower yesterday, before that I lived with my horse on a pack trail for five days and bathed in mountain streams—this is an improvement."

They headed out of the room and found the front desk clerk busy with another guest. They waited patiently in line while she finished.

"Is she the one that took your request for the car service?" Bernadette asked Melinda quietly.

"I'm not sure. There are two girls who work here later in the day that have similar hairstyles and build. It was Sabina or Nadia."

They stepped up to the front desk, and Sabina greeted them. "How may I help you ladies?" She was a young woman of twenty with a bright smile and her hair pulled back off a pleasant round face.

Melinda stepped forward. "Hi, Sabina, I ordered chauffeur pickups from the airport yesterday for both Ms. Callahan and my brother, Travis Cooper. Do you know who took the request and the company that did the pickup?"

Sabina went to her computer and pulled up the file. "Yes, I see the request right here. You ordered it last night, and they confirmed the request at seven this morning. Was there a problem with the pickup?"

Bernadette leaned on the desk. "Everything was fine, Sabina. Who took the request that evening?"

"That would have been Nadia. I hope everything is okay, she's my twin sister and only started last week," Sabina said.

"Everything is fine, Sabina. I left something in the car, and I wanted to see if they had it," Bernadette said.

Sabina picked up the phone. "I'll get them on the line right now. They're just down the street—they'll bring it right over."

Bernadette put up her hand and smiled. "You know, Sabina, we need to take a walk. If you'll just give us the address, we'll drop in to see them."

Sabina wrote the address and handed it to Bernadette. "It's only ten minutes. First Rate Tours and Shuttle, you can't miss it if you walk straight down the main road towards the center of town."

Bernadette and Melinda walked out of the air-conditioned hotel into the late-day heat. The rain had just ended and now the humidity felt like a warm sauna. A hedge of rose flowers by the front entrance tickled their nostrils with its scent and a double rainbow arched overhead in the billowy clouds. For a moment, all seemed right with the world.

"Are you heading out for a walk?" Travis asked, walking up behind them.

"Bernadette thought we should check out who arranged our car service this morning," Melinda said. "She thought we should do it now instead of later."

"I hope you don't mind, Travis. I don't want to crowd your detective tomorrow, but I'd like to see what the car service company has to say."

"You can't keep that inquisitive mind out of things, can you?" Travis said with a wink. He put his arm through Bernadette's as they walked. This time, she didn't move away.

They walked up the street, passing the fruit vendors and a few cafes on the road. Some kids played on the sidewalk as the sun's last burning rays scorched the pavement before the coolness of night fell. Some dogs followed them for a while, found them uninteresting, and left. Minutes later, they arrived in front of the car service office.

"I don't see anyone inside. Is it still open?" Travis asked.

"The sign says it's open until seven, maybe they're in the back," Bernadette said, pushing the door open and walking in.

A ceiling fan spun overhead, a radio played an island tune, and a cat wandered out from behind a desk. It mewed softly, as if it was lonely. Bernadette noticed a coffee pot on a burner. A thick sludge rested on the bottom. The stench of burned coffee wafted into the air.

An office door was slightly ajar. Bernadette pushed her head inside. She surveyed the room for a minute and stepped back. With a slow shake of her head, she approached Travis and Melinda.

"What's wrong?" Melinda asked.

"There's a dead man in that office."

"How do you know he's dead?"

"He's got a hole in his forehead, dried blood around him, and he's got flies giving him his last rites. We need to exit this scene and call the police," Bernadette said.

Melinda put her hand on Bernadette's shoulder. "Look, Travis and I will do it. This isn't your concern; you need to stay out of it. We'll tell the police we came to find a jacket. You go back to the hotel."

"But it is my concern. Whoever tried to kidnap Travis and me murdered that man in there. I need to take my chances with my police force. If they boot my ass out for trying to do the right thing, then they're not the ones I want to be involved with."

"You sure about that?" Travis said.

Bernadette sighed and looked at Travis. "Yeah, I am. Let's call the police. They have to know what is going down here."

11

BERNADETTE SAT in a wooden chair and winced slightly at the dent the wood was making on her butt. She'd sat in the same small room for two hours. One junior officer had taken a statement at the crime scene. They were in the Royal Saint Lucia Central Police Station, which was close to the tour and shuttle office.

The police station was a colonial-style built by the British in the nineteenth century. The paint peeled off the walls, the floors creaked with the weight of countless officers and felons who'd trod the boards, and Bernadette sat ready to be interviewed.

Finally, the assistant superintendent walked in. He was of medium build, with a balding head and patches of gray, and worried wrinkles around his eyes. He looked somewhere north of fifty, but his weary complexion had aged him even more.

He wore an open white police shirt with epaulets and a small paunch that protruded over his dark blue pants. When he sat in the chair in front of Bernadette, he looked like he'd let himself fall into the effort. The wall clock showed past eight o'clock and the shadow of whiskers on the man's face was evidence he'd been at work for a long time.

"Good evening, I am Assistant Superintendent Vernon Charles. I've read your statement and I want to know what you are doing here. Ms. Cooper stated you arrived to help her find her parents. Are you an investigator?"

"No, I've completed four years of university police studies in Canada. They have accepted me into the Royal Canadian Mounted Police Force starting next month. Ms. Cooper is a dear friend of mine —when she called to tell me what had happened to her parents, who are also dear to me, I offered my help," Bernadette said.

"And upon your arrival, two men attempted to kidnap you, but you escaped? Is that correct?" Charles asked.

"Yes, that is the statement I made," Bernadette replied. She kept her voice even and relaxed her body. She'd taken a class in interrogation, but this was the real thing.

"Rather than report the incident to the police, you handcuffed the kidnappers to a tree and took their car? Is this correct?"

"Well... yes I did. There was no traffic on the road, and I decided I needed to get to Castries. I reported the two men to the police later."

"But you did not leave your name?"

"I'm sorry about that—I wanted to ensure my friend was okay. I thought if they had attacked me, perhaps they'd attempt something on her as well."

Charles made a note on the file. The reasoning seemed to make sense. He looked up. "Then you went back to the airport in a rental car to pick up Mr. Cooper?"

"Yes, I was afraid the men might have slipped away and tried to kidnap Travis. My fears were right. The man, who called himself Steven, was leading Travis to a car. I intervened," Bernadette said.

"I see from a report made by the parking attendant that you used a car door to stop this man," Charles said with a raised eyebrow.

Bernadette shrugged her shoulders. "I had to separate him from Travis."

"At no time did you ever think to involve our police force?" Charles asked.

"I didn't know what I was dealing with. I needed to find out who knew about my arrival details..."

"You thought perhaps it involved one of our own police with the men who tried to kidnap you? Is that it?" Charles asked. He didn't raise his voice. It was a matter-of-fact question.

Bernadette nodded her head. "I have no experience with the police on this island or anywhere in the Caribbean. I was told by an acquaintance from this region I should be wary."

"Where is your acquaintance from?"

"Jamaica."

Charles shook his head. "You cannot compare Jamaica to our little island. They have over two million people, their police commit half the crimes. We are a small island of less than a tenth their size."

"Well, my bad, as they say. I should have reached out to your force."

"Yes, you should have. We could charge you with interfering in a police investigation," Charles said.

"Which investigation is that? Did any officers actually check for the men I handcuffed to a tree?"

Charles leafed through the report. "The officers in Vieux Fort did not attend the area until hours after your report. They found no one there."

"Therefore, I did not interfere with anything," Bernadette said.

Charles let the beginnings of a smile edge his lips. He wrote something else in the file and looked up at Bernadette. "Your story is quite remarkable. The body you found had been dead since late last night. All of you have firm alibis and we do not consider you suspects. However, if you'd have let us know earlier, we might have discovered the poor soul sooner."

"I apologize for that," Bernadette said. "Who was the deceased?"

"His name was Steven Charles, no direct relation to me, but he may have been a distant cousin. I have numerous relatives on the island," Charles said.

"I'm sorry for his loss to the family. I wish I could have done more."

"You helped us by looking at the pictures of known criminals on the island. I see you could not identify the person who claimed he was Steven."

Bernadette shook her head. "No, none of the pictures your constable showed me resembled the man I saw. I wish I could have provided more help."

"So, do we. Now, I must request that you not leave the island until we have some closure on this matter. I know this might affect your plans with your future police academy, however, this is now an ongoing investigation, and I'm sure you understand this."

Bernadette swallowed hard. "Yes, I totally understand, and I'll help in any way I can. I thank you, Assistant Superintendent Charles, for forgiving my missteps in dealing with your department and not reporting my incident sooner."

"Please, do not trouble yourself. We all make "rookie" mistakes. If you pass your academy training with your illustrious Canadian police force, I'm sure this will be the least of them. Now, enjoy the rest of your stay on our island—and stay out of trouble," Charles said with a smile.

Bernadette left the room. She felt drained. Melinda and Travis were waiting outside. She hugged them both.

"How was your interview?" Travis asked.

"Kind of draining," Bernadette replied. "Looks like I really screwed this up. I should have called the police sooner. We might not be in this mess."

"Did you get the same message as us?" Melinda asked.

"That we can't leave the island?"

"Yeah, I got that. Sorry, I did not know my intuition would be so bad," Bernadette said.

"No one gets everything right—you did your best. You saved me from being taken by them," Travis said. "I don't know what we'd do without you being here." He put his arm around Bernadette again and hugged her.

"Thanks," Bernadette said. She pushed herself out of Travis's hug and patted him on the chest. "Now, how about if we find some food?

An English tourist once told me he felt so hungry that he thought his throat had been cut. I thought that was a funny saying, but that's how I feel right now."

They wandered down a street that led to the waterfront. A small café with wooden benches and a hole in the wall for ordering from the kitchen that had a limited menu of beer and wine. Travis bought some local beers from the window and ordered for them.

"They had three Rotis left," Travis said. "Two chicken and one goat. I hope you like it."

"I'm happy to have the goat," Bernadette said. "I love Roti. A friend of mine from St. Thomas introduced me to it. It's kind of like an English meat turnover but filled with curry and vegetables. Goes great with beer."

"You think everything goes great with beer, Bernadette," Melinda said. "And, on that note, I need to find the ladies' room. I'll be right back."

Melinda left the table as Travis stared at his beer, then looked up at Bernadette. "Can you tell me what all this means?"

Bernadette put her beer down. "If you explain the sentence that was going on in your head before your statement—I'll try."

"The men who tried to take us this morning and the dead man— what does it point to? I don't want to have this conversation in front of Melinda. She's got this positive image in her head that mom, dad and Uncle Max will be found safe and sound in a few days once I pull a few million dollars out of a hat—but I know you don't see that."

Bernadette sipped her beer. "Why wouldn't I?"

"Because you were always the most infuriating realist I've ever encountered. You see everything at face value. I'm asking you how you see this scenario playing out now that we have a dead man in the picture. I know you've got something churning through your head."

Bernadette raised her head to meet his gaze. "When criminals use deadly force, they establish a pattern. I'm sure your detective will tell you that when you meet him tomorrow."

"You think they might have murdered us both today?"

"That I don't know. But they murdered the man at the car service. How they knew who Melinda was going to call is something the police will have to investigate. Perhaps they wanted to be sure they had enough time to pick us up without someone alerting the police."

Travis leaned back in his chair as the server delivered their order of rotis. "Do you have any other revelations?"

"Someone has been watching Melinda the entire time she's been on the island. The people who kidnapped your family have someone watching your every move. They tried to take both of us to keep Melinda from having any resources. When your hired help arrives, get someone as a bodyguard to watch out for you."

"You think we're in that much danger?" Travis asked.

"Yes—yes I do... and why isn't Melinda back yet?"

"I don't know, maybe a lineup at the ladies...?"

Bernadette pushed back her chair and hurried to the toilet area. It was just around the corner. She'd seen a man walking there only seconds ago. Her senses were on high alert. Why had she let Melinda go on her own?

She rushed to the toilet area. There was no one there. The ladies' room was occupied. A door opened; Melinda stepped out.

"Hey Bernadette, sorry if I'm holding you up. I couldn't find the toilet paper in there, had to use a tissue," Melinda said. She stopped and looked at Bernadette. "Is everything okay?"

"I'm fine, the food arrived—it's getting cold."

"Sure, there was a lineup when I got here. And some man was lurking about making us ladies jumpy."

"What did he look like?"

"He was kind of slim with red eyes, I think it was the eyes that scared us. He stood over by the trees, just staring—kind of freaky."

"Do you think he was watching you?"

"Well... I'm not sure... oh my God, do you think that was the man from this morning?" Melinda said, holding her hand to her mouth.

"I don't know, all men can act weird sometimes, but let's get back to our table."

They walked back to the safety of the glow of the café and the streetlights. Bernadette whirled around to look behind her. A man disappeared into the bushes. The feeling of dread hit her again. They would have to be careful from now on—she would have to have another conversation with Travis.

12

ASSISTANT SUPERINTENDENT CHARLES lied to Bernadette Callahan. He knew Steven Charles. His family was from Gros Islet. Steven's mother had gotten in trouble over some merchandise she'd claimed she purchased from a local vendor—the vendor stated she'd stolen it.

Charles was a constable then, and the woman was all of twenty years old. Steven was hanging on her side in dirty diapers. Charles couldn't see the value of her spending time in jail with such a young child. He made it right with the vendor and asked her to never get into trouble again. But now her boy lay dead so someone could assume his identity and steal his Mercedes.

Charles would drive to Gros Islet tomorrow and visit the mother. It was the least he could do for her. Now, as he pushed his papers to the side of his desk, he wished for a cigarette. He didn't wish—he craved one from the depth of his soul, or at least that's where he thought the desire came from.

He picked up a pack of chewing gum, exhaled, and put a piece in his mouth, and chewed with resolve. He was thirty-six months clean of cigarettes and thirty-eight clean of the cancerous spots that had appeared on his right lung as if an alien life form had dropped in to destroy him.

Pouring himself a glass of water, he considered what the young Callahan had told him. He couldn't be entirely cross with her for not contacting the police. She didn't understand the island and acted on instinct to protect her friend. He admired her. He wished he had more like her on his force. She had real intuition—but it made her act instead of analyzing a situation.

Charles had been in law enforcement for twenty years. At fifty-seven years old, he was only a few ranks below the highest in the force, and now, with two major crimes involving tourists, he doubted he'd want the top job.

The head Superintendent was still on the cruise ship investigating the mystery of the missing passenger. The case had fallen to Saint Lucia, as they were the next port of call for the ship. How unlucky was that? The news was having a field day over the three Canadians and the local crew taken hostage. Now, here was a second citizen—an American, no less, who'd gone missing off their coast.

Saint Lucia had no Coast Guard, only Marine Police Units. They were small patrol boats with little ability to do an effective search in the deep ocean. If the man had gone overboard over fifty kilometers off their island, they had little hope of finding him.

Charles knew his boss would make a diplomatic show to prove their concern about any tourists that landed, or almost landed, on their island. Tourists were now the most important commodity on Saint Lucia. In 1997, the government decided that tourism and not bananas would be the principal crop the island would cultivate.

In the past three years, Castries had opened its harbor to a flotilla of cruise ships. They churned up the waters, made the fishermen angry and the shop keepers happy. The ships brought joyous vacationers who spent money on tours, trinkets, and food, and ventured to another island.

The islanders had not witnessed such activity since the pirate raids of the eighteenth century, and this time they were less hostile. Charles was both happy and sad to see the influx of tourists. The people of Saint Lucia benefited from the income, but he didn't like how it made them more dependent on the ships.

His family had grown bananas on a farm near Soufriere. The farm wasn't big, but they sustained themselves. Charles had worked the farm until his early thirties. That was when his father told him he should do something different with his life, and perhaps get married. His father saw no future in bananas and their hardscrabble life.

Charles chose the Royal Saint Lucia Police force. He moved around the island in different posts, then settled in Castries and got married. His wife was from Vieux Fort, raised in the country like himself. Right now, Charles would like to find a small farm and give all this up.

Picking up another report, he gazed at it with interest. A constable had found a link between the lady on the front desk of the hotel and the dead man, Steven Charles. He'd made a note to investigate this in the morning. Right now, he needed some food, the sweet voice of his wife, and to see his children before they went to their rooms and ignored him with their cell phones.

13

BERNADETTE TOOK a long shower and realized Melinda had lied to her. She smelled bad. There was something about long plane rides that made one's body take on the chemical aroma of the inside of the airplane. It took her a few washes and rinses to rid herself of the mix of stale air and the plastic seats.

She put on a bathrobe and wrapped a towel around her hair as she entered the bedroom. Melinda was lying on the bed, still dressed and fast asleep. Bernadette walked as quietly as she could to the little desk with Melinda's laptop.

Melinda had given her the password to log in to her computer and told her to use it whenever she wanted. Bernadette logged in and waited for the modem to boot up. She'd only just begun using a state-of-the-art wireless system before she left university and she was now one of those who found a cable modem slow.

She watched the system boot up and clicked onto the Google site that the older gentlemen named Fred had mentioned this afternoon. In her last year in university, she'd almost lived on Google. If she needed to review a conviction file or an arrest file for a strange case she wanted to use in her studies, invariably she found it here.

Now, she wanted to find out something about the man who'd

gone missing off the cruise ship. She entered the name of Valdis Kalnins and found a site called Caribbean Dreams. Valdis was the president of the company. A further search of a Miami court's legal site showed multiple legal actions against this same Valdis Kalnins.

She sat back in the fancy art deco desk chair, which offered as much comfort as the chair used for a confessional in church and wondered how this connected to the Coopers. Something tugged at her very foggy brain that was fighting jet lag, lack of sleep, and not enough downtime to make sense of everything. Then it hit her. Max was the key.

Bernadette grabbed her room key, padded softly out of the room, went across the hall, and knocked on Travis's door. He answered the door in his underwear and looked like he'd just woken up.

"What's up? Are you okay?" Travis asked.

"I'm fine. I had to ask you a question about your uncle Max," Bernadette said, trying not to let her eyes wander to his six-pack abs and that nice "package" his underwear held hostage.

Travis saw Bernadette's eyes and looked at himself. "Oh my God, so sorry, I'll get my bathrobe." He disappeared and returned to the door. "I apologize, you startled me when you knocked on the door." He took a deep breath. "Now, how can I help you?"

Bernadette's hand adjusted her own bathrobe. She became self-conscious of standing in the hotel hallway in front of a man she'd once had an affair with.

"I'll only take a minute. I just read a bio of the man from the cruise ship who is missing. His name was Valdis Kalnins."

"Yes, that's great, Bernadette. What's your point?"

"He was from Latvia," Bernadette said.

"And... how does this affect... wait a minute, my uncle Max was from Latvia—is that what you're getting at?"

"Yes, that's exactly it. Tomorrow, find out if your uncle and this Valdis crossed paths somehow."

"Once again, you're of the opinion that nothing is random? It's all connected?"

"You know it," Bernadette said.

Travis stood at the door. He moved from one foot to the other. "Did you want to come in for a little while? Maybe have a tea...?" His eyes dropped to her robe and then hit the floor.

Bernadette clutched at the front of her robe. It had fallen open. She turned and marched back to her room. "I'll talk to you in the morning."

She re-entered the room. Melinda lay awake on the bed. "Hi, I just had to speak with Travis for a moment."

Melinda rubbed the sleep from her eyes. "In a bathrobe? Must have been urgent."

"I'll fill you in tomorrow," Bernadette said. She walked back into the bathroom, put her bathrobe away, and dressed in her panties and t-shirt for sleeping. She told herself from now on she needed to control her urges to tell Travis things. Their mutual attraction was still there. They'd touched on it several years ago at the lake. How do you extinguish that? It was obvious they were both still attracted to each other.

The silly move with the bathrobe—what the hell was she thinking? She climbed into bed and tried to put the vision of him, half-naked, out of her mind. If she was ever going to be an efficient cop and eventually a detective in the Royal Canadian Mounted Police, she was going to have to make better judgment calls—that had not been one of them.

Travis Cooper lay awake. He was trying to push the image of Bernadette Callahan out of his head. God, she not only looked good, but there was this scent that emanated from her. It was fresh and clean—it made him want to lean in and breathe her in. How could he have forgotten that night on the dock by the lake? Everything about her was so wild, free, and the epitome of what he wasn't. Was that why he'd fallen so hard for her?

He'd spent years trying to get her out of his mind to focus on his business. There were countless girlfriends and even a few lovers. But none of them had ever measured up to how he imagined Bernadette. Now, here she was in the flesh, and it was an amazing package at that. She looked all suntanned, strong, and confident.

He'd wanted to take her in his arms, kiss her long and hard, and throw her on his bed. All of that was in his imagination. He had to block all these thoughts out as he tried to think about his family. He was here to rescue them, Bernadette being here was a gift to both his sister and him. She was a wonderful human being that he just wished he didn't want to sleep with the moment he lay eyes on her.

"Listen, you bloody idiot, tomorrow you will investigate the link between Uncle Max and the guy, Valdis, something or other to discover if there's a link. The next time you speak to Bernadette, you will apologize for inviting her into your room..."

Travis sighed deeply, placed the pillow over his head, and mumbled, "You are such a dumb ass, Travis Cooper."

He finally fell into a deep sleep and did not see the note that was slipped under his door.

14

BERNADETTE WOKE up at six a.m., she didn't want to, but her body clock was back in Western Canada. She got out of bed and opened the closet. Melinda had neatly hung up all her clothes and arranged her shoes in a tidy row.

Until now, she had only an idea of what her aunt Mary packed for her. There was a pair of running shoes, socks, and a pair of shorts with a few t-shirts.

"Well, this is a pleasant surprise," she whispered to herself. She looked over to see Melinda still sleeping.

Bernadette hadn't run in several weeks. The past three months had been riding horses, setting up camp, taking care of horses, and helping with the tourists. On her one day off a week, she tried to fit in some trail running in the town of Banff, but invariably the mountains called her. She couldn't resist long hikes into the backcountry with a fly rod to fish for trout in the hidden lakes.

The trout were feisty up there. They fought hard on the lure and Bernadette always released them. She felt as if they were special and earned their hidden place. Only once did she not release a fish. It was when a large grizzly bear came ambling by. She left a large trout for him by the lake to feast on so she could pack her gear and leave. The bear enjoyed the meal.

She dressed in her running gear and softly closed the door behind her. The air conditioner hummed in the hallway and a housekeeper dressed in a t-shirt and shorts pushed her cart towards the exit.

Bernadette saw two police officers in the lobby sitting with a young lady that looked like Sabina. As Bernadette got closer, she saw the name badge, "Nadia," on her dress. The young lady was holding back tears. Another man, he looked like a manager, was sitting beside her with a tissue.

The doors opened automatically as Bernadette walked outside. She would have loved to have lingered to find out what the situation was, but she had an idea. Nadia was the one that made the car service reservations.

The assistant superintendent she'd met last night was following the chain of events. Bernadette's police studies had drummed that into her. Follow what came next. Now, they'd have to find out who intercepted the call to the car service.

Bernadette began a slow jog out of the hotel driveway and back to the street they'd walked the night before to the car service. They parked a police car outside the car service with caution tape draped across the door.

She knew the forensics team would have been in there. Bernadette had allowed herself to be fingerprinted last night. She'd suggested it before they asked. They had taught her crime scene investigation 101, to always eliminate potential suspects. They'd find her prints on the front door but not on the office door. She'd smelled dried blood at the office door. It had a metallic smell that was unmistakable. To open the door, she used her elbow.

The lecture from Dr. Ramesh, the city coroner, came back to her. "Human blood contains water and iron. It has a smell similar to rust. This is an olfactory illusion, smell a paper clip. It does not smell the same," the doctor had said while they'd stared at a line of corpses in the morgue.

That odor alerted her a dead body or human in severe distress was behind that door. The abundance of flies on the body told her without a doubt the body was in decay. Dr. Ramesh had an entire lecture about flies and maggots on the human body. Bernadette kept the doctor's words out of her mind so she could enjoy things like food and the touch of a fellow human being. Sometimes you had to block things—that was one of them.

She continued her run up the street, dodging around food stalls and street vendors and watching out for the cracks in the pavement. The sidewalk dropped off sharply into a deep storm drain that took care of the rainy season's sudden deluges.

Bernadette had read on her flight down that the best season to be here was December to May. This was not the season, but then again, she wasn't here for the sights; the goal was to get the Cooper family back.

She found a steep hill and charged up it. Her heart pounded, and she felt better. After she'd run for a good forty-five minutes, she turned around and ran back to the hotel. She stopped occasionally, not to catch her breath, but to see if anyone was following her. There was no sign of a tail. She kept going all the way to the hotel.

The police had gone from the car service company and from the lobby of the hotel. Bernadette made it back to the room and took a shower. She dressed in a pair of shorts, a t-shirt, and flip-flops, and headed back out the door. There was a small restaurant beside the lobby where Travis and Melinda were sitting.

"You enjoy your run?" Travis asked.

"Yeah, haven't been able to get one in for some time," Bernadette said. The server came with coffee into which she spooned two sugars and a sizeable amount of cream.

Melinda looked at Travis, then back to Bernadette. "Travis found a note under his door this morning."

Bernadette stopped and put her coffee down. "What did it say?"

Travis pulled a piece of paper out of his pocket, unfolded it, and read, "We will deliver all your family and crew to you in five days.

The price is ten million US dollars. We will deal only with you. Get rid of your detective."

Bernadette read the paper while sipping her coffee. "The note is a print copy of an email."

"What do you think we should do, Bernadette? Do we take this to the police or wait for our detective?" Melinda asked.

"I think it's obvious you need to let the police know," Bernadette said. She turned to Travis. "Any idea what time this note arrived?"

"No, I went to bed after you left my room—my door, I mean," Travis said as his face turned a shade of red Bernadette hadn't seen before.

"It could have happened anytime during the night. The police will have to investigate who worked last night and who had access to the hotel. I don't see any CCTV cameras, so it's going to be the old-fashioned interviews of people. Your detective doesn't have the personnel for that or the local knowledge of the people who work here," Bernadette said.

"You're right, Bernadette, I'll take this to the police station right now," Travis said.

"I'll go with you; I need to get out of this hotel for a while and I like to see how the police will react to this," Melinda said. "Will you be okay on your own, Bernadette?"

Bernadette looked up from her coffee and smiled.

"What am I saying? Of course you'll be all right," Melinda said. She picked up her handbag and walked out of the hotel.

They left Bernadette alone at the table with a large pot of coffee, cream, and sugar. She couldn't be happier for the moment. When the server dropped off a basket of sweet rolls, the day got even better.

The thoughts of the kidnapping occupied her thoughts as she munched through her third roll. She was about to dig into the fourth when a man came through the door and walked towards her.

He was in his late twenties and wore a pair of dark blue dress trousers with a light blue short-sleeve shirt. A silver pen shone brightly in his shirt pocket, his right hand gripped a spiral notebook. He had reporter written all over him.

Bernadette dabbed at her lips with a napkin and pushed her plate away. She'd been warned not to get involved in anything. This was the worst-case scenario coming to visit.

"Good morning, I understand you are Bernadette Callahan. My name is Lucas David. I'm a reporter at The Saint Lucian Daily Press. I am led to believe you discovered a dead man last night," he said as he stopped in front of her table and looked down at her with a smile.

"Well, you have my name right," Bernadette said. She took her napkin off her lap, placed it on the table, and stood. "I can confirm that I discovered the body of the unfortunate man, but that's all the police will allow me to say. If you need more, you'll have to ask them."

"But the police sent me to talk to you," Lucas protested.

"I doubt it. You got my name from one of the police who heard my name and gave it to you. You came here to do a little fishing. Nice try Lucas."

"Yes, but—"

"Is this person bothering you, madame?" a large man asked as he placed a hand on Lucas's shoulder.

"Yes, I'd like him to leave," Bernadette said.

"I'm Andrew Xavier, the hotel manager, and I'll escort this man out of the hotel."

"Thank you, Andrew," Bernadette said. She couldn't have been happier with the intervention of the manager. He escorted the reporter out the door.

"I'm sorry that he bothered you. I'll inform the front desk. The reporter will not bother you again," Xavier said on his return.

Bernadette left the table and headed for her room. On entering the room, she turned on Melinda's laptop and checked her email account. It took her only a few minutes to see Lucas David had filed a report for his paper last night.

"Looks like you were making a name for yourself, Lucas," Bernadette said. Her Aunt Mary had forwarded the newspaper's account of the death in Castries.

"Nice move, you little shit," she muttered as she continued to look at the news reports from Caribbean News, Reuters International, and several Miami newspapers. Saint Lucia already had a spotlight on it from the missing Canadians. Now Bernadette Callahan, a Canadian and law enforcement student selected to join the famous Royal Canadian Mounted Police in September, was on the scene and had discovered a dead body—what was the connection to the missing Canadians the articles asked?

Bernadette sat back in the chair and opened a bottle of water. She had to admire the reporter. He'd done his work and found her from her class list at university and dug the RCMP connection out of one of the police in Castries. That was his job, and he'd done it well. She wanted to kick his ass, but that was her natural reaction.

She breathed a sigh of relief, seeing no email from the RCMP academy in Regina. But as she scrolled down further, there it was. A memo from the human resources department in Regina, Canada, asking to clarify her involvement in the investigation into a murder investigation. The request was for a full written report of her involvement and the incident report from the police in Saint Lucia. The depot commander of the academy would review the report and let her know if they would continue to welcome her as a recruit.

"Aw shit, Bernadette, you knew you'd step in it, and you did." She slumped in the chair, took a long drink of her water, and prepared to write the email that would have to save her career in the only police force she'd ever applied to.

15

BERNADETTE STARED at the laptop and pondered what she would say to the human resources department of the RCMP. Could she get a favorable police report from the Saint Lucian Police? She bit her lip as her finger hovered over the keys.

She felt stuck in a void of analysis paralysis, a definition she hated. One of her mentors had said, it's better to move than hesitate in a crisis. With that thought in mind, she dialed the number of her friend, Detective Linda Myers, in Edmonton.

Myers picked up on the second ring, "Detective Myers speaking."

"Hey, it's me, Bernadette,"

"I hope you're calling me to tell me you need a ride back from the airport," Myers said with a sound of disapproval in her voice.

"Ah.... no, I'm still in Saint Lucia. I can't leave until the investigation finishes," Bernadette replied.

"Want to guess how I found out you were in Saint Lucia?"

"No... I..."

"An officer comes over to me, drops the Edmonton Journal on my desk this morning and says, hey Myers, isn't that the smart-ass kid you saved from the gangs years ago?"

"Sorry, I should've told you, Myers, I was kind of in a rush."

"Really? Is that why you didn't call? Or is it because this is the dumbest thing you've ever done in a bunch of dumbass things? I thought you got over saving the world and taking matters into your own hands when you joined the RCMP?"

"Yeah, well, Melinda and I go a long way back—so I kind of have a question for you on this," Bernadette said in a quiet voice. Myers had saved her from the gangs back in her high school days and got her into karate that helped her take care of herself. She'd also inspired her to join the police. Bernadette had chosen the RCMP instead of the city police. It was not a choice Myers condoned, but she respected Bernadette's decision.

"You need to make it right with your force because you received an email from them requesting an explanation of your involvement?" Myers asked.

Bernadette slumped in her chair, "Yeah, that would be it. I screwed up big time, but I couldn't let it go. There're some killers loose down here and I may have seen them when I arrived."

Myers paused, "Damn it, girl, I can't fault you for your moral integrity. I just wish you were joining our force; I got strings I could pull here. Do you have anyone on the inside of the RMCP you can reach out to?"

Bernadette ran her hand through her hair. "Not really, the only guy I know was my trail boss in Banff, but he's been out of the force for twenty years."

"Then write your little confessional to human resources, tell them what happened and how you were exercising your judgment. And get the investigating officer in Saint Lucia to write something—if you haven't pissed him off—then pray."

"I guess I couldn't have asked for any better advice. Thanks again, Linda, you've always had my back."

"Well, I would have had your back had you called me before you went—I would have told you to stay home."

"Yeah, that's why I didn't call."

Myers laughed, "You're still a righteous little shit."

BERNADETTE HUNG up and got busy with the email to the RCMP. She did exactly as Myers had suggested with the chain of events and how she'd been able to save Travis. She hoped this letter might save her job.

An hour later, she emailed the RCMP and Assistant Superintendent Vernon Charles. She felt exhausted and needed to get out of the room. A large swimming pool on the side of the hotel would be the right thing to relax.

Pulling open a drawer, she found the two swimsuits her aunt had packed for her. She rolled her eyes as she picked them up—bikinis. For a moment, she'd hoped for the nice swimsuit she trained with back at university.

Competitive swimming had saved her sanity back then, and now, she could have used a nice tight-fitting Speedo swimsuit, a pair of swim goggles, and a good hour of doing lengths. A bikini was good for suntanning and hanging by the pool.

She took a quick shower to rinse herself off and slipped into a little yellow number that revealed more than it concealed. As she adjusted the top and looked at herself in the mirror, she tried to remember where she'd last worn this. The memory escaped her. Throwing on a cover-up, she grabbed her hotel key and headed for the pool.

There was no one there. Bernadette found a lounge chair under an umbrella, threw a towel over it, and slipped into the pool. The water was refreshing and only slightly cooler than the heat of the day.

At first, she tried to do the crawl. The bikini was next to useless. The top took on water in the fast strokes she made. She changed into the butterfly, and that was just as bad. In desperation, she flipped over and did the backstroke.

She made long strokes with her arms and lazy kicks with her legs. It felt great. Reaching the end of the pool, she was about to do her quick roll and return when she saw Travis.

Travis stood at the end of the pool, staring down at Bernadette with a vacant look on his face. As Bernadette swam towards him, he snapped out of his trance. He shuffled from one foot to the other and stuck his hands in his pockets.

"Hey, Travis, how was the meeting with the police?" Bernadette asked. She put her hands on the end of the pool and looked up at him.

"Well, not great. We couldn't meet with Vernon Charles as he was out for the morning, so we showed the note to one of his constables. He said he'd pass it to Charles when he returned to the office He wanted nothing to do with it."

Bernadette put her hands on the pool ladder and pulled herself out of the water. "Sounds like you ran into the one guy on their force who didn't want to be involved in the responsibility of a chain of evidence. When is Charles back?"

"He's back around two. Until then, I guess we just wait for my detective to show up," Travis said as he averted his eyes from Bernadette to look out over the harbor.

Bernadette followed Travis's gaze and wondered what his problem was. She looked down at her top to see it had fallen quite low. With one hand, she pulled it up and reached for her towel on the chair. As she toweled herself off, a flash of memory came to her. She'd worn this bikini on a deck by the lake when she was eighteen. Travis had been beside her—they'd drank a few rums and fallen into each other's arms.

Dr. Luke Cooper discovered them intertwined in the boathouse with Bernadette straddling Travis and doing a dive in his throat with her tongue. That was the end of the summer fling that left a small ember of desire burning between them all these years. A red tinge spread over her cheeks with the memory.

Bernadette shook off the vision and wrapped the towel around her. She walked over to Travis and stood a few feet from him. "I need to get my head around the ransom note you received. I think I'm in jet lag brain fog."

"What do you need to understand?"

"How would the kidnappers learn you'd hired a detective? Did you tell the media?"

"I only told Melinda and you when you picked me up yesterday," Travis said. He pulled his sunglasses out of his shirt pocket and put them on.

"Let's sit under an umbrella, you are too fair-skinned for this heat," Bernadette said. She took him by the hand and led him to a table with two chairs under an umbrella. The pool was still empty of anyone but them.

Bernadette threw off the towel. It was too hot to wear. She noticed Travis's eyes flicked down and over her swimsuit. She suppressed a smile and got back to the subject. "You said you only told Melinda and me about the hiring of this detective, and yet the note said you had to get rid of your detective. Is that correct?"

Travis pulled off his sunglasses. "Why didn't I think of that? Of course, that's right."

Bernadette shook her head. "If we're the only ones who knew, how would the kidnappers find out? Did you tell anyone else? You need to think hard about this. There's a key here to how the kidnappers knew we were arriving yesterday."

Travis closed his eyes for a minute, then opened them wide. "I made a phone call back to Vancouver last night. I spoke to my legal advisor and told him we'd be adding some personal protection for us and that the head of the detective agency was arriving today."

"Did you give your lawyer your detective's name?"

"Yes, I told him about Thomas Davina."

"Did you tell him when he's arriving today?"

"No, why would I do that?"

"Just asking," Bernadette replied.

"I had a voice mail in my room from his detective agency that gave me his flight number and that he'd be renting a car at the airport."

"Do you still have the voice mail?"

"Yes, I haven't cleared it yet."

Bernadette got out of her chair. "When you called Vancouver, did you use your cell phone or the phone in your room?"

"I used the phone in my room. It's clearer than my cell for making a long-distance call. Why do you ask?"

"We need to check your room right now. Let's go," Bernadette said.

16

BERNADETTE GRABBED Travis's hand and pulled him out of his chair. Her strength amazed him. They ran hand in hand to the hotel, entered the lobby, and nodded at the front desk clerk. She smiled at the sight of them.

They looked like two lovers about to indulge in a "nooner." She gave a wink at Bernadette and continued about her business.

Bernadette ignored her—they hurried down the hallway. Travis put his key card into the door and opened it. "What are you looking for?"

Without replying, Bernadette picked up the phone receiver beside his bed and took the back off it. She cautioned Travis to not make a sound—she showed him a small metal disk, then closed the phone and replaced it on the nightstand. They walked out of the room and stood in the hallway.

"Is a mini recorder?" Travis asked.

"Yes, it's a bug—a listening device."

"Damn it, I'm in the software business, I should have checked for this when I arrived," Travis said.

"You're not wired for deception and bad guys; you look for glitches in programs. Whoever these guys are, they learned where

Melinda was staying and placed that on your phones. Let's check Melinda's room. I'm sure there's one there as well."

They stood at the door to the room and Bernadette flushed as she took her key card out of her bikini top. Travis watched her, then averted his eyes.

Bernadette knocked on the door to alert Melinda she was coming in. She walked past Melinda to the phone on the desk and checked the back. She found the same small disk and closed the back of the phone and carefully closed the phone, and turned to face her friends.

Melinda was about to speak—Bernadette put her hand to her lips.

Travis shook his head and said, "How about we meet in the hotel lounge?"

"Good plan," Bernadette said. "I'll change and join you there." She went into the bathroom, got out of her bikini, did a rinse in the shower, and changed into shorts and a t-shirt.

Ten minutes later, she found Travis sitting with Melinda at a small table.

"I filled Melinda in on our conversation," Travis said. "And I ordered a round of rum punch."

Bernadette dropped into her chair, "Well, now you know how these guys found out when we were arriving and the car service we used. When the police get here, you can show them what we found."

"I've never been more frightened in all my life," Melinda said. "The kidnappers are listening to every plan we've made on the telephone."

The server brought the round of rum punch. Melinda took the drink and almost downed it in one gulp.

"Easy there, girl," Bernadette said. "You'll need to be coherent when the police arrive." She turned to Travis. "Can you contact Detective Davina when he lands?"

"Yes, he gave me his cell number. I'll let him know they've tapped all our conversations?"

"Good idea. Now we need to look around the hotel to see where the recorders for the transmitters are. Those things aren't sophisticated, they only transmit one hundred to three hundred meters. Someone has to come in and take the tapes away."

"Why not wait for the police?" Melinda asked.

"We could save them some time," Bernadette said with a wink, while she sipped her drink and looked around the hotel lobby to see where someone might hide a remote recorder.

"Hold that thought. I'm going to call Davina," Travis said. He walked away from the table and called Davina, letting him know about what they found in the hotel room and that the kidnappers were aware of their movements—and perhaps he might be careful on arrival.

Detective Thomas Davina didn't get Travis's message. By the time he'd turned his phone on, he had three urgent messages ahead of the one from Travis. He moved slowly through customs, then grabbed his bags.

His man, Ezra Williams, met him in front of the rental car kiosk. They immediately began discussing the case and didn't see the man they'd cut in front of in the rental line.

"Hey, what are you doing?" A heavy-set man, with gold chains around his large neck, asked in an angry tone.

Thomas looked up, seeing the man for the first time. "I apologize. I didn't see you there. Of course, please, after you."

"You cannot just cut in front of me. Who do you think you are?" the man asked, working himself into a fury. His voice was deep and with a Spanish accent.

"Again, I apologize, and to make it right, how about I give you my rental car? They've given me an upgrade. Please take it with my compliments."

"Yes, now you're showing me respect. Good, I will take your car. Now get out of my way," the man said. He completed the paperwork, took his keys, and strutted out of the airport as if he'd just won a major battle.

Ezra watched him walk away. "I could take that guy down if you like. A big turd like that would have given me a bit of exercise after my flight."

Davina smiled. "I don't need to worry about any more people on this island. You screw with him; you screw with his friends. We've got work to do." He grabbed his keys. "And besides, this fine lady gave us an SUV. Should be good on the bad roads here."

They walked out the sliding doors of the airport just as a car exploded in the rental parking lot. Ezra grabbed Thomas and pushed him back inside. "That was your upgrade, boss!"

17

THE SMOKE CLEARED. Sirens sounded in the distance as they approached the airport. Thomas and Ezra stood there for a moment to assess the situation. Security guards tried in vain to douse the flames with handheld fire extinguishers. The fire engulfed the car.

"What's the plan?" Ezra asked.

"Did the explosion destroy our vehicle?"

"No, I can see the Suzuki SUV at the end of the row, away from the wreck. We could go around the side, get in, and be off. You think we should leg it?" Ezra asked.

"If that's your English term for get out of here—I'm in," Thomas said, picking up his bag. "We could be here for hours—someone tried to kill us. I don't want to wait around to see who comes by to check if we're dead."

"Copy that, boss. Let's go—I hate giving long-winded reports to coppers."

They walked quickly towards their rental by using the exit road from the airport, then angled back into the rental parking lot. Ezra opened the back hatch, threw in their luggage, and got behind the wheel. Thomas jumped into the passenger seat.

No one attempted to stop them. All eyes were on the burning car. In minutes, they'd left the flames and smoke behind them.

Ezra kept the SUV at the speed limit and repeatedly looked in the rear-view mirror for someone following them. Thomas turned and looked behind them, then opened his cell phone.

"I have a message from our client," Thomas said as he listened to the voicemail.

Ezra kept his eyes glued to the road, watching ahead in case someone might try to attack them on the route. He'd spent his entire working life in the army, with a long stint in special forces in Belize. He was adept at jungle fighting. This long highway with multiple ambush points made him uneasy. They had no weapons. He could evade or outrun another vehicle, but he didn't like either option.

Thomas listened to the message and closed his phone. "Well, that confirms it, the kidnappers had our clients' rooms bugged. They knew we were coming—the car bomb was our welcome committee."

"I didn't see a spotter," Ezra said.

"Neither did I, but in the blast's confusion, whoever was there to ensure we're dead couldn't get close enough. That was one hell of a big bomb."

Ezra chuckled, "yeah, a bit of overkill as we used to say in the army. A bit of a waste of good gelignite, to my thinking."

"Ah, the British humor," Thomas said. "But we must realize how sophisticated they are. They discovered our arrival last night, tapped into the car rental reservation system, and planted the bomb."

"Or they bribed someone at the car agency to give you an upgrade when you came in. They could have said they wanted to do it as a surprise."

"No, too much face time on that one. They must have come to the airport this morning with a laptop, did an easy hack by accessing the rental car agency's website and getting into their reservation system. They waited for the car to be serviced, then they placed the charge," Thomas said.

Ezra nodded in agreement, "that's pretty much what my unit

would have done in Guatemala when we wanted to rid ourselves of a target."

Thomas looked at Ezra, "Really, I didn't know the Brits did such clandestine operations?"

Ezra shook his head, "You're joking, right—you Canadians never did that?"

Thomas smiled, "Only when no one was looking." He took out his phone again. "Now it's time we take the fight to our kidnappers. I'm calling Ramirez."

"Who's he?"

"Ex-US Army Ranger. He arrived yesterday. I sent him to get some supplies and to get any intel from the locals on our missing persons."

Ezra winked, "Yeah, so you hired me, an English black man, and a Spanish guy—so we'd fit in with the locals—nice one."

Thomas patted Ezra on the shoulder. "You get my methods. This country is over ninety percent black and I'd stand out like a proverbial sore thumb as I made the rounds to question the locals. You two can work together and hit every dive bar and backwater community on this little island."

"You think this job is going to be a breeze, don't you?"

Thomas turned to look at the road. "You bet; I've made reservations at Sandals Resorts in Rodney Bay for six days from now. My wife is flying in, and the kids are staying with their grandparents at the lake north of the city."

"Must be why they pay you the big bucks, boss, and I'm living with the wife and kids in Dangriga, one of the worst shit holes in Belize," Ezra said.

"Why do you stay there?"

"The wife is Spanish, and all her relatives are there. I do some work for a Canadian expedition company and the few jobs with you to tide me over. It's not bad, keeps me occupied."

"Well, after this little job, you'll be doing fine. I'll give bonuses to both you and Ramirez if we wrap up in six days. Maybe you should bring your wife to Sandals to celebrate."

"Nice offer, but me wife, she's a simple lady, no airs and graces for her, as we say back in the old country. We have a nice roof over our heads, time with the kids, and a big family dinner every Sunday. She doesn't want much," Ezra said with a sheepish grin.

"Well, suit yourself," Thomas said. He punched in the number for Ramirez. He listened for a moment and put the phone away. "That's strange, the phone rang and didn't go to voice mail."

"Maybe he's already made some contacts," Ezra said.

"Yeah, that must be it. I'll call later," Thomas said, closing his phone. It was strange that Ramirez hadn't checked in with him. He should have done it yesterday when he landed. He didn't do that. Thomas had a feeling this contract would not be as easy as he hoped. These hostage-takers were not playing by any rules he was used to. He'd need to be careful.

18

FRIDA COOPER PACED the tiny room while Luke took his turn lying on the bed. They'd lost track of their days in captivity—was it a week? She paced in her bare feet to keep the noise down as Luke napped.

A door slammed outside. A low muffled voice that she recognized was approaching. Her name for the little man who was their caretaker was Tony Montana.

The man reminded her of Al Pacino's character in the movie Scarface. He wore his shirt open all the time, with a habit of raising his eyebrows as he spoke. His English wasn't good, and Frida's Spanish was worse, so they used some words and hand gestures to communicate.

The key rattled in the door. Frida rushed over to Luke to get him up—she didn't want to face Tony on her own. Luke understood a little more Spanish than her and somehow, they pieced together the conversations.

Tony pushed the door open and stood inside. His eyes moved from Frida to Luke as if he was doing inventory. The door closed behind him, and he stepped in.

He thrust a folded piece of paper towards Luke. "You—write letter—do it now!"

Luke opened the paper and read the instructions.. "They want me to write Travis a letter."

"What do they want you to say?" Frida asked.

"They want me to request ten million US dollars for our release."

"Si, ten million," Tony said with a smile. It was the first time he'd smiled, with a gold tooth that sparkled while his eyebrows danced up and down.

Frida turned her back on Tony and whispered to Luke, "Can Travis raise that kind of money?"

Luke sighed and whispered, "Perhaps Travis can bargain with them. I'll write the letter. This is the start we've been looking for." He looked at Tony, "Yes, I will write the letter."

Tony smiled even more. He knocked on the door and shouted for a pen and paper. The door opened, and another man walked in. He was the total opposite of Tony. He had a thick build with enormous arms and hands. His head looked like an extension of his neck, everything about him suggested violence.

"I am glad you do this," the man said in an accent that sounded vaguely Slavic. "This will go well for you—you must tell your son we deal only with him—you understand?"

"Yes, I understand. I will write the letter," Luke said as he took the paper from the Spaniard and wrote.

"Make it simple words, nothing fancy. I will check this later. You understand."

"He understands, he's writing..." Frida said in frustration.

"Good, and tell him, if I don't get money—I kill you —Understand?"

Luke swallowed hard, Frida grabbed his arm to steady him, and he wrote.

"Dear Travis, our captors want ten million dollars for our release. Please do as they say, or they will kill us."

"Your loving mother and father."

The big man took the paper and looked over it and scowled as he mouthed the words. He shoved the paper back at Luke.

"You must sign the paper—both of you sign!"

Luke signed his name and gave it to Frida. She signed it and handed it back to the man. He looked at it and nodded.

Both men left the room. Frida and Luke collapsed on the bed. Neither of them spoke. In all their years together, they'd experienced nothing like this. Frida hoped they had signed a note for their freedom, but somehow, in the back of her mind, it felt like a death sentence.

19

EZRA PARKED the SUV away from the hotel and grabbed the bags. Thomas took a moment to survey the surroundings, several unoccupied cars lined the street opposite the hotel. A small park across the street was empty. A two-story office building a short distance down the block faced the hotel. His eyes flicked from one window to the other to see if there was the flash of binoculars or a camera lens—there was nothing.

He turned and followed Ezra into the hotel. A group of tourists clinked glasses in hearty cheers in the lobby lounge bar. The sound made his mouth water. He craved a large vodka with enough ice to cool him off and quiet his nerves.

The near-miss at the airport had put him on edge. He was used to hunting captives and finding people who didn't want to be found. Someone had made him a target. He didn't like it.

Ezra stood in the lobby waiting for him. "Who am I bunking with?"

"I put you in with Ramirez. Let me see what room he's in," Thomas replied, hoping Ramirez hadn't answered his phone because he was sleeping.

He walked to the front desk. "Could you please call Mr. Ramirez and let him know Thomas Davina is in the lobby to meet him?"

The desk clerk gave him a quizzical look, then went to her computer. "Mr. Ramirez has not checked in with us, sir. I see he was to arrive last night."

"Thank you. I'm the one who booked it. Please put Mr. Williams in that room, and I'll check into mine," Thomas said. He looked over his shoulder to see Ezra looking at him. Now he'd have to explain the absence of Ramirez.

He collected the key cards and turned towards Ezra. Travis Cooper walked into the lobby and walked towards him. Thomas drew in a breath and let his own problems recede into the background. He had a client to think of.

"Mr. Cooper," Thomas said, shaking his hand. "So glad to see you. Have you had any news we can discuss?"

"I've been expecting the police to come by at any moment. We've had a note from the kidnappers, and we found recording devices attached to our phones in our room. I left you a voicemail to warn you that someone might harm you as they tried to do me and my friend Bernadette Callahan," Travis said. The words rushed out of him so quickly he needed to catch his breath.

"We need to find somewhere private to speak," Thomas said. He ushered Travis into the lobby bar and ordered coffee for Travis and himself. His large vodka would have to wait.

"When did you find these devices?" Thomas asked, leaning forward across the table.

"Only a few hours ago. My friend Bernadette clued into it when I found a note under my door from the kidnappers."

Thomas arched an eyebrow, "Ah, you have a note—what did it say?"

"They want ten million US dollars and they said I have to get rid of the detective I hired. When my friend Bernadette noticed they used the word detective, she knew someone must know of your arrival. I tried to warn you with a phone call and left a voicemail."

Thomas winced. "I never got your message until after they tried to get rid of me with a bomb in my rental car. Luckily I gave it to someone else." He smiled at the server who delivered his coffee, and continued, "Sometimes it pays to be as polite a Canadian as the world believes we are."

"Oh my God, someone tried to kill you?"

"Well, it seems they tried. And sadly, Mr. Ramirez has not shown up as well, but we must get to the problem at hand. Let's have a visit with the little bugs in your room."

Travis led Thomas down the hall to his room. He showed him the phone. Thomas opened the back of the phone, examined it, and put it back, and the two men exited the room.

"Is the one in your sister's room the same?" Thomas asked.

"Yes, the same. And none of us have touched it in case you're wondering about fingerprints."

"That's fine, but I doubt they'll be able to lift anything off it. It's a simple device that needs a wireless recorder of no more than three hundred meters away. That's about its range."

"That's what Bernadette said as well."

"Who is this, Bernadette? Is she some other security you hired as well as me?" Thomas asked. He looked slightly put out by someone second-guessing what he knew.

Travis shook his head, "No, she's a good friend of ours who Melinda brought down to help us. Unfortunately, Melinda didn't know I was going to hire you. She arrived yesterday and has become involved in the investigation. She's a graduate of university police studies and enrolled in the RCMP this fall."

"Excellent, I'll have to meet with her later to discuss her views on this investigation."

"You can speak to me right now," Bernadette said.

Thomas whirled around to see Bernadette standing in the hallway.

"I'm Bernadette Callahan and happy to help in any way I can," she said, extending her hand.

"I'm delighted to meet you. I understand you're quite the amateur sleuth." Thomas said as he shook her hand.

Bernadette didn't bat an eye at the slight putdown, "Whatever I can do to help." She looked at Travis, "Do you want me to show you where they've been receiving the recordings from the telephones?"

"You found it?" Thomas asked.

"There's an air vent in the hallway. I noticed it had marks on it—made it obvious someone had tampered with it. There's a recorder inside with an antenna. I didn't mess with it as they'll be back to retrieve it," Bernadette said.

Thomas smiled at Bernadette, "You must have graduated top of your class. That is excellent investigative work."

Bernadette shrugged. "Not that hard. I walked up and down the hallway and wondered where I'd hide a receiver that can only be one to three hundred meters from the rooms. The air vents are an obvious choice. It's at the end of this hallway."

"Can you show me?" Thomas asked

Bernadette nodded and walked down the corridor and stood over a vent. She took out a ten-cent Canadian coin and unscrewed the vent. Sitting inside was a small device with a cassette and an antenna.

Thomas kneeled beside it. "Pretty simple, you could buy this at most spy stores in North America. These are easy to manage and cheap. You don't need anyone with a scanner nearby who might be noticed. But they need to come in every morning and change the tape."

"When I went for a run early yesterday morning, I saw a woman in shorts and a t-shirt pushing a maid's cart. All day I've watched the other room cleaners. None of them dressed like that. I enquired with the front desk if any cleaners came in at six in the morning. They told me none of them started until ten. That must be who was retrieving the recording."

"How about if we set up a watch for the early morning and put a tail on whoever comes to pick it up?" Bernadette asked.

Thomas looked up at Bernadette. "That's an excellent idea, I love how you think, young lady."

"Ah, the police are here," Travis said, motioning with his head towards the lobby. "I'll go meet them."

Thomas and Bernadette stood in the corridor while Travis spoke with several uniformed officers. Travis walked back with one of them. He was a round man of thirty-five with sergeant's stripes on his short-sleeve uniform.

"This is Sergeant Alphonse; he is taking over the investigation from Assistant Superintendent Charles as he's taking command of a car bomb incident at the airport."

"I understand you have had a note from the kidnappers. I've given the note to our forensics unit," Sergeant Alphonse said. "Please show me the recording devices you have found."

Thomas pointed to the register. "The recording device is in there, and the transmitters are in the rooms of Melinda and Travis Cooper."

"Excellent, my men will dust them for prints then take them into evidence."

"No, you can't do that," Bernadette said. "You could set a trap for the kidnappers when someone comes to pick up the tape tomorrow morning."

The sergeant smiled and shook his head, "We practice police science on this island, not some kind of detective work you see in American movies. Thank you for pointing this out for us. I will have one of my men posted outside the hotel in case the kidnappers contact you. Thank you and enjoy the rest of your day." He returned to his men, gave his orders, and they marched back with equipment to dust the recorder and bag it for evidence.

Travis watched the police as they entered his room, took the devices, and left. Bernadette stood beside him. He put his arm around her. "What do we do now?"

Bernadette put her head on his shoulder, "It's time to dig for clues."

20

TRAVIS WALKED with Bernadette to the lobby area and found a place on a sofa. The police moved around with dusting powder and evidence bags. They watched with interest as they sat close to each other. Bernadette had given up caring about Travis's increased advances. The attention felt nice. If she got to her training academy in time, this would be the last man she'd be this close to. The next six months would be in a barracks with other women and in training with a bunch of over-hyped men trying to show how they were superior to the women.

"What did you mean by dig?" Travis asked. He looked at her, his eyes searched hers. Bernadette had to swallow hard not lose her focus.

"The police took away our one lead, we could have followed whoever came for the tape back to their drop. That would have been a slam dunk, as they say in basketball. And the sergeant is placing a police cordon around the hotel. That will keep the kidnappers from getting in close to observe you."

"But you said we need protection," Travis said with a confused look.

"Yes, you do, but not so tight and obvious you can't draw them in to make a mistake. The kidnappers won't come near us now and they won't send anyone to retrieve the tape. The sergeant says he's going to use police science to catch the people who have your family—you need instinct and science."

Travis shook his head. "You've always baffled me, Bernadette. You're so damn intelligent, you could have been a doctor or a lawyer, done anything you wanted in politics. If you desired—"

"—And I chose the police force, is that what you mean?" Bernadette said, leveling her green eyes at him.

"Yeah, sorry if it sounds like a putdown, but I never understood why you followed that path," Travis said, resting his hand on her leg.

Bernadette took Travis's hand in hers. "Maybe by hitting the streets with the law as my guide, I'll do more than I could have in other careers and I have an entire life to find out. Let's find Melinda—I've got some questions to ask her, and you'll want your detective in on this."

They met in a bar down by the dock. Fans blew overhead to keep them cool as the last rays of sun left the sky. The place was busy with passengers from the stranded ship.

Bernadette noticed several tables of cruise passengers commiserating over the ports they were missing, the sights they wouldn't see, and how unfair their luck was with the passenger going overboard. She sipped her drink and tried not to judge them. But it was hard. The man who'd gone overboard was missing everything.

Thomas jotted down notes as he listened to Travis across the table. Melinda sat beside Bernadette with a solemn look on her face.

"How you are holding up, Melinda?" Bernadette asked.

Melinda stirred a mint tea she ordered. "I thought you had something today. I was so hopeful, and now that the police took the evidence away—I just don't know. It feels like they have thrown us backward."

"Hey, we'll catch up, and we'll find your parents, uncle, and the crew. I've got a feeling this will turn out okay," Bernadette said.

Melinda wiped her eyes, "A feeling? How's that going to help?"

Bernadette placed her beer on the table. "I have this strange sixth sense I picked up as a child. When something went incredibly wrong, I'd do this thing where I'd take some time to assess whether it would right itself or continue to be wrong. Whenever I had a feeling it would turn out well, I was usually right."

"What about the times you were wrong?"

"I was bluffing on a pair of twos in a game of poker," Bernadette said.

"What does that mean?"

Bernadette put her hand on Melinda's, "Sorry my friend, my attempt to lighten the mood. The genuine answer, and this will get spooky, is my Grandmother Moses on the reservation taught me to dream cast when I was a child."

"What is a dream cast?"

"When I go to sleep, I let myself dream about people I know or care about. If they don't come into my dreams, I know they are no longer here. It seems simple, but it's worked for me ever since my childhood," Bernadette said as she sipped her beer and put it down. "I actually knew the day my father passed away—I couldn't see him anymore."

"I'm sorry, I didn't know that," Melinda said.

"Let's move on to something else. I want to go back to the day of the hostage-taking," Bernadette said.

"Why, what more can I tell you, I put everything in the police report." Melinda said, the subject seemed to distress her.

"Yes, you did, but I want to get a sense of the day, and how you felt as the whole thing took place. Police reports are wooden; they sometimes look like a person describing their summer vacation because it's done in a barren room, under duress, and just after the event. You've had several days to reflect and think about that day."

Melinda sipped her tea. "I wished I could have given the police more information about that day. They rushed me to write the description of the kidnappers and the boat, but I really had little to tell them."

"But you had lots to tell them, didn't you—you had your senses and your fears? They were on overdrive that day, but you couldn't put them into words. You had to print them legibly on a police report—those senses didn't make it to the page—did they?"

Melinda lowered her head and then raised it. "You're right, there was so much more about that day that I wasn't able to express."

"So, tell me. What really happened that day?" Bernadette asked. She turned to Thomas, "I need a piece of paper and your pen."

Thomas looked up from his conversation with Travis, "What's this about?"

"Melinda is going to give us some insights into the day of the kidnapping—I think we'll want to hear this," Bernadette said.

Thomas passed the pen and paper to Bernadette, he looked taken aback by the request. He watched with interest as Bernadette began.

"Let's go back to your swim. You said you went in just before lunch. Why? How come you weren't trying to get a tan on that pasty white body of yours?" Bernadette asked.

"Uncle Max and dad were having an argument over a real estate deal Max had them involved in. Max said it was sure a thing and dad wanted to back out. There was talk about a one-million-dollar deposit they'd put down. They had a week or ten days to back out of it. Dad wanted out, he thought it was a scam."

"Do you remember the name of the real estate deal?" Thomas asked.

Melinda shook her head, "No. I know I heard them mention it several times, but right now the name escapes me."

"Don't worry, it will come back to you. What happened next? Just give me the shortened version of the highlights," Bernadette said.

"I saw the motorboat approach our boat, then I heard a scream, a gunshot, and splash. That's when I swam back to the boat," Melinda said.

"And that's when someone shot at you from the sailboat?" Bernadette asked.

"That's right, I turned and swam back to a reef and hid behind it until they left."

"You say someone shot at you. How close were the stream of

bullets that entered the water? Were they really close, somewhat close, or quite far away?" Thomas asked.

"They were quite far away," Melinda said. "Like maybe three meters."

"He wasn't shooting to kill. He was scaring her away," Bernadette said, looking at Thomas.

Thomas nodded. "My thoughts exactly. Tell us what happened next."

"I swam back to the boat after they left and walked around, saw no one, then the kidnappers returned. I jumped back in the water and headed for shore. They got back on board, looked for me, and left," Melinda said. She ran a shaking hand through her hair.

Bernadette put her hand on Melinda's shoulder, "I know this is hard, but try to remember the scream, gunshot, and splash. I want you to think hard about the exact order you heard them."

Melinda put her hand to her forehead and closed her eyes. "Now it's coming back to me. I heard the splash, the gunshot, and the scream. I don't know why I wrote it down the other way in the police report."

"Do you remember anything else that was strange about that day?" Bernadette asked.

Melinda pursed her lips and frowned. "Yes, I wondered why the captain waved to the kidnappers on the boat—it was like he knew them."

"I think we have something to work on," Bernadette said, looking at Travis and Thomas.

"Why, what did you discover?" Travis asked.

"Someone must have escaped from the boat. Melinda heard a splash and gunfire, but the police have no report of a body found in the bay. Also, the kidnappers didn't want to kill Melinda, but to warn her away. No one can fire several shots in a pattern that many meters from a target. They must have found out it was Melinda they'd left behind and came back for her." Bernadette said.

"Wait, you think someone escaped from the kidnappers?" Travis asked.

"That's exactly what I think. And Melinda stated she saw the captain wave to the kidnappers. Would you wave to someone on a boat you didn't know? I suggest we check the profiles of the two crew," Bernadette said.

"This is going to get interesting." Davina said. "I'll start on their profiles tonight."

They ended dinner early. Bernadette entered the room and fell into bed. She smiled at Melinda before she fell asleep and gave her a knowing wink. As if she was keeping the Coopers and the uncle alive with her dreams. It was only partially true. Sometimes she had few dreams, and those were the worst ones. In those, she sensed she'd lost her way. She hoped she'd see something tonight. After tossing and turning, she fell into a deep sleep. She saw a man with an enormous face; he looked evil. It woke her up.

21

BERNADETTE WOKE UP LATE. The sun was blazing through the window and Melinda had already left the room. She rubbed her eyes, spread her arms, stretched and yawned, then glanced at the clock. It was past nine.

"Oh crap, I should have been up hours ago," Bernadette said, heading to the bathroom. She jumped in the shower, did a quick rinse of what she called the "naughty bits," and toweled off.

As she pulled on her t-shirt, she saw the paper on the desk. They'd worked on it over dinner. It was the description of the two crewmen on the boat. The captain was Pierre D'Abboville, he was a Frenchman from St. Pierre/Miquelon who rented near the Castries yacht club. And the chef was Javier Sanchez from Miami, but he'd listed a place in Gros Islet as his residence in Saint Lucia.

"Did one of you escape the kidnappers?" Bernadette asked the paper as she slipped into her sandals. The burning question is, how did he do it? Perhaps the gunman on the boat really was that bad a marksman, or he didn't care about one of the crew escaping. But why hadn't the crewman reported himself to the police? Was he in on the kidnapping? Thomas and Travis thought the idea was a stretch, but they had nothing else—for now.

Grabbing her key, she pushed open the door and made her way towards the lobby and the breakfast lounge. The only one there was Ezra. He had a newspaper spread before him with a coffee.

"Mind if I join you?" Bernadette asked.

"Please do," Ezra said as he pushed his paper off the table.

Bernadette sat and welcomed the server who brought her coffee, "Am I too late or too early for everyone?"

Ezra winked, "you've slept like a lady of the manor. Melinda and Thomas were up at the crack of dawn and made plans to roam the city to see if Captain Pierre swam back here."

"And they left you behind, for what, to hold down the fort should the kidnappers appear?"

"Travis is staying in the hotel in case the kidnappers call, but I'm going out to look for Javier. You can join me if you like, I have the car for the day," Ezra said.

"Who's looking after Travis?"

"Ramirez is on his way here from the airport. He arrives in an hour. It turns out someone ran his car off the road on the way to the airport."

"Is he okay?"

Ezra laughed, "I doubt if Ramirez will complain about a car accident, Thomas told me he served in the Gulf War. You still want to come with me?"

"I'd love to get out of the hotel," Bernadette said. "I'll grab a coffee and rolls for the road. Give me a few minutes and I'll meet you outside."

Ezra was waiting in the SUV at the front door when Bernadette came out. She got in, positioned her breakfast on the console, and strapped in, "let's go, I could use a road trip. I'm tired of all the waiting around."

Ezra put the car in gear and pulled into the busy street, "waiting is a lost art. I learned the hard way in the army. When I was your age, I was full of me self, always wanted to get out there and get the job done. I almost got me arse shot off in battle before I realized that waiting wasn't a bad thing."

"Hilarious, Ezra. How long did you spend in the army?"

"Too long. Joined at eighteen, ready to take on the world. Did some tours in Ireland, then the Gulf War. I decided I'd put in for Belize. Marvelous country, English-speaking, and lots of pretty ladies, but I didn't realize Guatemala wanted to invade. Had to do lots of recon to keep 'em out. At forty I'd me fill of it, and took my wife and kids down to a little fishing place called Dangriga and that's it."

"So, why do this personal protection job? I mean, if you're happy in a fishing village..."

"Oh, you are the direct one you are," Ezra said with a smile.

"Kind of my nature. Hope you don't mind."

"But you ask anyway? I like that." Ezra slowed behind a large transport and looked at Bernadette. "Yes, the sleepy life of a fishing village is not quite my style. It's got some good things, nice beaches for my kids with brilliant weather. I have a twenty-foot Panga boat, and I can spend all day fishing for kingfish and wahoo on the most beautiful barrier reefs anyone has ever seen. You'd think I'd be in my piece of heaven with my lovely wife—."

"—You miss the action, isn't that it?"

"Ha," Ezra said, slapping the steering wheel. "You got it—I tell the wife it's for the extra money. But we've got enough to last us for years to come. I built us a delightful house with a two-car garage and put a little pool in the back with a garden. It's cheap to live there, but it's too quiet for me. I miss having the thrill of the hunt—looking over your shoulder. I crave it like a junkie craves his fix—you appreciate what I mean?"

"I know exactly what you mean. I realized that was the reason I wanted to join the police force over anything else. My goal is to be a detective."

"I understand you're headed to join Royal Canadian Mounted Police. Will it be as romantic as the name sounds, or will you be writing traffic tickets on some highway in the freezing cold?"

"That's probably my lot in life for my first few years. They move the officers all over the country. I'm hoping to spend some time in the far north, I'm part native, so they might give me a shot."

Ezra put his head to one side, "My army unit did joint exercises with your Canadian Army in the far north, I froze me arse off. That's the reason I put in for Belize, I never wanted to be that cold again."

"I've frozen more than once, I understand," Bernadette said with a laugh. She looked out the window at small farms and roadside businesses. The traffic was light, a few commercial trucks and local vans that carried passengers from one town to another streamed past them. The sea was calm, with a few boats moored in the bays.

A sign for Rodney Bay appeared, they drove into a roundabout and turned down a large street. On the left were small hotels and a wide road with signs of construction.

"Looks like this place is getting a makeover," Bernadette said, looking at the cranes and construction workers.

"Oh yes, everyone wants the cruise ship dollars. We're doing the same in Belize. The entire Caribbean gave up bananas and sugar cane crops to have the tourists flood the islands and deposit their cash," Ezra said.

"You don't sound convinced," Bernadette said.

"No, I'm not. In my small village, the average person gains little from the tourist dollars. The tour groups pay their graft to some government lackey to get the business. I don't have a lot of faith in developing an economy out of having people drop in for a look-see at your sights. Doesn't do much for the kids."

"My grandfather used to say the same thing, and he was a guide," Bernadette said.

They drove in silence as they passed Rodney Bay, the yacht club, and into the town of Gros Islet. The place looked run down. Houses were weather beaten, poorly built, with bare dirt front yards and broken pavement.

"Any idea how we'll find Javier's home?" Bernadette asked.

"I've got a rough idea. He's close to the fresh fish market near the canal. I asked the police officer who was on duty outside our hotel about Javier. He said he was living with a lady known to the police."

"How well known?"

"I'm not sure. I did a background on Javier, he's got an

outstanding warrant, it's small stuff, but he wouldn't want to fly into Miami airport without a lawyer helping him."

"Don't the yachts do any background checks on their crew?"

"I've never known yachts to do a police background check for the crew. It could be he'd done some thefts from kitchens he worked for. If they prosecuted every chef who did a business out the back door to make some extra cash, there'd be no restaurants," Ezra said. "They pay the chefs shite and the servers like they're movie stars."

"Once again, you've got some hard and fast opinions," Bernadette said with a laugh.

Ezra winked, "Well, get a beer in me and I'll solve the world's problems."

He stopped the SUV in front of a small house with wooden shutters that hadn't seen paint in so long, it was a distant memory.

"You want me to come with you?" Bernadette asked.

"Absolutely. A young white woman showing up might rattle them, make them slip up."

"You think so?"

Ezra turned to Bernadette, "look, I'm a black man, you rattle me, just follow my lead."

They walked up to the home, stepped onto the concrete blocks used for steps and Ezra rapped on the door. Steps sounded inside. Someone looked out the window. There was a muted conversation inside and finally, the door creaked open.

A slim lady wearing a printed red dress opened the door. She looked about thirty, with wiry red hair, light-colored skin, and freckles. Her eyes darted from Ezra to Bernadette. They were green with little flecks of white.

"What can I do for you?" She asked.

"We're here about Javier, are you his girlfriend?" Ezra asked.

The eyes flicked back to Bernadette, "Sort of, we met at a party, he stayed with me for a while... have you found him?"

"What if he's not missing?" Ezra asked.

"What do you mean?" the woman asked. She crossed her arms

and moved from one foot to the other. It looked like a defensive stance to Bernadette.

"We heard he's an excellent swimmer," Bernadette said.

".... I don't know what you're saying."

"Was Javier an excellent swimmer? That's just a question," Ezra said.

She shrugged her shoulders. "He might have been—why do you want to know?"

"Because that's how he escaped. Who is he hiding from?" Bernadette asked.

The woman touched her hand to her face and stared hard at Bernadette. "Who are you people? What do you want?"

"They kidnapped my friends on that boat. If Javier escaped, we need to find out if he can help us," Bernadette said. "He's not in any trouble, we're only looking for information."

The woman put her head down. A child's voice called to her in the house, she turned and told the child to hush. Bernadette and Ezra waited for her to speak.

She attempted to close the door. Bernadette placed her hand on it.

"The children of the hostages are trying to find them. If you don't help, these people might die," Bernadette said.

She put her head down, then raised it back up to stare at Bernadette. "I heard a rumor he might be in Soufriere." The door closed.

They stared at the closed door. Ezra turned to Bernadette, "I knew you could get it out of her."

"I have a feeling she thinks someone is after him. She trusted us. Should we make tracks for Soufriere?" Bernadette said.

They walked back to the SUV and Ezra stopped at the door, looking at the fish market.

"Are you thinking of bringing some fish back to the hotel, or have you seen some interesting people to question?" Bernadette asked.

Ezra laughed, "You read me well. I see some fishermen hanging out by the dock. Let me have a talk with them." He reached into the back seat, opened a cooler, and pulled out six Piton beers.

"And you want me to stay here?"

Ezra nodded, "Yes, I'll be speaking in Creole French with them. I'm not great at it, but I can get my point across. They'll trust me more than you. And besides, those guys would just be making eyes at you and getting all hard. We don't need that."

"My, you are to the point, Ezra," Bernadette laughed. She wandered down the street for a bit and came back a half-hour later when she saw Ezra return to the SUV.

Ezra turned to her as she got in the passenger's side. "That was an interesting talk. The men saw a motorboat come alongside a large fishing boat midway between here and Martinique, the same day they kidnapped your friends."

"Why didn't they report it to the police?"

"Most of them have had a run-in with the police in the past. They've probably offloaded goods from Martinique for sale at the market. It's hard to make money just on fish."

"Did they mention how big a fishing boat?"

"Yes, it was a large inter-island boat, they said, over fifty meters in size. Those types can travel anywhere."

"We just widened the search," Bernadette said.

"Yes, we did. We'll stop in at the hotel to meet with Thomas, he'll want to be in on the search for Javier. We have a busy afternoon ahead of us. It looks like you got your wish of going on a road trip."

Bernadette fastened her seat belt. "I couldn't be happier, it's time we found out what the kidnappers looked like. If we find Javier, we might have something to go on."

22

Ezra and Bernadette pulled into the hotel in Castries to see several police cars in front. "You think something has happened?" Ezra asked.

Bernadette got out of the car and stopped. "I think before we go in, we have a talk about what we uncovered."

Ezra nodded, "You want to hold off on telling the police because you think we might find where Javier is?"

"Just for a while. If we find nothing in our search of Soufriere, we turn the information over to the police. If he fears going to the police, he'll run like a rabbit if he sees them doing a house-to-house search."

"Nice style. You'd make a good private detective if you tire of writing tickets on those frozen highways in the north," Ezra said.

"I'm just trying to keep the Coopers safe," Bernadette said.

"You got my vote," Ezra replied as they walked into the hotel.

Travis was sitting with Assistant Superintendent Vernon Charles in the main lobby with two police hovering over them. Melinda sat in a chair off to one side. Her head was down, a tissue clenched tightly in her fist.

Bernadette moved past the police officers to get to Melinda. One of them attempted to stop her. She put her hand up and motioned him away. The determined expression on her face was one of a momma bear protecting its cub. Neither of them wanted to mess with her.

She kneeled beside Melinda. "What's up? Have you had news?"

Melinda pulled her head up. "Oh, Bernie, thank God you're here. We got a message from the kidnappers."

"Do you want to tell me what they said?"

Melinda choked on a sob and pulled herself together. "The note was in my dad's handwriting, it said we have to give them ten million dollars or they'll kill them all."

Bernadette squeezed Melinda's hand. "I realize it's tough to read, but all kidnappers say that—they need to scare the hell out of you to get the money."

Melinda wiped a tissue over her eyes. "Well, it's damn well working."

"How did Travis get the ransom note?"

"The police found the note stuck under the windshield wiper on their patrol car. They'd seen two kids on skateboards by their car earlier, but they can't be certain if it was them."

Bernadette shook her head, "And they wonder how the criminals can make the police seem so foolish, they get the kids to help."

"It seems so serious now," Melinda said. "I thought these people were just trading our parents and Max for money—but they're threatening to kill them. I didn't realize this before."

"Hey, where's that positive blonde I know and love? We'll get this done—don't collapse on me. We'll bring them back." Bernadette said.

"Are you sure?"

"Yes, I'm sure. Now go to the ladies' room and wash your face—your mascara has run, and you look scary," Bernadette said as she wrapped her in a hug.

"I do not know what I'd do without you," Melinda said. She got up, straightened her dress, and headed for the ladies' room.

Bernadette watched Melinda walk away and wondered to herself if all that she said was true. This was a real kidnapping. All she knew was from textbooks and university classes. This was real life with people she loved and cared about. She saw Thomas in a conversation with Ezra. She waited for them to finish speaking before she approached him.

"What's the situation?" Bernadette asked Thomas after Ezra left.

"The hostage-takers want ten million US dollars in five days. They seem to have put us at a disadvantage as they've not opened the door to communication," Thomas said.

"Did they say where they'll make the exchange?"

"No, that's just it. We still have nothing to go on. Of course, this is a classic strategy for kidnappers. We won't find out an exchange location until the last minute. But it makes it impossible to negotiate the terms or the amount," Thomas said, shaking his head. "It's impossible to play this hostage game when our opponents won't throw us the ball."

"We have five days, perhaps we can catch a break," Bernadette said.

Thomas rubbed his face. He looked tired. "I hope you're right, we could use one. Ezra told me about the cook, Javier. I agree, we keep it to ourselves for now. Once the police leave, we'll head for Soufriere and see if we can find him. If we don't, we'll inform the police of our findings."

"Sounds like a plan, but what about locating the kids on skateboards?"

"How would that help—?"

"—Use them to send a message."

Thomas's eyes opened wide, "You are brilliant Bernadette Callahan. You'll waste your talents with the RCMP. I could pay you three times what you'd make as a lowly constable."

Bernadette put her hand on Thomas's shoulder. "Thanks, but I'm set on the force. If writing traffic tickets gets boring, I'll call you."

"Suit yourself. How should we go about getting a message out?"

"There must be a place where kids hang together to skateboard in this little town. Ezra and I can scout out the streets and find them. You decide the message and we'll get it out."

"Sounds good. I'll let Travis in on it when he's finished with the police," Thomas said.

Bernadette poured herself some water and waited for Vernon Charles to finish his conversation. She'd never seen Travis look so worried. This was his family, any misstep on his part would put them in jeopardy.

Charles got up, shook Travis's hand, and left. Bernadette approached and sat beside him, taking his hand. "How are you holding up?"

Travis managed a weak smile, "Not well, but I guess that's to be expected in this scenario. I feel like it's a bad episode of the Price is Right. I'm hoping everything aligns and my parents, uncle, and the crew pop out somewhere."

"I have a feeling we can help with that," Bernadette said. "We might have a lead on the missing person from the boat and a way to contact the kidnappers."

Travis took Bernadette's hand. "I appreciate you're ready to help on this, and I'm happy you're with us, but I want you to turn everything you have over to the police."

"But they're overwhelmed with everything," Bernadette protested. "We could be an extra hand. Ezra, Thomas, and I will track down the kids that dropped off the message."

Travis shook his head, "I can't let you do that—we've just received a ransom note with a threat they'll kill my parents. I'm calling my office to put the funds together and wait for their instructions."

"But they've already murdered two people."

"Yes, and they made their message perfectly clear they'll do the same to my family."

"My instinct tells me there's more to this than we see. This isn't just a kidnapping, there's more. How about if I work in the background for a few days to see what I can come up with?"

"No. I don't want you doing anything. I just read my father's handwriting. He's in the hands of killers. I want you to take care of Melinda and stay out of this. Do you understand me?" Travis said. His face had turned red. The note in his hands trembled.

Bernadette put her hand on his knee, "Okay, I got it. I promise I'll stay out of the way of the police..."

Travis squeezed her hand, "I'm sorry for blowing up. Seeing my dad's handwriting... it's shaken me to the core. I don't think I've ever been so afraid to lose them."

Bernadette wrapped her arms around him, his head fell on her forehead. She could feel his tears falling. She held him for a time and kissed him on the cheek before heading back to her room.

Bernadette found Melinda in the room lying on the bed staring at the ceiling. Bernadette sat on the bed and brushed her forehead.

"Did your father mention the name of the real estate company your uncle and father were dealing with?" Bernadette asked.

Melinda took Bernadette's hand off her forehead and sat up. "Yes, I think so, but Travis told me he wanted us to give everything to the police. He doesn't want to jeopardize our family."

"He told me the same thing, and I promised him I wouldn't get in the way. I just wanted to find out, for my curiosity," Bernadette said.

Melinda blew out a breath, "I really can't remember, this is all a bad dream... wait that's it, the name had something to do with dreams."

"Caribbean Dreams?"

"... that sounds like it...yes, that's it exactly." Melinda said.

"That's great, Melinda, thanks," Bernadette said. "I'm going for a little walk. I'll see you later."

Bernadette left the room and headed down the hall to find Thomas. Caribbean Dreams was the name of the company of the man missing from the cruise ship. She needed to find the connection.

23

BERNADETTE FOUND Thomas and Ezra in the lobby bar drinking coffee with a man who had bulging muscles and a dark complexion. Thomas looked up and smiled as she approached. "Well, how does it feel to be pulled out of the loop with the rest of us?"

"Has Travis taken you off the case as well?" Bernadette asked.

Thomas motioned for her to join them, "We're now officially on bodyguard duty only, and waiting for the kidnappers to give the date of exchange. There's not much to do, really. I'm here for my client, and Travis has spoken." Thomas turned to the man, "This is Ramirez by the way, he had a bit of delay, but he made it."

Ramirez nodded to Bernadette, "Pleased to meet you." His eyes flicked over her with an approving smile.

Bernadette sat down and leaned forward, "I discovered the Coopers had money invested in the same real estate company as the man who went missing from the cruise ship?"

"I'd say that's one hell of a coincidence that needs to be investigated," Thomas said.

"My thoughts exactly. I need access to your computer to find where they have offices and how much the Coopers had invested."

"You won't need my computer for that," Thomas replied. "They have an office in Rodney Bay. The Coopers deposited one million dollars for a stake in a two-hundred-million-dollar complex with hotels and shopping. Travis asked me to investigate the connection between their brother Max and the man named Valdis something... they are both from Latvia, that's all I could find out. No idea how this relates to the Cooper kidnappers."

Bernadette glanced at her watch. "It's just past two-thirty, I could be there by three-thirty latest and ask some questions."

Ramirez said, "These are the islands. It's Monday, they've probably closed by now."

"I'll call ahead, say I want to get in on this hot deal I've discovered. Real Estate Agents will work any hour to make a commission."

Thomas looked at Ramirez, "Bernadette's got a point. If she can make the appointment, you can drive her there."

"But I don't want to take you away from Travis and Melinda, they're your clients," Bernadette protested.

"And I promised personnel protection to Mr. Travis Cooper, which extends to anyone he cares deeply about." Thomas took out his phone, punched in a number, and handed it to Bernadette. "I have the number to their office keyed in, it's ringing."

Bernadette took the phone just as a voice answered. She made a convincing appeal that she had only a day left on the island and had heard about the development from a friend. "I just have to get in on this deal. I've heard it's the chance of a lifetime," were the words that got the meeting.

She handed the phone back to Thomas. "I told them I'd be there in an hour."

"Good, do you have a dress to wear? I doubt you'll be convincing in those shorts."

"I'll go change. I'll be back in five." Bernadette shot out of her chair and ran down the hall to her room. She opened the door as quietly as she could. Melinda was napping. She pulled off her t-shirt and dropped her shorts to the floor and pulled on her dress and found the pair of high-heeled sandals her aunt had packed. She kicked the clothes she'd taken off into the closet.

It took her another minute to apply some quick makeup, and she was out the door. Four minutes later, she was back in the lounge in front of Ramirez, Ezra, and Thomas.

"A *dios mio*," Ramirez said. "You get ready faster than my Ranger unit."

"Ah, Ramirez, your Ranger unit never looked as well put together," Ezra said with a wink at Bernadette. He couldn't help but admire the low-cut dress with the high hemline that exposed her tanned legs.

"Never has a truth been more aptly spoken, gentlemen. Now, if you'll get over admiring this young lady, perhaps you can get on your way. And, Ramirez, I'm sure you can act the surly and rich Spanish boyfriend with tons of money."

"I'll try my best," Ramirez said with a wink at Bernadette.

"Hey, what if I'm the surly rich Canadian girl with a Spanish boy toy in tow?" Bernadette asked with a grin.

Thomas waved his hand, "Do whatever works, go see what you can find out."

RAMIREZ DROVE the SUV on the crowded highway. There wasn't much point in passing anyone, as the traffic was bumper to bumper as far as they could see. He relaxed and put the radio on and tapped his fingers to the island music.

Bernadette turned to him; he was a good-looking man in his mid-thirties with well-defined muscles. He was what the girls would call "eye candy," back in her class. Easy on the eyes.

"Can you tell me how you got in an accident back in Miami?"

"Why do you want to know?"

"Was it just a fender bender? Did you get hurt?"

Ramirez shook his head, "Someone ran me off the road."

"Does that happen all the time in Miami?"

"I don't think I want to get into the details. That's something for Thomas to tell you about," Ramirez said.

"Why is that?"

"He didn't want it causing any more concern than you already have."

"So... it was a setup, you know it and don't want to talk about it."

Ramirez looked at Bernadette. "Thomas said you were good. You're very good. Yeah, it was a setup. Two cars came at me, they worked together to push me off the road. I didn't see them coming. I rolled a few times and got knocked out."

"I'm surprised they didn't kill you."

"Might have been in their plan, but when the highway patrol came by, they got out of there fast."

"Something serious is going down here. No one would attempt to kill Thomas and you if there wasn't."

"Ten million is a lot of serious."

"I think there's a lot of players for ten million," Bernadette said.

RAMIREZ SHRUGGED HIS SHOULDERS, "Maybe you're right, hope we find out before it's too late."

They drove in silence until they reached Rodney Bay. The office was on a side street in a larger building beside a construction site.

Ramirez parked and locked the SUV. He eyed some little kids playing nearby and stared at them for a second. They looked back, then ran away.

"Is that the tough guy stink-eye you just gave them?" Bernadette asked.

"That's the look that says, if you mess with my ride, I'll find you. I use it in my home country and parts of Miami."

"Very good, now when we walk into the real estate office, I know you want to play the Spanish boyfriend part. That's all fine because you're cute, but if you run your hand down my ass, I will break your fingers when we leave the office," Bernadette said.

Ramirez opened both hands and spread his fingers wide, "My dear lady, my fingers will obey your command."

"Good, but you can play the boyfriend, just don't go over the top."

"You make it hard on me. But sure, we'll be arm in arm and my hand will not wander," Ramirez said. "I think I'm asking Thomas for a pay increase. This is the hardest job I've ever done."

They walked into the real estate office. Bernadette saw someone she recognized. She whispered to Ramirez, "Quick—put your arm around me."

24

THE PERSON BERNADETTE saw looked like Steven when she first arrived. She'd seen only a glimpse of him as he stepped into a back office. If it was him, her cover would be blown. They'd need to play the happy couple. She needed to use Ramirez as a screen, so Steven couldn't identify her.

They had painted the real estate office in blue and pink pastels with pictures of villas, low-rise apartments, and swimming pools covering the walls. It displayed cheerful people in each of the pictures engaged in various activities of sheer pleasure that could only exist in such a wonderful paradise.

A tall black man wearing a pink polo shirt and white trousers greeted them with a gleaming smile, "Welcome to Caribbean Dreams, how may I help you experience our island paradise?"

"I'm Denise Howard, this is my fiancé Carlos, we spoke on the phone. We have to fly back to Toronto tomorrow, and I've heard so much about your development. I just had to see it before we return home."

"Why, of course. I'm Winston Taylor, I'll be happy to give you as much information as you need." He paused for a moment and lowered his voice, "Now, I must let you know, we are almost sold out. But I have a few choice villas available."

"Well, aren't we lucky," Bernadette said.

"Yes, I can show you some lots on our board over here," Winston said. He motioned them to follow him to the center of the room to a layout of villas and lots on a topographical board. "The development sits on a hill overlooking Laborie Bay on the southern tip of our lovely island," he said with a wide smile and open arms.

Bernadette moved with Ramirez, so their backs were to the back of the room. She let her hand wander down his back and squeezed his butt. Ramirez looked at her with surprise—she motioned with her eyes to the back room. He got the message.

"Now I have this wonderful villa with an ocean view that someone could not close on. Too bad for them, but a marvelous opportunity for you. The price is two hundred and seventy-five thousand US dollars. With a ten percent deposit, this can be yours," Winston said. His eyes opened wide, and his hands made a gesture of how lucky they were.

"This is all very nice. And we'll buy it, but we heard we could get in on the overall development. Isn't that right, sweetie?" Bernadette said, looking at Ramirez.

"Yes, we heard there's some big money to be made by being in on the investor pool," Ramirez said. He gave Bernadette's butt a quick squeeze to relay he got her message.

Winston's smile fell from his face like it had dropped off a cliff, "we reserve this for a few of our select investors."

"Why is that?" Bernadette asked.

"The cost is very high. Investors must have one million to invest."

Ramirez stepped towards Winston, "Are you assuming we don't have those kinds of funds to invest?" His eyes were wide, and his chest protruded as if Winston had just insulted this man called Carlos and every Latino on the planet.

Winston raised his hands, "please, I did not mean to offend you. It's just that the project closes for investments in five days, which means you will not have the customary ten days to back out if you wish."

"We don't need that. My friend explained all the details of the offering. If you give us the paperwork and the bank you use, we'll transfer the one million when we return home to Toronto," Ramirez said.

".... Well, of course. If that's what you wish, I'll get the paperwork for the villa and the investment project. We reduce the villa by ten percent for all project investors. Would you like me to do a full run-through of the project? It will take about a half-hour with just the highlights," Winston said.

"That's unnecessary, a friend of mine gave me a full outline of the development and the money we could make. What bank do you use?" Bernadette asked with the best poker face she'd ever used to bluff a pair of twos against what she knew was a pair of jacks.

"We use the First National in the Bahamas," Winston said. He dropped his voice again, "We find the local banks quite unsuitable for our needs."

"I understand, you must have a good bank, isn't that right sweetie?" Bernadette said, turning to Ramirez.

"A good bank with competent bankers is essential," Ramirez said. "Especially those who know how to make things happen."

"I'm so glad you understand the world of finance," Winston said. "This will make things happen so much faster. Please remember, our project closes for investment this Friday at five p.m." He did his dramatic salesperson pause again.

"Thanks, we'll make it happen. My friend told us we had to get in, and we're in," Bernadette said with a wide smile.

"That's wonderful, who is your friend? I must thank him—he's done all my work for me," Winston said.

Bernadette waved her hand and gave Ramirez a knowing smile. "Oh, our friend hates compliments and just loves to help people. We'll let him know you appreciate him."

Winston glanced at the two of them, his eyes narrowed. Bernadette wondered if he was doubting their story.

Bernadette held up her watch, "Oh my, is that the time? We've got to be back at the hotel for another meeting. Winston, we need the paperwork and some of your lovely brochures to take back to Toronto. We can have a certified cheque and the signed documents returned to you by this Thursday. Would that be alright?"

Winston snapped out of his gaze, "Of course. Let me get them, I'll be right back."

"That was close," Ramirez said. "I thought he made us for con artists."

"You mean more than him?" Bernadette asked. "Now I know why the kidnappers want their money in five days. This thing closes on that same day. If none of the investors get their deposits back—we're talking over fifty million dollars. That's a lot at stake."

"Big bucks means big crime. There's has to be multiple players in this," Ramirez said. He moved closer to her, "What's our next move?"

"You need to keep me out of sight from the back office. I'm sure that's Steven, the guy who tried to kidnap me. That's why I grabbed your ass. You didn't need to grab mine—by the way."

Ramirez blinked his eyes, "That was my sign for 'copy that,' it's what we do in the Rangers."

"You grab the other guy's ass to tell him you understood his message?"

"No, but I wanted you to know I got the message we had a potential threat in the back room."

"Okay, got it. Now, watch the back room and make sure you block me from the sight-lines of whoever might come out of there. If it is Steven, he might come out armed."

"Copy that," Ramirez said. He moved behind Bernadette and pressed against her to block her from anyone looking out the back.

"Okay, Ramirez, you don't have to press on me like I'm your first date since overseas," Bernadette said.

"Oh, sorry," Ramirez said as he backed away to leave some room.

The door of the backroom opened. Winston came out with a large sheaf of documents and brochures. His look was one of the eternal hope that all salesmen have that the sale will go through and the client is totally honest with him. He was blocking all the strange signs these two had that this was a bullshit meeting, and he'd wasted his time.

"Well, here we are. These are the documents to purchase a ten percent share of Caribbean Dreams that will allow you an equal share of revenue of the property for the next fifty years. And, we will discount the villa by ten percent as a reward for being a valued investor. And may I suggest you drop in to view our show home at Laborie Bay? It's only a twenty-minute drive from the airport."

Bernadette looked at Ramirez. "We'll do that. If it's that amazing, with the profits we'll make on this, our little villa will cost us almost nothing. We can't wait to look at it."

"Well, my love, it will cost something, but with the write-offs we'll get from using it for clients and our own personal use, this is a steal," Ramirez said. He leaned in and gave Bernadette a big hug, a kiss, and a generous ass grab. Bernadette returned the gesture.

Winston laughed, "I see you have some celebrating to do. I will wait for your documents. Thank you for making your dreams with our development."

They shook hands and walked out the door. Bernadette and Ramirez walked as quickly as they could without looking like they were in a hurry. They made it to the SUV, Ramirez hit the gas and motored out of there without passing the sales office.

"Do you think they bought it?" he asked.

"Well, we did enough ass grabbing to sell it," Bernadette said.

"But I thought you said--?"

"Forget what I said, we had to go with the moment. Besides, Winston loved our show."

"Yeah, I noticed he was watching your ass the moment we walked into the showroom. I couldn't make out his accent. Where do you think he's from? Ramirez asked.

"I'm pretty sure he's a Jamaican." Bernadette said, "he had a tattoo of One Love, that's a Reggae song on his left wrist."

Ramirez smiled, "did you notice the tattoo on the inside of his left arm? It reads Rastafari. The Rastafarians are mostly from

Jamaica... so I think you're accurate. Now, let's figure out what we've found out."

"We have a bank and a project that's collecting over fifty million in deposits, which closes in five days. We need to figure out what to do next."

"That's easy, we ask every construction company on the island who has the bid to start on the project," Ramirez said. "All of my family is in construction in Florida. A project this size must go into the ground as soon as the rains stop at the end of December. If no one has seen an offer to bid on construction, this is a total scam."

"We need to visit Laborie Bay tomorrow and see if they have anything built there," Bernadette said.

"I'll let Thomas know, I'm sure he can have one of us get you there."

They headed down the highway towards Castries; the sun was setting in the west over the ocean. The birds were nesting in the trees and the waves lapped lazily on the shore. Neither of them observed the black SUV following behind them, with Steven at the wheel.

Steven wasn't sure if the woman he'd seen in the real estate office was the Bernadette Callahan, that had embarrassed him two days ago. He'd tried to confirm it several times from the back room, but the big Latino had stood in the way. Now he wanted to find out.

After following them to Castries, he stopped two hundred meters from the Hotel Macambo. Through a set of binoculars, he saw Bernadette get out of the SUV and walk into the hotel. He smiled.

25

BERNADETTE WOKE to the sound of thunder. Rain pounded outside the windows as if the deluge would penetrate the room. She got out of bed and opened the curtains to see the sheets of rain obliterate the harbor.

Melinda snored softly in the bed beside her. Bernadette moved quietly to the bathroom and changed into her shorts and t-shirt. She slipped on running shoes as they were the only footwear in the bag other than sandals.

On the return from Rodney Bay, there had been several discussions with Thomas on how to tell Travis she'd be away for the day. In the end, after evaluating ideas—she would lie. That was her plan.

She stepped into the hallway to see Travis coming out of his room. She'd hoped to avoid him this morning, but here he was.

"I missed you at dinner last night, Bernadette. You weren't out investigating, were you?" Travis asked.

Bernadette walked up to him and put her arms around him in a warm hug. "Of course not, Travis. Ramirez took me to a store to buy some extra socks for running. We got back late and had dinner in the harbor. I felt you could use some time on your own."

Travis hugged her harder, "You know I'd never tire of you. Melinda and I missed you last night."

Bernadette pulled her head back and looked in his eyes, "That's really nice of you, Travis, I'm so glad you both think that way."

"I think that more than Melinda," Travis said. He moved forward and kissed Bernadette on the lips.

Bernadette pulled her head away.

"—I'm sorry, Bernadette, I don't know what got into me—I shouldn't have," Travis said.

"No—it's perfectly fine—you just surprised me," Bernadette said.

Travis closed his eyes for a moment. "Everything is spinning out of control. I'm not sure of my own feelings or my own actions. All I know is I must meet the demands of criminals who've taken my family."

Bernadette hugged him hard and kissed him on the cheek. "We'll get through this. We'll get your family back. I have a good feeling about this."

"You do?"

"Yes, I do. I'm heading out to Anse Cochon with Ezra today. I'm going to do an old-fashioned tracking method used by my Cree ancestors. They would go to an area where a disturbance happened and call upon the ancient spirits to tell them what happened."

"You can actually do this?" Travis asked with a look of amazement.

"I'm not as good as my grandmother, but I helped find a boy who'd wandered off a hiking path. The spirits guided me to him. I'm going to give it a shot and Thomas said you wouldn't need Ezra today."

"Let's have dinner together tonight and catch up. I'd like to hear if you find out anything from the spirits." Travis said. His eyes searched deep into hers, as if he was trying to believe her.

"Sure, I'll see you tonight," Bernadette said. She patted Travis on the chest and walked down the hall. In the lobby, she met Ezra, who was holding her coffee and sweet rolls.

"You ready to go?" Ezra asked.

"Yeah, let's get out of here, it's a three-hour return trip and I need to make up a story for Travis tonight of how my native ancestors speak to me about missing people."

Ezra opened the hotel door and escorted her to the SUV. "What? He bought that mumbo jumbo? When you said you might use that as a cover last night, I was sure he wouldn't believe you."

"Say every lie like you mean it," Bernadette said. "I heard that said one time. I understand it's a tactic used by the police to tell criminals you know everything about their crime to get them to confess. I used it so Travis will assume I'm using something other than old-fashioned investigation techniques. I sold it, he bought it."

Ezra put the SUV into gear and drove out of the hotel parking lot. "You are something else to sell that story."

The rain subsided as quickly as it came. Gigantic clouds that threatened another downpour loomed overhead. A gentle wind blew, and sailboats dotted the harbor. The SUV climbed out of Castries to the highlands above the town as Bernadette sat back and wondered if she might ever communicate with her ancestors.

The evil man came again in her dreams last night. She could almost detect an aroma from him this time—there was a scent of sulfur. The dream woke her up; it was the same time the thunderstorm arrived. A chill went through her—like she was having a foretaste of hell.

All her Catholic teachings of the nuns telling her of fire and brimstone for those who did not tread the path of righteousness descended on her in the night with thunder, flashes of light, and the stink of sulfur had to be brimstone. She looked around, realized she hadn't left her bed, and went back to sleep with a shake of her head for allowing such crazy things to creep into her dreams.

The smell and the images lingered. She focused on the view and drank her coffee. Never once did she look in the side mirror to notice if anyone was following. A black SUV, three cars behind, followed them.

26

FRIDA COOPER HAD LISTENED to Max's cough for the past twenty-four hours. She pleaded with the Spanish man she'd nicknamed Tony Montana to let her attend to him. The little Spaniard finally relented and led her to Max's room.

He didn't look good. Max had a constant cough and a high fever. It soaked his bed in sweat. Frida had Tony bring her towels and cool water. She mopped his brow and tried to comfort him.

"You're going to be fine, Max," Frida said. "Travis will pay the ransom. They will set us free. You need to rest, and we'll be out of here."

Max pulled Frida's hand off his head and opened his eyes, "Oh Frida, I got us into this mess. My greed brought us here... if I hadn't brought us to Saint Lucia for this deal..."

"But we wanted to believe in the dream. I saw early retirement for Luke, a way to pay off all our debts, and have a home in Saint Lucia. You didn't drag us here. We came of our own free will."

"But the man who sold us on the deal, I know him. We were in school together," Max said. "His name is Valdis."

"Where? In Canada?" Frida asked. "Wait, you immigrated to Canada in your twenties. Did you meet him in Latvia?"

".... Yes, that's it. I never told you. He reached out to me—said I'd never lose money on the deal. But Luke wanted us to back out. I phoned Valdis in Miami and said we wanted our money back. I told him Luke thought this might be a scam and we should call the newspaper."

"Were you and Luke arguing about that the day they kidnapped us?"

"I told Luke he should never have told the real estate people the deal might be fake. I'm afraid of Valdis, he could be cruel when we were kids—he might do something to us."

"You think he had us kidnapped?"

"His voice is unmistakable—he was in the hallway last night," Max said as he broke into a coughing spasm.

"If it's him, why don't you call out to him, perhaps you can reason with him?" Frida said.

"I overheard him say he will have us all killed once they transferred the money... I'm so sorry, Frida..." Max broke into sobs and fits of more coughing.

Frida mopped his brow and let the words of Max wash over her with sheer terror. Her faint hope shattered—there was no escape unless Travis found them. She drew in a breath and let it out slowly, she said a prayer and then said one more, "Oh Travis, I hope you called Bernadette."

27

THE CLOUDS OPENED several times on the trip to Laborie Bay. Sheets of rain kept the windshield wipers busy, and the other times the rain fell as if they'd turned the tap on in a shower stall.

Ezra put the wipers on high and leaned forward to find the road. Bernadette sat in the passenger's seat watching the highway for road signs. They came to Hewanorra Airport and took a left onto the St. Jude highway. Little stores and shops dotted the side of the road. Real estate signs promising future development sprung up in clusters like flowers in bloom.

Bernadette could witness the island's tourism coming to life with the increased tourist traffic and interest in this beautiful little paradise. She decided not to comment about it to Ezra, least he unleash another tirade regarding the skewed economics of tourism for the Caribbean.

They followed the signs for Laborie Bay and found a large sign for Caribbean Dreams with a red sticker saying, "70% sold!"

"I thought they had only two or three villas left," Ezra said.

"Either the sign is not accurate or Winston is one hell of a salesperson," Bernadette said. "Be interesting to discover what the salesperson at the show home has to say."

Ezra followed the directions to the development up a narrow dirt road that wound its way up a hill overlooking the bay. At the end of the road, in a barren parking lot, they arrived at a single show home with shuttered windows. Ezra parked in front, and they got out.

"There's no one around." Bernadette said as she tried the show home door, "The doors are locked."

Ezra walked along the road and surveyed the area, "There are no survey stakes in the ground or lot stakes. You'd think there'd be sold signs all over the place."

"I hope Thomas and Ramirez come up with something when we get back. They were going to check on local builders in the area and Thomas was going to investigate the First National Bank in the Bahamas," Bernadette said. "Right now, this doesn't look like very much."

"Ah, because you haven't looked inside," a voice said.

They turned to see Steven coming out of the forest, holding a gun with a silencer attached.

"Why did I think I'd cross paths with you again?" Bernadette said.

"Because you left me tied to a tree and tried to run me over?" he replied. "That got my attention."

Bernadette shrugged, "I guess it's too late to say I'm sorry."

"Had you behaved yourself, we would have left you in this nice little home and let you out when we released the Coopers. You've made things complicated," Steven said.

"That happens when you hold people I love for ransom. I thought you might know that, Steven. By the way, is your name really Steven?"

"Sure, if you want it to be, I can be Steven. Now walk towards the home." He turned his head towards the forest, "Michael, come out here."

Michael stepped out of the shadows. He gazed at Bernadette with a nasty look in his eyes. Every bone in his body wanted revenge for the humiliation he'd suffered at her hands. He held a large knife.

Steven walked around them and opened the door of the home and waved for them to step inside. Bernadette walked up the steps to the home and entered. A wall of heat hit them, all the windows shuttered. It felt like no fresh air had passed through the home in some time.

"Michael, check them for phones," Steven commanded.

"... I didn't see any in their hands," Michael said.

"Check their pockets. In case they have one."

Michael made a visible shudder. He placed his knife on the hallway table and advanced on Ezra. "Turn around, face the other way."

"Don't be afraid Michael, I will shoot them if they try anything," Steven said.

"I'm not afraid," Michael replied. He moved behind Ezra to pat his pockets but did it by standing as far away from him as he could. He went to Bernadette—she gave him a look that made him wince.

"If you can't see a phone in these pockets, you're legally blind. And if you pat my ass, I'll break your arm," Bernadette said with a glare. "You understand me?"

"She's okay, boss, no phone," Michael said. He stepped back and picked up his knife.

"Okay, so this is what's going to happen. We lock you in here. There is no way out. There is enough water and food here to last you until Friday. After that, someone will come to let you out."

"Why take us hostage at all?" Bernadette asked.

"Very simple, when you do not return to Castries, the police will spread their forces out to find you. It will take the heat off us, and we can go about our business. Just a simple diversion," Steven said.

"If this is all so simple, why did you kill Steven Charles at the limo company? And you blew up a man you mistook for Thomas Davina. Those seem like deadly diversions to me."

Steven cocked his head to one side, "I don't decide. If I did, no one would have died." He turned to Michael, "Make sure all the windows are closed properly."

Steven and Michael stepped out of the house and slammed the door shut. They heard them walk off and the sound of their SUV start up and drive away.

"Sounds like they took our vehicle," Bernadette said. "Let's check this place out."

They did a survey of the home and returned to the living room. "They shut the windows. The front door is heavy metal with four locking bolts. They've left us water and some energy bars for about two days," Ezra said.

"Yeah, that's great, but I discovered something disturbing in the laundry room."

"What's that?"

"Ten bags of lime and two shovels. The perfect method for burying bodies. I get a feeling when that door opens again—we'll be dead," Bernadette said.

28

Thomas Davina felt frustrated. Travis Cooper hadn't fired him —he'd changed his job from active investigator to bodyguard. That was easy enough to handle, with two police officers stationed outside the hotel. All he had to do was wait for the kidnappers to make a move. He disliked waiting, but it was a part of the game.

Ramirez was in the front lobby with his cell phone. He'd called all the construction companies on the island to see if any of them knew about the Caribbean Dreams project.

Thomas positioned himself in his room with a large carafe of coffee, his computer, and his phone. He began an investigation of the First National Bank in the Bahamas, but became frustrated as the morning wore on.

The bank had no website and no listing in the Bahamian banks. His search on Google turned up nothing. Out of desperation, he called a detective agency in the Bahamas. The man he ended up talking with had been a former British Intelligence Agent named Randal Preece.

"How may I assist you?" Preece asked.

"I've a problem locating a bank on your island. It's called First

National Bank," Davina said. "Perhaps I could hire you to track it down for me."

"I can save you the money," Preece said. "They run the place out of an industrial park. One bank I do security work for claims the place is a scam. I've driven by there a few times and seen no cars parked in front and no activity inside."

"I didn't know banks could operate like that in the Bahamas," Davina said.

"They call themselves an offshore trust. Their building's sign is illegal, and the police haven't issued a fine because they can't reach anyone. The office looks vacant," Preece said. "I checked into the place for a client and it had scam written all over it. I'm sure our local bank authority will shut them down, but things take time when you have no one to speak with."

Davina shook his head. "Did you find out any of their principal owners?"

"A holding company in Toronto has an affiliation with a company in Romania, I'll email you the file. I saw your name on the news, Mr. Davina, I'd like to help in any way I can to locate the hostages. If you need my professional services, there's several qualified personnel I can send you," Preece said.

"That is most kind of you. I will call you should I need some help. Right now, we're waiting for our kidnappers to make their move. I hope it's not too long," Davina said. He put his phone down and checked the email Preece had sent.

There was only one way forward at this moment. He needed someone to get him inside information on this so-called offshore trust. And he knew just the person. A young man in Belgium named Noah Olieslagers had done time for computer hacking. Davina used him for jobs where there was no theft, only the gathering of information he needed for cases.

His email asked for all files the company had on Caribbean Dreams and closed his computer. After a yawn and a stretch, he went in search of Ramirez.

Ramirez was on the phone when Davina approached him in the

lobby. He had the local telephone book out with a notepad at his side. He looked up at Davina, nodded at him, and finished his call with a thank you to the person on the other end.

"You find out anything?" Davina asked.

"Yes, I found the company that built the show home in Laborie and that's it. One construction company told me the land they built it on might not belong to them in a few days."

"How's that?"

"Final closing on the property comes due this Friday. If they don't pay the full balance, they lose it," Ramirez said.

"I'm getting the same information I'm digging up on the bank, everything about this seems like a front to fleece investors," Davina said. He looked at his watch. "What time did Ezra and Bernadette say they'd be back?"

"Ezra said the return trip would be about three hours. They might stop somewhere for a quick lunch. They left at 0800 hours."

Davina looked at his watch, "It's been six hours, I wonder what's keeping them?"

29

Sweat dripped from every pore of Bernadette's body. She sat on the sofa in the living room. Ezra lay on the carpet with his shirt pulled up. The temperature in the room was over forty-five Celsius, it felt like the Sahara Desert. Bernadette was so hot she reached back, unhooked her bra, pulled it off from under her shirt, and threw it onto a chair with a sigh of relief.

"At this temperature, we will cook to death," Ezra said.

"You sure the air conditioning doesn't work?" Bernadette asked.

"I tried it several times—I found the unit in the hallway closet, it doesn't seem to be connected, or they shut it off. No idea how they had people come to view this place. They build these island homes to be cooled by the winds off the ocean. With the shutters buttoned up, we've got no chance of cool air. We're going to be slow-roasted," Ezra said.

"Did you notice any cleaning supplies in the bathroom—could we make a bomb and blow a hole in the door?" Bernadette asked.

Ezra shook his head in a lazy motion, "No, I didn't notice a thing. This place is clean of everything but what's in the refrigerator, and I'm thinking one of those precious few bottles of water they left us might go down real good right now."

"Bring me one while you're at it. I'm too hot to move," Bernadette said. She realized her brain was getting fogged from the heat. The first sign of heatstroke and exhaustion. If they remained in this airless home for over twenty-four hours in this heat, they might be dead by tomorrow.

Ezra dropped a bottle of water in her lap and sat across from her in a plush armchair. They decorated the entire home in a Tommy Bahama Caribbean motif, with overstuffed chairs in soft pastels, accented by piles of throw cushions, and pictures of island natives frolicking in the waters.

Ezra spun the top off his bottle of water and slowly put it to his lips. Bernadette did the same. She lifted it up, looked at it for a second, and sniffed it. Almonds—that was the smell—her brain searched for almonds. She knew what it was.

Launching herself off the sofa she landed on Ezra. She whispered, "It's cyanide."

"What the hell?" Ezra replied in a whisper. "Why are you whispering?"

Bernadette put her hand on her lips and whispered, "That's why Steven didn't shoot us, he doesn't have to. He turned the A/C off and laced the water with cyanide. There's a color in it, but it's smells like almonds—that's cyanide."

"You better be sure about that, because I'll die of dehydration by morning if you're wrong."

"I'm totally sure. They added flavoring in the water to hide the taste, but cyanide has an overpowering odor."

"So, what do we do? Sit here for two more days and wait for them to come and pick up our roasted corpses?" Ezra asked.

"Let me check something," Bernadette said. She got on her hands and knees and checked under the sofas and the coffee and end tables. Then she looked under the lamps. She came back and sat beside Ezra. "There're listening devices all over this room."

Ezra nodded slowly and asked in a hoarse whisper, "What do we do now?"

"Did you ever do any acting?" Bernadette asked.

"No, not at all. Why?"

"You need to act like you ingested all this bottle. You'll have trouble breathing, and you'll go into cardiac arrest. It would be good if you fell on the floor for a big and convincing finale."

"Then what do we do?"

"Lay here and see if our boys return."

Ezra shrugged, "Can't be any worse than me getting myself out of latrine duty in the army, I'll give it my best shot."

"Follow my lead," Bernadette said.

"Thanks for the water, Ezra. Man, this is nice and cold." Bernadette said in a loud voice.

"Don't chug it all down, girl, we got to save some for later—but it tastes good."

Bernadette held up her fists and threw up one finger at a time. She went from one to ten, then screamed. "Ezra! What the hell, you're foaming at the mouth. Oh my God, I feel faint. I want to throw up. My heart is racing."

Ezra moaned and pounded on the floor. "What was in that water?" He jumped up and landed hard on the carpet.

Bernadette dropped to the floor, followed by Ezra. They lay there whispering, "Do you think it worked?" Ezra asked.

They heard a car come to a screeching halt outside. Doors slammed and footsteps approached.

"Do you know where the main circuit breaker for the house is?" Bernadette asked

"It's in the hallway."

"Quick—turn it off and get back in here." Bernadette said.

30

"WAIT UNTIL THEY GET REALLY CLOSE," Bernadette said.

"Won't Steven put a bullet in us to be certain we're dead?"

"He doesn't want the mess, that's why he chose the cyanide."

"Good point," Ezra said as he tried to look dead.

The door opened slowly. Steven pointed his gun through the door and waited for his eyes to grow accustomed to the darkness.

"I thought it would take longer than this," Michael said.

"They probably drank an entire bottle. I put enough in each one to take down an elephant. The stuff is very potent, it kills quickly," Steven said.

"Where's the light switch?"

"It's behind the door. You get the shovels from the laundry room and start digging, then we'll drag the bodies out and bury them. I want to get it done before they stink up the place, we might need this place one more time before Friday."

Bernadette and Ezra waited on the floor, taking shallow breaths, and hoping the darkness would hide any telltale signs of life. They heard the men approach them.

"I can't see if they are breathing—can you?" Michael asked as he kicked Ezra's leg.

"Get down close and check vital signs," Steven said. "I'll put my hand on her chest and check for her heartbeat. You do the same for him. If they're still breathing, we smother them with a pillow from the bedroom."

Bernadette lay there waiting. She felt Steven kneel beside her, his big hand moved slowly and did a massage of her breast. Bernadette shot her hand upward in a palm heel strike. It connected with his nose. He screamed in agony and fell back and dropped the gun.

Bernadette jumped up and threw a reverse elbow smash into his temple. She picked up the gun and pointed it at his forehead.

She turned to see Ezra making quick work of Michael. He'd grabbed Michael by his shirt collar and his waistband to flip him over and land on him. Ezra threw a punch to Michael's forehead to subdue him.

"What a pleasant surprise," Bernadette said. "I thought you wouldn't be back until Friday and here you are. Did you miss us?"

Steven lay on the floor with his hands in the air. "We meant you no harm, we were keeping you safe."

"Really, then how about I get you a bottle of water out of the refrigerator. I'm sure you're thirsty. Wouldn't you like a nice cold drink right now?" Bernadette asked.

"No—no thank you—I'm fine," Steven said.

"How about you, Michael?"

"Oh no, just fine...."

Bernadette smiled. "Now we know why you didn't shoot us, why would you when cyanide would do the trick? Keep the house nice and hot and put some poison nearby. Such a wonderful way to dispose of people."

"Not my idea. I only do what I'm told," Steven protested.

"And who told you to do this?" Ezra asked.

Steven went quiet. He looked at the floor.

"Well, I guess we'll just leave you here then," Bernadette said.

"You can't do that, this place will kill us," Michael protested.

Bernadette turned to Ezra. "Don't you love this? Now, they're stating the obvious." She looked back at Steven. "If we knew who masterminded the kidnappings and where the hostages are being held, we could have the police come find you. If not, it might be some time... like maybe Friday until they find your bodies."

".... it was Javier," Steven said. "He told us what to do—we are all working for him—he won't tell us where the hostages are. Our job was to keep you from interfering with Javier's plans."

"Javier the cook?" Bernadette asked.

"He pretended they kidnapped him with everyone else, but he jumped off the boat. He set everything up and now he commands us on the island. You must protect us from him. Javier killed the man in the shuttle service. He planted the bomb at the airport. He will kill us if he finds out we turned him in," Steven said.

Bernadette nodded her head, "That's the chance you take when you're a criminal. Maybe you didn't read the job description." She turned to Ezra. "Cover them, I want to check out the vehicle."

Ezra stood over them, "Please make any movement you like, it would be my pleasure to shoot you. That young lady is going into police training—I am not."

Bernadette returned a few minutes later with several bottles of water. "I found our phones and some water." She looked down at Steven and Michael. "I called the police and told them where to find you."

"Why don't we take them with us and drop them at the police station in Vieux Fort?" Ezra asked.

"There's nothing to tie their hands with. I don't like the idea of even twenty minutes with these two in a car. They loaded the 9mm gun with hollow-point shells. Those kill with maximum damage. I'm done with this guy—he's a police problem now. I called Vernon Charles to send his police officers in Vieux Fort to pick these guys up."

"You want to wait until they get here?" Ezra asked.

"If we do, we'll be sitting in the Vieux Fort police station for hours writing up statements. I told Charles we're on our way back to Castries, where we can make a statement. We need to hunt for Javier.

If he is the key guy that Steven claims he is, we find him, we find the Coopers—does that work for you?"

"The math sounds about right," Ezra said. He turned to Steven and Michael. "Okay, gentlemen, move to the center of the room and lie on your bellies. Any failure to do so will allow me to shoot you in your legs."

"He's joking," Bernadette said.

"No, I'm not. These bastards intended to murder us, a bit of bloodletting would do me good," Ezra complained.

Bernadette shook her head, "Just do as he says before he shoots you." She winked at Ezra, "He's out of control."

Steven and Michael scurried across the floor on their knees and fell on their stomachs. Bernadette and Ezra locked the door. They left the key on the steps for the police and got into the SUV. Ezra started the engine and Bernadette handed him a bottle of water.

Ezra took the bottle, twisted off the top, and downed most of it. He gasped and wiped his mouth. "I really hope that was safe and not a double-cross from those two bastards."

Bernadette stopped mid-swallow, "I did a smell check already, we're fine."

"Good, now all I'll need is several beers to wash away the stench of those two from my nostrils and my mind and I'll be fine. Do you have any idea how we find Javier?"

"Yes, I do. I saw a mountain bike rental shop on my run yesterday. If we hurry, we can get there before it closes."

"What do you need with a mountain bike?"

"I'll let you know when I rent one," Bernadette said. She looked at her watch, it was four, they had an hour to get there.

31

BERNADETTE STRADDLED the mountain bike in the rental shop. It was a bit too large for her, but she could make it work. She'd ridden a soft-tail, full suspension bike with disk brakes back in the Rocky Mountains. The rental bike was a hard-tail, no back suspension, and side pull-brakes that could get wet and fail in the rain, but it had a good frame with front suspension and road-worthy tires. This would have to do.

"This will be fine. We need it for two days, and I'll need some bike shorts with full padding, a bike jersey, and a helmet," Bernadette said.

"I take it you've done some mountain biking?" the owner asked.

"I did the trans-Rocky Mountain Challenge last year for seven days. I don't think my butt, or my legs, have forgiven me for it yet, but it was pretty exceptional," Bernadette said.

"This bike will be pretty simple for you then." the store owner said.

Bernadette smiled. "Not a problem, you keep your bikes in good condition. This will be fine for my needs."

"It would be my pleasure to see you ride it," the owner said. He was in his late twenties, dressed in shorts and a muscle shirt. From where Ezra stood, the testosterone was oozing out of the man. It was obvious he took an interest in Bernadette.

Ezra stepped forward, "Thank you. If that's everything, let's load this bike and get back to the hotel. I'm sure Thomas and the rest are looking for us."

"Yes, we'd better get back," Bernadette pulled out her credit card and paid the deposit on the mountain bike. The bike shorts and top she'd use back in Canada once she got settled somewhere in her new RCMP post, or so she hoped, if the next forty-eight hours worked out as planned.

"I'm thinking we stop at the hotel first, then make our way to the police station to make our statements." Ezra said.

"Sounds good to me." Bernadette said.

They loaded the bike into the back of the SUV and drove to the hotel to see several police cars parked in the front. Vernon Charles was standing in conversation with Thomas. Ramirez was in a cluster with Melinda and Travis.

"I hope this is a welcoming committee and not a what-the-hell-have-you-done-now type of reception," Bernadette said

Ezra parked the SUV, "Let's hope it's the first. How about if I talk to them while you change into some other clothes?"

"What do you mean? I'm wearing clothes..." Bernadette looked down at her t-shirt, "You're right, I left my bra back in the house, I'll change and be with you shortly." She shot past Charles and Davina with a smile. "I'll be right back."

She ran down the hallway, entered the room, and stripped. As her clothes came off, she realized how badly she smelled. Running the shower and pulling a clean outfit out of a drawer, she multi-tasked a shower and change inside of five minutes. With a quick comb through her hair, she ran back out the door.

"Sorry, had to use the bathroom after the long drive. What did I miss?" Bernadette asked as she approached Thomas, Ezra, and Vernon Charles.

Ezra had a scowl on his face. "Assistant Superintendent Charles just told me the men we left in the show home in Laborie are dead."

"Wait—that's not possible," Bernadette said. "I gave the information to you only two hours ago. Your police at Vieux Fort are only ten minutes away. When did they respond to the call?"

"The Vieux Fort police arrived thirty-five minutes after I received your call," Charles said. "The victims were shot in the back of the head. We will do a ballistics test on the gun you turned over and you will have to submit to a GSR test."

"I have a feeling the gun we took from them will be a ballistics match for the murder of the man at the car hire shop. I didn't buy what Steven told me about Javier being the gunman. They'd planned to smother us with pillows if we weren't dead from the cyanide," Bernadette said.

Charles looked at Bernadette and Ezra, "Yes, I heard the story Ezra gave about there being cyanide in a refrigerator in the show home, but my police officers found nothing in the home. You are the last to see these men alive. My superintendent will want a full report from you."

Charles waved his hand toward the police officers, "These men will accompany you to the police station to make your report and I'll speak to our crown prosecutor to see if we can let you go in the next twenty-four hours."

Thomas Davina stepped forward, "I'll have a lawyer get you out in time for dinner."

"I'll make damn sure it happens, Bernadette," Travis said. He held her hand and squeezed. "I know you lied to me about where you were. But I'm glad you're safe."

"I'm sorry, Travis. I couldn't tell you what I was doing, I had to follow my instincts." She sensed his disappointment in her.

Bernadette extended her hands, but they didn't place handcuffs on her. She got into the back of a police car with Ezra. They made the short five-minute drive to the police station where they read her the British legal system's version of her rights and took a gunshot residue test. She knew everything would come back negative, but she was being drawn into the police system. This is how it worked.

She let herself go through the process without judgment and

wondered, deep in herself, if she could actively do this to people. Because, if she made it out of this—she would do this for a living.

One hour later, a policewoman led her into a cell that had seen over a hundred years of inmates and personal angst. Her cellmate was an elderly black woman in a shapeless dress with bruises on her arms. The old lady moaned and spoke in Creole, then fell asleep and snored with loud gasps that woke her up with a start as if she'd seen a ghost.

Bernadette lay on a thin mattress and tried not to think of the bedbugs crawling on it and the several showers she'd need. She realized how deep she'd dropped into this situation. Detective Linda Myers had warned her not to get too embroiled in the case. There was no way back from this.

She'd be brought before a judge in the morning and charged with murder if Thomas Davina couldn't get a lawyer. Her time on the island had devolved into this. She'd spiraled down a long chain of consequences to the note on a file that said she was a criminal.

She fell asleep on the cot. A policewoman woke her up, "You are free to go."

The old woman was snoring soundly as Bernadette stepped out of the cell. She turned to the policewoman and asked, "What is this woman in jail for?"

The policewoman shook her head as she looked at the old woman, "She murdered her husband. But everyone knows he beat her all the time. I do not think it will go well for her. Her husband's family is out for her blood. You do not need to concern yourself with her, go now, your rich friends hired the best lawyer on the island to set you free."

Bernadette walked outside into the humid night to see Thomas, Ezra, Melinda, and Travis standing there with a short man in a dark suit.

"I told you we'd get you out of there," Travis said. "This is Paul Florent, the best defense counsel in Saint Lucia."

"Mr. Cooper is most kind," Paul Florent said. He had an elegant Caribbean accent tinged with upper-class English. "I presented the crown prosecutor with the facts in the case. They really had nothing to go on other than you were the last ones to see the men alive. Who would bring a murder weapon to the police?"

"Are they dropping the charges?" Bernadette asked.

"Well, no, not at the moment. But they couldn't hold you any longer on suspicion of committing a crime. The men were shot with a .22-caliber weapon. You turned over a 9mm. That gun had never been fired. In the end, they had to accept your story. Both of you are free now." Paul Florent said.

Bernadette turned to Thomas, "Do you think the police will search for Javier now?"

"Hard to say. Ezra gave Vernon Charles the same story account of your conversation. They now must solve the murders of the two men in Laborie. I have a feeling they are at maximum with manpower," Thomas said.

"You must be hungry," Travis said. "Let's get you some dinner and a few beers to wash away that jail cell."

"Actually, I could use another shower, and I'll pass on dinner. I'll order room service and get an early night. Ezra and I have a bit of biking to do in the morning."

"Bike riding? Where are you going to go?" Travis asked.

"I have a tour of the town I want to do. I'll let you know about it later tomorrow," Bernadette said.

She turned to walk to the hotel and stopped beside Paul Florent. "I was in a cell with an elderly woman. The jail guard told me she was in for murdering her husband. Do you know anything about it?"

Paul put his hand to his chin, "Yes, a sad case really, the woman's name is Marie Louise Lucien. She is from Soufriere, with no children or family. The police knew her husband had beaten her for years, but did nothing about it. Today she fought back and killed him with a knife."

"Are you representing her?"

"No, she has no money, a public defender is looking after her. A man named John Nelson, who is fresh out of law school but I'm sure he'll get the charges dropped to one of manslaughter and she'll receive five to ten years."

"What about self-defense? I saw her bruises in the cell, she looked pretty beaten up."

Paul shrugged, "That's something Nelson will have to present to the judge at sentencing. It's not my case."

"You don't think it will go to trial?" Bernadette asked.

"These rarely do. The facts are straightforward," Paul said. He looked at this watch, "I really must go, I have dinner reservations. Please enjoy the rest of your evening."

Bernadette watched Paul Florent walk around a corner with hurried steps. She wondered why she cared so much. The woman in the cell looked so helpless, that was why. Shaking her head, she said goodbye to the others and headed back to the hotel.

Tomorrow she would make a last-ditch attempt to find the man responsible for the kidnapping. Her time was running out to solve this, and so were her options to make it to her RCMP training.

32

BERNADETTE WOKE up with a start the next morning. She'd dreamed about the strange man again. This time, she was in an underground cavern. There was that same evil smile and crooked grin. It was hard to get his face out of her mind.

Melinda was already up, "Are you okay? You look like you've seen a ghost."

Bernadette ran her hand through her hair and lowered her eyes, "I dreamed I was in that house again in Laborie."

Melinda sat on the bed and stroked Bernadette's cheek. "I'm so sorry you had to experience that. I spoke with Travis last night. He thinks he can get the Saint Lucian Police to drop any suspicions they have regarding any wrongdoing. We could fly you back tomorrow."

"I can't leave until you find your family—that's not an option. I can join another training session with the RCMP. If they get pissy with me, I'll get into one of the police forces in Vancouver or Edmonton. There are officers retiring all the time, they need personnel and I'm qualified," Bernadette said.

"Yes, you are, but your heart is set on getting into your training this fall. I've ruined it for you," Melinda said.

"You ruined nothing. Some greedy bastards who've taken your family have. I'm here to correct that. Let's get this straight, you called, I answered. That's how it works. You'd do the same for me. Now, I need to get up, pee, get dressed, and down several cups of coffee before I get started."

Bernadette headed to the bathroom, did her morning routine in a few minutes, and threw some clothes on. Melinda was still standing there as if she was in shock.

Bernadette walked over to her and hugged her, "Sorry, was I too harsh?"

"No, I just realized what an amazing friend you are. When I called you, I thought you'd come here and just hold my hand. I didn't realize how involved you'd get. You've gone all the way into this investigation to the possible detriment of your own career."

"Please, you're making me sound like a hero. I'm here to do what's right. Now, I'm going for coffee, you want to join me?"

"I'll be with you in ten minutes," Melinda said. "I'm not as quick as you in getting myself put together in the morning."

Bernadette winked, "I put nothing together, I just let all the parts fall back in place." She walked out the door as Travis was coming out of his room.

"How are you doing this morning?" Travis said. He walked up to her and stood close, putting his hands on her shoulders.

"I'm fine, I had a good sleep—"

"You lied to me yesterday, didn't you?" Travis said, looking into her eyes.

Bernadette held his gaze. "Yes, I did. I sensed this was a scam. What I saw in Laborie and heard from the man who tried to kill us proved I'm right."

Travis narrowed his eyes, "Thomas told me about all the other investors last night. There's fifty million on the line, you think they'll murder my parents, don't you?"

"That's how it looks to me. Everything about this development leads to a Friday closing for investors. I think your father and uncle found out something they shouldn't have. They're being kept alive until this Friday. You can pay the ransom if you want but my instincts tell me you won't see Luke, Frida, and Max."

Travis lowered his head, "You're right. I've been stupid to think otherwise. I've been holding out in blind hope these people were telling the truth. What are we going to do?"

"I'm going to find Javier. I want Melinda and you to stay here. Ramirez will take care of you. I'm going out on a hunt with Ezra."

Travis hugged her, "What would I ever do without you?"

Bernadette kissed him on the lips. She let the kiss linger long enough until his eyes fluttered, then pulled her head back. He stood there in a daze.

"You'd probably miss me terribly. I must get a coffee, then change into some bike gear. I'll meet up with you when I find something."

Bernadette found Ezra in the breakfast lounge. "Did you find anything out?"

"Yes, it's like you said. There's only one area where kids can skateboard in this town. I found a little park with a flat concrete pad," Ezra said.

Bernadette poured herself a coffee and added her two sugars and cream at the self-serve area. "I knew there couldn't be many around. The streets and sidewalks are cracked with deep drainage ditches for skateboards. I'll down this coffee and take one to go. I'll meet you back here in ten."

She grabbed the bag of bike wear in the room, threw off her underwear and pulled on the bike shorts. The Lycra with the padding felt cold to her bare skin, but she'd learned long ago, the only way to wear bike shorts was to go commando. Underwear became sopping wet and chaffed like hell. Next, she slipped on the sports bra and pulled on the bike jersey. A quick look in mirror satisfied her—she looked like a tourist on a mountain bike.

To finish her outfit, she pulled on athletic socks and slipped on her running shoes. She would have preferred proper bike shoes with clips, but this would have to do. Ezra was standing in the lobby with Thomas when she returned.

"Ezra says you have a plan to find Javier. I can't say I like it." Thomas said.

"What's not to like? Ezra meets up with the skateboard kids, the same ones we assume left the note on the police car for you. He'll give them hard cash if they take a note to Javier—I follow the kids," Bernadette said.

"What if they don't remember the man or woman who gave it to them?" Thomas asked.

Bernadette tilted her head to the side, "I have a feeling they do. This island is tiny and I think whoever gave it to the kids banked on the odds they wouldn't tell the police. And the police don't offer big money—only threats."

"You seem sure of yourself, Bernadette, for someone who's spent four years at university learning about police science," Thomas said. "I don't mean to be critical, but I'm just saying your reasoning might be off on this."

"My reasoning comes from my childhood. I wasn't the best kid. I was good at school, but I observed the gangs and how the kids thought. We've got a shot at this. Vernon Charles has an all-points bulletin out on Javier as a person of interest. He only half-believed the story I told him. You and I both realize an APB does nothing. You need a house-to-house search to find this guy. I intend to narrow the search."

"We need to get going," Ezra said. "Those kids won't be there all day."

"Promise you'll call for backup the moment you have contact," Thomas said.

"Absolutely, there's no way I'm having another gun pointed at me. I have a cell and so does Ezra. This is an explore only," Bernadette said.

Bernadette followed Ezra to the SUV, they got in and drove into the inner part of the city to Constitution Park. It had a wide expanse of cement a skateboard could move over.

"Let me out here," Bernadette said. They pulled the mountain bike out of the back. Bernadette strapped on her helmet and threw her leg over the bike and checked the brakes.

"I'll signal you by rubbing my forehead when I make contact and have a courier," Ezra said.

"You know what you're going to say?"

Ezra smiled, "I have kids, I'll be asking them if they want to make some more money for dropping notes to people. And they'll only get money when I get a reply. They'll get the message. If they don't, then these are the wrong boys, and this is a bad idea. You and I will take the bike back and go for beers."

Bernadette nodded, "Let's hope my crazy idea is right. I'd like to see the look on Vernon Charles's face when we find Javier."

Ezra walked away and reduced his gait to the style of a Caribbean male enjoying the late morning sun. He angled his way towards the boys as if they were the least interesting people in the world, then stopped just on the outside of their group.

Bernadette watched him as he approached two of the boys. One was in a red t-shirt, the other in white. They chatted for a while, with the boys shaking their heads. Ezra pulled out a handful of Eastern Caribbean dollars, fanned it in his hand, and put it back in his pocket. The mood of the boys changed. They nodded their heads in agreement.

Ezra handed them a note and a small bill. That was the deal, they got twenty Caribbean dollars for taking a note, and two hundred and fifty for bringing back an answer. The twenty EC was worth about ten US dollars. The return note would net them just under one hundred US dollars. A small fortune for any kid.

The kid, wearing the long sleeveless red t-shirt with white board shorts, took the bill and stuffed it in his pocket with the note. He dropped his skateboard to the pavement, jumped on, and took off. His friend was right behind.

Ezra put his hand to his head and massaged his forehead. Bernadette took off after the boys.

33

THE BOYS HIT the road fast. Bernadette was wrong about the pavement—the skateboards worked well if they stayed in the center of the street. The kids were good. They rode the center line and did kicks and glides with expert precision.

At one point, they caught the back of a truck's bumper. They dropped down to coast with the truck, then peeled off onto a side street. Bernadette had to stand up on her pedals to keep up with them.

The easy recon mission was turning into a hard-core challenge of her ability to keep up with them while dodging traffic. A taxi came up on her fast, blaring its horn. She'd moved into the center of the road to follow the kids. As she swerved back to the side, she hit the deep drainage ditch on the road.

The bike flew into the air. She rode it out as she careened onto the sidewalk, missed a vendor, and back onto the road. The kids had disappeared.

She pedaled fast, changing gears to get more speed. At a crossroads, she saw the red shirt—cutting off the same cab that had blasted its horn at her. She made the turn and was back on their trail.

Sweat dripped into her eyes from the bike helmet. Her wet hands had a hard time gripping the handlebars. Why she hadn't bought a pair of bike gloves was only a dark thought now. Pedaling hard got her to within five hundred meters behind the boys—they hadn't noticed her. If they did, it was a lady on a mountain bike—why would they care?

There were twenty more minutes of following until the kids stopped in front of a little restaurant. They picked up their skateboards and walked inside. Bernadette did a slow ride past the place and hid behind a large sign for tires.

A small man wearing kitchen whites and an apron came out of the shop with the kids. He slapped them both on the head. He had the profile of Javier. It was obvious what they'd done was wrong. The man looked up and down the street before going back into the restaurant.

Bernadette pulled out her phone and dialed Ezra. "I've got him. The place is the Carib Bar and Grill. How soon can you be here?"

"What are you near?" Ezra asked.

"I'm on Bishop's Gap Road, hiding behind the Come To Me Tyre Shop," Bernadette said.

"Great, I found it on the town map. I'll be right there," Ezra said.

Bernadette put her phone down and hung out behind the sign. The two men inside the tire shop looked at her with interest. She made like she was adjusting her seat, smiled, and waved at them as if she didn't have a problem in the world and was enjoying her day. They waved back and resumed their work.

Ezra rolled up five minutes later and got out. Bernadette opened the back of the SUV and stowed the bike. She pulled off her bike helmet and put on a baseball cap. She stripped off her bike jersey and slipped a t-shirt over her fitness bra. The two men in the tire shop let out an approving whistle.

"You have admirers, Bernadette," Ezra said.

Bernadette waved at the two men and smiled, "Happy I can provide some visual relief—now what's our plan?"

"Do you think you saw Javier?"

"I'm not sure, I only had a description of him from Melinda, who told me he was a short, light-skinned Latino. I also know he was a cook. The man who came out of the restaurant fit that description and slapped the kids for bringing him the note. That makes me want to whack him across the head a few times," Bernadette said. "But I don't know if it's Javier."

"I called Thomas on the way here. He said he'd call Vernon Charles. We should have the local police here in a few minutes. I say we sit in the vehicle and wait for them to arrive. Then we turn this over to them," Ezra said.

"What if he slips out of the back?"

Ezra's head rocked back, "You think he'd do that?"

"He looked like a scared rabbit when he stepped back into the restaurant. Let's go in and do a recon. I could use a beer," Bernadette said.

"Okay, but the police will be here any minute now," Ezra said as he got out of the SUV. They walked across the street and opened the door.

Two patrons sitting at the bar with early morning beers turned their heads to look at the middle-aged black man and young white woman enter. Ezra made a slight nod to the men and walked with Bernadette to the bar.

A young black woman in a tight-fitting tank top and yoga tights that showed her curves sauntered towards them as if she'd all the time in the world.

"Two Piton beers," Bernadette said.

"I'm not sure if I want a beer," Ezra said.

"They're for me—did you want one as well?" Bernadette asked.

Ezra shook his head and ordered a ginger beer. He watched the girl walk away, then turned to Bernadette. "I don't see anyone in the kitchen, do you?"

"No, and I hear nothing in there either. Let's wait for the girl to come back and see if you can order anything."

The girl came back with the same slow walk as if she found an additional time dimension and needed to remain in it if she could. She popped the tops off the beers and slid them across the bar.

"Is your cook making breakfast today?" Ezra asked.

The girl looked back at the kitchen. "No, he ran out the back ten minutes ago. Said something came up."

Bernadette shot off the barstool and ran to the kitchen. She saw a door leading to the outside and pushed it open. A narrow path led down a hill towards the town.

"Damn it, he's gone," Bernadette said.

Ezra turned to the young girl behind the bar, "What was your cook's name?"

"He said his name was Rafael. He started last week."

"Did you know him—was he a local?" Bernadette asked.

The girl shook her head, "I've never seen him before, he spoke a 'patois,' and some Spanish. He's a strange one, I hope he does not come back."

The door of the bar opened; Vernon Charles walked in with two other police officers. "Where is he?"

Bernadette exhaled, "Gone, he slipped out the back door. This girl here can probably do an ID if you have a picture of Javier. But he's gone."

Charles produced a picture of Javier and laid it on the bar. "Is this the man that was your cook?" She moved slowly forward, as if she was approaching a forbidden object. After studying the picture for a moment, she backed away.

"Was he a killer or something like that?"

"We don't know. He is a person we'd like to interview," Charles said. He lowered his voice to a softness you'd use for a small child, "Now my dear, is this the picture of the man who just ran out the back?"

The girl put her hand to her head, "Yes, that is him. That is the man who worked here. My momma will be so angry, she will tell me I cannot work here if this place hires criminals."

Charles put up his hand and spoke in an even tone, "My dear, we do not know that. We only wanted to speak with him. Tell your momma to call me, I will be happy to speak with her directly if you wish to keep your job."

Charles impressed Bernadette with the way he handled the interview. He handed the young girl his card and turned to Bernadette, "It seems you flushed him out, but this has done us no good. You might have told us what you'd planned to do."

"I'm sorry—again. I was going to call you the moment we made a positive ID on him."

"Perhaps you could let us do our jobs." Charles said. His frown said it all. He whirled and walked away.

For a moment, Bernadette wanted to respond, then she stopped. She realized in that moment they had put the two kids they'd bribed in danger. If Javier was a killer, their plan had put them within arm's reach of him. He might have been responsible for the killings in the show home in Laborie and the other two as well. An icy chill traveled down her spine as the simple words Charles spoke broke over her.

Bernadette turned to Ezra, "We have to go." She walked out of the bar and swung the door open.

Ezra threw some cash on the bar. "Give our drinks to the two men at the bar," he said as he followed her out into the street.

Bernadette whirled around. "God, I screwed that up. I was so certain my instincts were right. But look what I did. I had no backup plan. What an ass I am, what a total rookie." She stopped for a moment and threw her hands up in despair. "How in the hell will I ever be a police officer if I don't anticipate what these shithead criminals are going to do? Of course they'll run out the back door."

Ezra put his hand on her shoulder, "Don't be so hard on yourself. My first sergeant had to convince me of what an idiot I was. I thought if I shot at the enemy, they wouldn't shoot back."

"Thanks, but I've got work to do. I need to get my bike out of the back," Bernadette said.

"Wait, you're joking—right? You can't seriously be thinking of going after this guy after what Charles said? He'll throw you in a cell for obstruction of justice or anything else he can think of. You found the guy—they know he exists, now let them take care of it."

Bernadette pulled the mountain bike out of the back of the SUV, stripped off her t-shirt, put on her bike jersey, and strapped on her helmet. "I can't leave it alone. I started this and I'll finish it. I once shot a deer and wounded him. My grandfather made me track that deer for a day until I put him out of his misery. I'm going to run Javier into the ground."

She got on the mountain bike, checked the brakes, and jumped on the pedals. She disappeared down the road as Ezra watched her with a look of resignation. He'd seen someone like her only once before in the army—he was killed in action.

34

BERNADETTE HIT the pedals and changed the gears to increase speed. For a moment her mind raced about where Javier could have gone, then she let herself breathe deeply and relax. She slowed the pace of the bike and realized she needed to think like a stalker and not like one chasing prey.

Javier would seek out familiar places. The deer she'd once tracked for half a day was laying beside a stream with its head bowed, its body covered with sweat. She'd taken dead aim to make a clean kill. To find Javier; she had to think like him.

She dropped the bike's front ring to mid-range and did the same with the back. In this mode, she could cycle for hours. A small cloud-burst fell with needle points of cooling rain. She felt the rain and was happy she'd changed into the bike jersey; it would dry in seconds after the rain stopped.

After a tour of the inner town and square, she realized where he wouldn't be. Everything was too open and common. She found him in a little bar and grill on the outskirts of town, now he'd have to run to something as remote. She had an idea where he might be.

The perfect hiding place was open, but not common. With a few quick pumps of her pedals, she turned her bike towards the harbor.

In ten minutes, she came alongside the forty-foot sailboat, The Wet Dream, the boat the Coopers were taken hostage on.

The sailboat had a dark blue hull with a teak deck polished to a brilliant shine that gleamed in the late morning sun. A tall center mast and spinnaker with tightly wrapped sails rocked gently with the waves.

Bernadette got off her bike and laid it against a pile of ropes and walked towards the boat. There were no signs of activity, no coffee cups on the table in the cockpit, or cleaning products on the deck to show that someone might be there. The only way for her to find Javier was if she went on board.

She walked towards the sailboat—every few steps she stopped to listen for sounds. A thought crept into her mind. Should she call the police? What if Javier was there, watching her approach from one of the cabin windows?

"Can I help you?" a voice asked.

Bernadette whirled around to see a young man with the logo of the sailboat charter company and the name Julian on his blue t-shirt. He wore blue shorts and a pair of white running shoes and held a deck brush in his hand.

"I'm looking for someone. I thought he might be on this boat— you mind if I take a quick look?" Bernadette asked.

Julian shrugged, "Sure, I have seen no one on this boat, but I've been working in the office. Please go ahead."

She stopped and stared hard at the narrow windows that looked out from the low main cabin. Was there something there? Had a face appeared and then melted back into the shadows? A feeling of dread came over her, but she pushed forward. What if this was just her overactive imagination in hyper-drive? If she called the police to an empty boat, she'd be wasting their time. She'd didn't want to add to the annoyance she'd sensed from Vernon Charles for her latest actions.

Her hand almost shook as she grabbed the handrail to step onto the gangplank. She stopped, took a breath, and calmed herself. "Don't be a silly ass, Bernadette. There's probably nothing here and you're scaring yourself," she muttered... but in a whisper.

She stepped onto the deck and walked towards the cockpit, she picked up the sound of a voice. It sounded muffled. She stepped inside, pushed past the helm and around the center table. The muffled sound was more like a moan.

With her hand on the hatchway, she stood and listened. The moan sounded again—she saw the blood splattered around the side of the stairs and pooled at the bottom.

She leaped down the stairs and hit the bottom to find Javier lying on the floor of the cabin with an enormous patch of blood on his abdomen. All around him was a large pool of blood.

Bernadette pulled out her phone and dialed nine one one, which got her an ambulance. Then, she had to dial nine nine nine to get the police. She placed the phone down and found a towel in the galley to hold against Javier's wound.

"Hold on, Javier, the ambulance is on its way. You'll be fine," Bernadette said. He opened his eyes and looked at her. She could see from the flutter of the eyelids he was going fast.

"You know who I am?" Javier asked.

"Yes, I do, you're Javier, the cook on The Wet Dream sailboat you escaped from," Bernadette said.

"Yes... I did... I escaped..."

Bernadette patted his face, "Wake up, Javier. You helped the kidnappers—where did they take them?"

"Take who...?"

"The Cooper family. Where did the kidnappers take the Cooper family? You've been sending messages from them."

"I send messages.... what messages....?"

Bernadette could hear the sirens of the ambulance and the police coming. Javier's eyelids were fluttering, his pupils were dilating. Without a blood transfusion, he would not last long.

"Yes, Javier, you sent the messages. Where are the hostages?" Bernadette shouted at him. She felt like she was chasing his last remaining thoughts. He was the only link to the Coopers.

"They are safe. We put them under the Soufriere Hills in Patrick, no one will find them there..." His head rolled over to the side.

Bernadette laid him on the floor and began chest compressions. The paramedics arrived and took over. She got up and stood there, watching them as they tried in vain to revive him. He'd lost too much blood.

Three police officers climbed down the stairs into the cabin, with Vernon Charles behind them. The paramedics put their emergency kit away. A paramedic looked up at the police and shook his head, "There's no saving this one. He's bled out."

Charles cleared his throat and stood behind Bernadette, "You are covered in blood, did you find him this way?"

Bernadette looked down at her blood smeared bike jersey. Her white running shoes had splotches of red, and she looked like she wore the crime scene. "Yes, I thought he'd come back to the boat. I wanted to confirm he was here before I called you, I heard him in distress and found him several minutes ago."

"You didn't think to call us first?" Charles asked, crossing his arms and staring at Bernadette. "Our crown prosecutor may want to question you. He will want to know if you are involved in this crime."

Charles turned to his constable. "Take a swab of this ladies' clothes and send them to the lab."

"It's Javier's blood." Bernadette said. She extended her arm while the constable did a swab and placed it in a jar. Then he took several pictures of her.

"Once again, you are at the center of my crime scene." Charles said.

Bernadette sighed and dropped her shoulders, "Look, I know I should have called, but I had a hunch, you know what we call an instinct. And as for my involvement in this scene, Julian let me enter the boat. I did not know he'd be here, and besides, would you have raced here on a hunch?"

Charles rubbed his chin, "You are right. We would have put it on our list and come by later today. Did you find anything—now that you're wearing most of our crime scene you can tell us something?"

"Perhaps we should go on deck," Bernadette said. She didn't want the paramedics in on their conversation. They were probably very trustworthy, but she didn't want the whereabouts of the Coopers being known.

They climbed topside to see a group of people standing on the dock, craning their necks to see what was happening. As Bernadette emerged covered in blood, it sent the crowd into a frenzy of muttered speculation.

"Let's sit at this table," Charles said. "

Bernadette sat at the table in the cockpit, Charles sat across from her. The table dropped them out of the eyesight of the crowd and lessened their speculation regarding Bernadette's appearance.

"Javier spoke to me before he died. He said the captives were under the Soufriere Hills in Patrick. He must have meant with Patrick, the person who is keeping them safe. That's all I could get out of him," Bernadette said.

"That's enough. I'll send all available manpower to the town of Soufriere, there are over three thousand households there, it will take time, but we can do it," Charles said. He rose from the table, "Now, shower on the pier, you are scaring half the town. And I don't want you in our search, you have good instincts, but bodies seem to trail you wherever you go. My police think you are bad luck."

Bernadette got up from the table and felt her legs almost buckle beneath her. She steadied herself and walked to the gangplank. The police officers holding back the crowd looked at her with wide eyes. With measured steps, she walked to the outdoor shower on the pier and turned it on. A stream of cold water fell on her.

The blood flowed onto the concrete pier and washed down the drain. There was little she could do for the running shoes. They remained a patchy red. She used her hands to squeegee the water off her body and walked to her mountain bike. She saw Travis and Melinda running up the pier towards her.

They wrapped her in a hug and Bernadette did everything she could to hold back the tears. She finally pulled herself away from them.

"Look, I'm okay. I didn't die, Javier did. Someone murdered him before I got here. He told me your family is in Soufriere. I gave the information to Charles, and he's putting every available person he has on it," Bernadette said.

"Oh my God, Bernadette, you've found our parents and my uncle, that's amazing," Melinda gushed as she hugged Bernadette again.

Bernadette pulled herself out of Melinda's embrace. "I have a location that Javier gave me as he was dying. Charles told me he has over three thousand homes to check. That's going to take time."

Travis nodded his head. "I'm not sure how much time we have. The kidnappers left another note on a police car window. They want the money transferred to them by five o'clock tomorrow night or they will kill one of our family every hour that we delay."

"Then I was wrong," Bernadette said. "Javier may have been in on the communications, but he's not the key person. That person killed him or had him killed."

Bernadette walked over to her mountain bike and picked it up. "Travis, I need you to loan me two hundred and fifty Caribbean Dollars."

"Sure, Bernadette, but what's it for?" Travis asked.

"I need to see those skateboard kids again. They knew where Javier was hiding and drew us there. There's someone else on this island involved in this, those kids probably know who that is. I need to find out."

35

THE LATE-MORNING SUN was blazing down on Bernadette as she pedaled back to the square with the skateboard kids. The warmth dried her off, but her hair clung to her in a sticky mess under her bike helmet. She brushed it out of her eyes and kept going.

She weaved through traffic towards the square as she dodged tourist buses and taxis. The place was getting busy as the locals moved about the markets and businesses. It took Bernadette a half hour before she saw the two kids Ezra had met earlier this morning.

They were back, the red and white t-shirt boys doing jumps and tricks on their boards with their friends. For now, they were oblivious to Bernadette. She rolled up on them slowly and observed them from the edge of the crowd.

The boy in red did a quick kick turn with his board and stopped. He saw her. He froze for a moment and motioned to his friend in the white t-shirt. They stared at Bernadette.

Bernadette recognized the expression. Any second now, they'd make a run for it. She jumped on her pedals and cut off the only exit they had from the square. She pulled out the roll of cash, looked down at it, and then at the boys.

They walked towards her slowly. She felt like she was pulling two fish in on a line. Any sudden movement could make them bolt. Bernadette didn't move.

"What do you want?" the boy in red asked. He was the taller of the two, with a wide face and curly hair.

"I came to give you the money we promised you. And to say I'm sorry that man hit you," Bernadette said.

The two boys looked at each other and broke into smiles. The boy in red reached forward to take the money. Bernadette pulled her hand away. "Not so fast. First, you need to answer some questions."

"What questions?" the boy in the white t-shirt asked. He had close-cropped hair and two missing front teeth. They both looked all of twelve.

"Did you read the messages you were delivering to the police?" Bernadette asked.

The boys looked at one another, the one in red tried to do a hand signal to the one in white that he obviously didn't understand. The boy in red looked up to answer...

"I'll take that as a no," Bernadette said. "Did you realize the messages you delivered involved you in a crime?"

The boys shot each other sideways glances and stared at the pavement. Neither of them uttered a word.

"Okay, I'm going to be straight with you. I want to find out the identity of the man or woman who gave you messages to leave for the police."

The boy in red looked at Bernadette, "Will he come after us if we tell?"

"No, I'll make sure he doesn't. Can you give me a description?"

The boys lowered their heads and whispered to each other. The white t-shirt boy kept shaking his head.

"My friend says we shouldn't tell," the boy in red replied.

"I could turn you over to the police," Bernadette said in a firm tone. "They might want to charge you with being accessories for the crime."

"What's an accessory?" the boy in white asked.

"It means you helped. I understand you didn't mean to, but you did. Now, you can help me find this man who used you for this bad thing," Bernadette said.

They looked at each other, then back at Bernadette. The boy in red looked at the ground and shrugged his shoulders. The one in white said, "I think he was a Rasta man."

Bernadette blinked and looked at the boy, "Why do you think that?"

"He had the tattoos on his arms.," the boy explained.

It took Bernadette a few seconds to let the words connect, "What tattoos—can you describe them?"

"Like the One Love song. My mother plays Bob Marley all the time in the house. She says he was a Rasta man."

The boy in red shot an elbow into the side of his friend. It was obvious he was giving the right information. They both became quiet and looked at the ground.

"Was he tall or short?"

"He was tall and slim; he wore fancy clothes like he was a rich man," the boy in white said. The boy in red looked down at the ground and said nothing. His elbow to his friend had not sent the message of silence.

"That's extremely helpful, now tell me your names," Bernadette said.

The boy in white said, "I'm Vincent Simeon, and this is my cousin Henry Simeon. We live over on Cedars Road."

"Thank you," Bernadette said as she offered the large wad of cash to the boys. "Now, don't spend it all on candy, you could buy yourself some new running shoes."

Vincent took the money, unfolded it, and looked at his cousin. His eyes became wider as he leafed through the cash. "Thank you very much, lady."

Bernadette watched the boys jump back on their skateboards and push out of the square. She got on her bike and rode back to the hotel. Ezra was standing at the door with Travis to meet her.

"How about if I return the bike to the shop and you take a shower and get a beer?" Ezra said.

Bernadette rolled her neck and stretched out her arms, "A shower sounds fantastic, but I need to give you some information. I have an idea about who killed Javier."

"Who is it?" Ezra asked. He stopped in mid-stride as he pushed the bike to the SUV.

"I think it's the Jamaican guy we met at the Caribbean Dreams presentation center. The two boys gave me a description that matched him," Bernadette said.

"Thomas will want to hear this. He'll be back in ten minutes. Why don't you take that shower and meet us back here?" Ezra said.

Travis walked up to Bernadette and put his hand on her shoulder. "Take some time to collect yourself. If this man is still at the presentation center, we'll have the police pick him up. But please, take a few minutes and clean yourself up."

"Okay, sure," Bernadette said. Here she had a key element to this puzzle, and she was being told to hit the showers. She trudged down the hallway, ran her card through the door, and entered the room. Melinda wasn't there.

She ran the shower as hot as she could stand it then stripped the bike gear off and was about to step into the shower—her face had splatters of blood, there was blood matted in her hair, and a long smear of dried blood ran down her leg. No wonder they all wanted her in the shower. Her body looked like she'd been in a massacre.

With great care, she washed and rinsed herself multiple times until the water in the shower was clear. It took several minutes, but when she stepped out, she felt like she'd expunged the last of Javier from her body.

Fifteen minutes later, she was back in the lobby with her hair reasonably dry and wearing a fresh t-shirt, slacks, and a pair of sandals. Thomas was sitting in the lobby with Travis and Ramirez.

"We ordered you a beer," Thomas said, "We thought you could use one."

Bernadette looked at her wristwatch, "It's eleven-thirty, that's as close to noon as I need." She picked up the Piton beer on the table and downed half of it.

"I understand the young boys had some news you'd like to share," Thomas said.

Bernadette took a breath, "Yes, they gave me a profile of the Jamaican that Ramirez and I met at the presentation center. I didn't see anyone who looked like him in the square when Ezra contacted the boys. But someone was there. That person must have gone to the sailboat to wait for Javier."

"The murderer might have received a call from Javier. Once we blew his cover, he had to run. His killer was there to meet him," Thomas said.

"Sounds like a reasonable scenario. Now that I'm cleaned up and don't resemble a murderer, I think I best go down to the station and make a statement to the police," Bernadette said.

Thomas raised an eyebrow, "Hopefully they'll take you seriously. The tales of two young boys you gave money to may not sit well with them. How about if I send Ramirez to check out Winston in Rodney Bay? If you can get the police to move on him, we can give them his exact location."

Bernadette tipped the last of the beer and got up. "I'll do a quick mouth rinse, so I don't smell like I walked out of a pub, and I'll head down to the police station."

Thomas leaned forward, "Take your cell phone with you, and perhaps Melinda and Ezra as well... just in case you get yourself into a situation where you need bail..."

"So not funny," Bernadette said. "But Melinda would be splendid company and I have an idea I'll be there for some time."

36

BERNADETTE AND MELINDA waited by the pool for Ezra to return. They sat under the umbrella as the clouds dropped a sprinkle of late afternoon rain. Melinda was unusually quiet as she sat across from Bernadette.

"How do you process all of this and act normal?" Melinda asked, with her blue eyes focusing on Bernadette.

Bernadette looked across the harbor and back at Melinda. "You realize that all of this will pass. A friend from India told me everything gets washed away by time. In India, they use the great river Ganges as their metaphor. I like to think that every day I get up, I will put what just happened into a special compartment and let it rest."

"Is that how you see discovering Javier? Like you'll put him into a compartment?" Melinda asked. There was a tremble in her voice, as if she was about to lose it.

Bernadette sensed Melinda's distress and moved closer to her, "We can't carry everything with us. I had to learn that growing up. If you remember when I met you, they sent me from my home for fighting in my village. My life became one of moving through situations and letting the past go. You must do the same thing if you want to be a surgeon."

Melinda wiped a stray tear from her eye. "Thanks for the talk, I think I'm getting anxious about things unwinding—I never expected murderers amongst the kidnappers. I've been living in a strange reality of academic studies and social events with my family, with no idea a world of corruption and crime existed—well, I did, but I thought they over-dramatized it on television."

"Unfortunately, this is part of the reality we've become involved in," Bernadette said. She saw Ezra waving at them, "It's time to go."

They walked to the police headquarters and, as expected, it took time to find someone to take her statement. As it involved the Cooper abduction, no junior officer wanted to be responsible. There were several phone calls as a desk sergeant tried to reach Vernon Charles. They waited for someone to take charge as the large ceiling fans hummed overhead and they sweated on the uncomfortable wooden chairs that had seen weary bottoms for several decades.

Finally, a short, round male officer with a worried expression came out into the main lobby and waved to Bernadette. "I am Sergeant Norville, Assistant Superintendent Charles has requested I take your statement. Please follow me."

Bernadette followed the man, who had a distinct waddle as he walked into the same room she'd met Vernon Charles several days before. She almost sighed as she took a seat and realized how deeply she'd become involved in this case. There was a moment a few days ago when she thought she'd be clear of this—that hope was fading.

RAMIREZ TOOK his time on the drive to Rodney Bay. The tourist traffic was heavy, with tour buses from the cruise ships and vans full of locals returning from the morning markets. He turned off the air conditioning, opened the window, and let the humid sea air wash over him. This was a moment to enjoy being away from the hotel. He didn't mind the bodyguard duty, but he preferred doing it in a convoy of fast-moving cars with a lightweight machine gun at his side.

He'd spent most of his time by the pool while Melinda did laps or sat under an umbrella talking on the phone with her friends back in Canada. Now, he let the wind blow, found some Latin music on the radio, and thumped the steering wheel to the beat. This was nice.

He rolled up to the Caribbean Dreams office, did a slow drive-by, and parked a block away. He needed to make a visual on Winston, the tall, well-dressed Jamaican who'd given them the sales pitch. Ramirez knew a few Jamaicans in Miami. The good ones were very good, funny, and fun to be around. The bad ones, well, he stayed clear of them.

He hadn't made a visual on his drive-by; his next attempt would be a slow walk by the window and see if Winston was there. He donned his sunglasses and did his best island-time shuffle with a casual glance in the window. He saw no one inside.

He stopped at the next building, turned around, and walked by again. This time he tried the door. It was open. With his hand on the door, he hesitated. If Winston was there, would he remember their conversation? Would he know he was there to check on him? Ramirez decided he needed to find out. If Winston put up a fight, he'd kick his ass and get in a good workout.

He pushed open the door and walked inside. Light island tunes played from a sound system on a back desk. There were no signs of recent activity. He listened for any sounds in the back room. There was nothing.

Ramirez wished he had a gun with him. Thomas had refused to let him pick one up in Castries. Guns laws in Saint Lucia were like England and Canada. There were complex regulations to purchase one and he couldn't bring one into the country.

Right now, a nice Berretta 9mm would make opening the back door feel like he had control. He felt defenseless. Keeping his left hand close to his chest and ready to strike anything that came at him, he pushed the door open with a swift motion.

He waited. There was nothing. The backroom had one table and a chair. A single piece of paper lay on the table with some large lettering. Ramirez walked towards it to read the paper.

At first, he couldn't read it. The wording was upside down. He walked closer and bent over to look at it. Finally, he understood—but it was too late.

The sign read—HE IS BEHIND YOU.

The blow that struck Ramirez in the head sent him falling forward. His body collapsed on the table—he crashed onto the floor. His world faded to black.

SERGEANT NORVILLE TOOK out a pad of paper and a pen, "Now, what is it you want to report?" He adjusted himself slightly in his chair and looked at Bernadette.

"I had a discussion with two boys this morning. They gave me a description of another person who gave them notes from the kidnappers. I think this person killed Javier," Bernadette said. She realized her words sounded all wrong. Her class training had taught her to be more decisive, more direct. This was coming out all wrong.

"What has caused your suspicion?" Norville asked.

Bernadette paused, "Someone discovered we'd found Javier. They wanted to make sure he revealed nothing to the police."

Norville rubbed his hand over his eyes and looked at his blank piece of paper. It was obvious he did not know how to write this strange sequence of events.

He put his pen down and leaned back in his chair, "Can you start first by telling me who these boys are?"

Bernadette took out a piece of paper, "They said their names were Vincent and Henry Simeon. They claimed they are cousins who live on Cedars Road."

Norville clasped his hands together. "And who did they say might have murdered our deceased victim, Javier?"

"They said he was a tall black man with a Jamaican accent. They called him a Rasta man. Perhaps they think all Jamaicans are Rastafarians, but the man fits the description of someone I met the other day at the Caribbean Dreams development in Rodney Bay—they also identified his tattoos," Bernadette said.

"This is a delightful story you've been told by some skillful boys. Did you pay them for this information?"

Bernadette's face flushed, "Yes, I did. I promised them earlier if they returned with a message from Javier, I'd pay them. I felt bad, they were mistreated by Javier and used by my partner and me."

"I see," Norville said. "Would it surprise you if I know all the people who live on Cedars Road? This is a small city and I've lived here all my life. There is not one person on that road with the last name of Simeon. These boys have fabricated a story to take your money."

Bernadette paused, "Okay, maybe they lied about their names. I get why they'd do that, but I feel strongly they were telling me the truth about the Jamaican. The man in Rodney Bay is Winston. You'll want to bring him in as a person of interest."

"How will I find him interesting? We have quite a few Jamaicans on the island. I cannot bring him in on suspicion of being a Jamaican. I'd have the press in an uproar," Norville said.

"No, it's not that. I went to Laborie after meeting with Winston, he told me to check out the show home. We discovered the show home was a trap, and the men who tried to take us hostage were murdered. I think he might have had a hand in that as well," Bernadette said. Sweat dripped down her forehead. She realized how deeply she'd become involved in the events. The more she spoke, the deeper she dug the hole.

Sergeant Norville opened a file from the side of the desk and looked at it. "Our officers in Rodney Bay interviewed Winston yesterday regarding the deaths of the two men in the Caribbean Dreams show home. He claims he knew neither of the deceased and had an alibi for the entire day you were in Laborie. Winston also stated he did not know how the men you say took you hostage gained access to the show home. They have no keys missing."

Bernadette sat back in her chair and absorbed the information. "But I think the boys' description of the man they spoke with has connected Winston to the kidnappers."

Norville made a loud sigh, "Very well, I see you will not let this go.

I will have the police in Rodney Bay interview Winston again. I'm sure he will make a fuss in the newspapers and I will hear about it in the morning. As for your two boys, I suggest you do not give them more money."

"Thanks, I'll do that. Hopefully, Charles will find the hostages in Soufriere with the information I got from Javier," Bernadette said.

"Ah, the words of a dying man. They made no sense to me. They built only part of the town of Soufriere on a hill, the rest is very flat. I understand that as of this morning, our police have checked every home in the hills. They have found nothing."

Bernadette walked out of the interview room to see Melinda and Ezra standing on the sidewalk outside.

"Did they believe your story?" Melinda asked.

"Not really, but the Sergeant made me realize there's someone else pulling the strings for our kidnappers on the island."

37

"TELL RAMIREZ the police in Rodney Bay are on their way to interview Winston. I hope he hasn't made a run for it," Bernadette said to Ezra as they walked back to the hotel.

Ezra pulled out his phone and dialed. "He's not answering, it goes to voicemail. He might be somewhere he can't answer it. I'll leave a message and let him know."

"There's something we're missing in the people pulling the strings on the kidnapping," Bernadette said. "I have a feeling they're here on the island and they can lead us to the Coopers."

Thomas came out of the hotel as they approached, his lips were set in a tight line. "How was your interview?"

"Well, I was selling the idea of Winston being involved, and the sergeant wasn't buying it. I heard the search in Soufriere isn't going well," Bernadette said.

Thomas shook his head, careful not to make eye contact with Melinda, "I'm afraid not. They've done a house-to-house search of all the houses in the hills. Now, they'll need to go into the town itself—that could take some time. I hope they find something before they transfer the money tomorrow."

Melinda stepped forward to face Thomas. "they'll kill my parents when they get their money—is that what you want to say?"

Thomas held her gaze, "My advice has been to not release the money until the hostages are free, or we see proof of life. I've seen none of this. Your brother has proceeded—I hope he is right."

Melinda broke into tears and pushed past Thomas into the hotel. They watched in silence as she walked away.

Bernadette moved the hair out of her eyes and cleared her throat. "I've been speculating about the kidnappers and what they've been doing on the island. They've had Steven and Michael attempting to kidnap or kill anyone who came to help Melinda and Travis. And they had Javier hiding out, using him to send messages to the Coopers for ransom demands..."

"What's your conclusion?" Ezra asked.

Bernadette looked at Thomas. "There has to be someone else who is in control of the kidnap operations here in Castries. When you went searching for Pierre D' Abboville, the captain of the boat, did you find anything at his home?"

Thomas shook his head, "No, the place he'd listed as his residence in Castries was vacant. The people who rented it to him claim he'd moved out to take the job on the sailboat."

"The only notes I've seen from the kidnappers has been regarding the return of the Coopers and the uncle, I've never seen mention of the captain or the cook. We know the cook was here all the time, and perhaps the captain was as well. My best guess is he was living back on the boat when the police returned it to the harbor," Bernadette said.

"And, he was waiting for Javier when he came back?"

"That's just one scenario I can see. What if the captain came back to Saint Lucia after they took the hostages aboard the large fishing vessel off the coast? The speed boat could have returned to Gros Islet and the captain could have made his way back onto the sailboat when the police returned it to the charter company," Bernadette said.

"Wouldn't someone at the charter company notice there was a person on board the sailboat?" Ezra asked.

Bernadette rubbed her shoulder and looked up at the clouds, "... what if someone had placed a new charter on the boat?"

"And not take it out of the harbor. Wouldn't that be suspicious?" Thomas asked.

Ezra turned to Thomas. "It happens all the time in yacht clubs. Some clients don't know how to sail a boat. They do a live-aboard for a week, then wait for a captain to show up or just throw parties on the boat to show their friends how cool they are."

Thomas nodded. "It's worth checking out. I'll contact the charter company and see if the sailboat is rented—remind me of the name I'm asking for?"

"The Wet Dream," Bernadette said with a slight smile.

Thomas sighed, "Some yachtsman had a strange sense of humor when he came up with that name."

Bernadette laughed. "It probably just came to him."

Ezra groaned and shook his head. His cell phone rang, he opened it and put it to his ear to listen. His face looked like it had dropped. He said into the phone, "We'll be right there to pick you up." He ended his call and turned to Thomas. "It's Ramirez. He just woke up in a medical center in Rodney Bay. Someone knocked him out at the Caribbean Dreams sales center."

"Is he okay?" Thomas asked.

"He sounded a bit off his game, with slurred speech, but getting clocked on the noggin can do that," Ezra said. "The police found him when they came to do an interview with Winston."

"It sounds like Winston made a run for it and someone stayed behind to cover his tracks," Bernadette said.

"Ezra, take a taxi and pick up Ramirez, I'll stay here with the Coopers. It's best if you stay here as well, Bernadette—you'll be of more value here, looking after the Coopers."

"Sure, happy to help, but what are you going to do about Ramirez?" Bernadette asked.

"It depends on what Ezra finds out when he talks to the medical people. I'd like to send him to the United States and have him seen by a doctor. He told me someone had knocked him unconscious on his way to the airport coming here. A second time in a week is not good for the brain. My agency has complete medical coverage for all our contractors, we'll look after him," Thomas said.

Ezra hailed a cab, got into it, and left. Bernadette massaged a tight muscle in her neck and let the thoughts regarding their hostage takers roll around in her head. "There's a connection with these people. That's been the key that's eluded us."

"Give me a clue where your train of thought came from and I'll see if I can climb aboard," Thomas said.

"I connect everything to the Caribbean Dreams development. We know there are over fifty million dollars in deposits that Caribbean Dreams gets to access on Friday. What if this is just a scam to take the deposits?"

Thomas raised an eyebrow. "That's a real possibility. I already ran that by Travis, however, he's resigned to pay the ransom."

"But you and I both expect it's a smokescreen to hide the actual crime?"

"That we agree on. Everything my computer geek in Europe sent me tells me that."

"Good, and here's something else. Isn't it a strange coincidence that the man who was at the center of the Caribbean Dreams development disappears at sea the night before he was to get off the cruise ship?"

"Perhaps he decided they would discover his scam?" Thomas said.

"Or it was another distraction," Bernadette said.

"You figure he jumped overboard and had a boat pick him up off the coast somewhere at night? That's risky. I saw a picture of the man in his bio, he looked rather out of shape to be floundering in open waters."

Bernadette put her hands on her hips. "You can walk off any cruise ship disguised as another passenger or crew member. All you need to do is steal their cruise pass card, you show it at security and you're off. With the volume of people leaving those ships, the security doesn't have the resources to register who they're looking at."

"And he could have drawn some blood from himself beforehand and left it on the railing?"

"That would make it look like suicide. And he also made a lot of outrageous claims that night in the bar. The man I met in the Tiki bar in the harbor said he upset Valdis with pointed questions."

"Couldn't he have been embarrassed enough to commit suicide?"

"It could be it added to his show. He wanted to make a big scene about how well his investments were doing before he left. It drew more attention to his being missed off the boat."

"If your scenario has some truth to it, then this Valdis could run this crime under our very noses on this island."

"I have a strong feeling that's not happening. He'll need to be somewhere to get a good head start in his getaway when the money is transferred," Bernadette said. She turned towards the hotel, "I'm starving. Let's order lunch to your room and get your computer booted up. We need to put Google to work."

38

BERNADETTE JOINED Thomas in his room, it looked a mess in there. She had to move his clothes off a chair to sit beside him at the desk. Several pairs of shoes and socks lay beside the door, with the bed covered in papers.

"Sorry for the mess, I'm what I call a 'cluttered thinker.' The more clutter I have around me, the more I can think. My wife calls me a disheveled mess in progress when I travel. When she travels with me, I have to clean up my act," Thomas said.

Bernadette looked around the room. "I've never brought this much stuff with me to trash a room like this—but good job."

Thomas grinned sheepishly and opened his laptop as Bernadette went to the door to get the room service tray of two sandwiches and a large pot of coffee.

"What you're about to witness is the full power of the Thomas Davina Detective Agency at work, as I use some very clandestine websites to make background checks on our suspects."

"Is what you're using even slightly legal?"

Thomas winked at her. "As we're in the Caribbean and not in North America or Europe and you tell no one outside this room, we're fine. My friend in eastern Europe gave me a way to tap into the

Interpol, CIA, and FBI databases. He does a data dump from them every month and leaves me with the information. That way I'm never noticed when I access the files."

"But don't these agencies find out your guy is doing these downloads? Aren't they encrypted and secure?"

"Oh, they are, and my Eastern European computer geek helped build the firewalls that keep these guys safe, but all walls can be broken, and for our purposes, we're only after low-level criminals. Some of this stuff is just stored as excess in their servers. I doubt they'd notice my guy was in there. It equates to the police department having their traffic fine computer accessed."

Bernadette shrugged, "So I'm not seeing anything I'll have to report to my police department when I sign up or to my priest when, and if, I ever make my confession."

"Let's check our captain first," Thomas said. His fingers flew over the keys as he hit various websites. Bernadette took a sandwich off the tray on the bed and poured herself a coffee. She didn't want to see what site Thomas was on.

"There, we have him. Our Captain Pierre D 'Abboville was born in Calais, France, and immigrated to Martinique when he was twenty-one. He spent time on cruise ships for several years while making his home in Montserrat."

"Isn't Montserrat off limits right now because of an active volcano?" Bernadette asked.

"Only parts of it, half the island is off-limits, the other half is habitable. They are still evacuating the island with every new eruption."

"What about our Latvian developer? What does his bio have to say?"

"Valdis also spent several years on cruise ships... this is interesting, the same cruise lines and the same years as Pierre and he also owned property on Montserrat. He had a hotel he was trying to build on the south side of the island that he abandoned several years ago when the volcano erupted."

"Did you find out about the sailboat rental?" Bernadette asked.

"Yes, I did. Someone chartered The Wet Dream... and I still find that name preposterous for a boat..." Thomas said with raised eyebrows. "They chartered it the day after the Saint Lucian police released the boat back to the charter company."

"Any idea if there's a connection to Valdis or Pierre?" Bernadette asked as she swallowed a bite of her sandwich.

"It was a private individual who put it on their credit card," Thomas said as he rifled over the small desk covered in a pile of papers. "Yes, here it is. A female by the name of Esmeralda Vasquez from Miami, Florida. I'll run her name in the system and see what I get."

Bernadette drank her coffee and watched Thomas work. At that moment, the world of being a private investigator was appealing. She was feeling more and more removed from the very idea of joining the ramrod straight and by-the-book Royal Canadian Mounted Police in Canada. They were going to put her through six months of training—to do what? Would it be as cool as what she was doing now?

Thomas punched more keys and leaned into the laptop as the data showed on the screen. "I'll be damned—she's related to Emilio Vasquez. He's the guy that was killed in the car explosion at the airport this week."

"He's the guy you gave your rental to?" Bernadette asked.

"Yes, and from looking at his profile, he was one nasty guy. He ran offshore gambling and money laundering for the drug cartels in Miami. The FBI has been after him for years. Looks like Senor Vasquez ran out of luck."

"He got car bombed by the one intended to kill you—that's crazy," Bernadette said.

"Yeah, that is crazy, but this brings the idea of a syndicate you thought might be involved in this kidnapping. It looks like our Valdis has some very heavy muscle in the Miami Cartel. They could have fronted the money to do the initial land assembly here in Saint Lucia."

"But why the kidnapping? Are they the type that has it as part of their business plan?" Bernadette asked.

"There's no record of Vasquez being a part of a kidnapping. I'm not sure how this came about, or if they connect to Valdis."

Bernadette sipped her coffee and looked at the screen. "Something has bothered me about the disappearance of Valdis."

"What's that?"

"I figure it takes less than four hours to fly from Miami to Saint Lucia. Valdis came on a cruise ship. Why would he do that?"

"Yes, that's been something I've wondered about as well..."

"How about if the cartel gave the money to Valdis for the fraud and sets him up for the fall? He double-crosses them, slipping off the cruise ship and taking out Vasquez at the airport."

"But they meant the bomb for me," Thomas protested.

Bernadette set her coffee cup down and leveled her gaze at Thomas. "If the bomb was radio-controlled, the bombers saw who got in the car. Also, the car rental counter gave the keys to Vasquez—you didn't."

"That's a possibility I never thought of... I thought the kidnappers wanted me dead."

Bernadette raised her eyebrows. "You could have appeared at a convenient time; you hid the murder of their competition. With Vasquez out of the way, Valdis takes all the money, and since everyone thinks he's dead, he makes the perfect getaway."

Thomas shook his head, "My, you have a fantastic mind. I wish you'd consider working for me."

Bernadette smiled and winked, "The stuff in my head is weird, so it's easy for me to understand the criminal mind."

"I still don't understand the kidnapping," Thomas said.

"My guess is the Cooper's uncovered something. The kidnappers are holding them until the development closes. It's a way of keeping the attention off the Caribbean Dreams scam."

Thomas nodded his head, "Your scenario makes sense. I think Vasquez came to the island to take charge of the operation. If it was going off the rails with the kidnapping, he may have wanted to take over."

"We won't know until the police get them all in that tiny interview room to hear their stories," Bernadette said. "What should we do with this information about Vasquez? Should we give it to A.I. Charles?"

"He'll wonder how we got it. I'll send a message to one of my FBI friends. He'll do a back channel to the FBI in Miami. I'm sure they've learned about Vasquez by now, but they may not have shared it with the Saint Lucian police. This happens all the time in the world of police work."

Bernadette stood up and stretched. "I'm going to see how Melinda is doing and check on a few leads of my own. If your FBI friend has any insights into the Miami Cartel, I'd like to hear about it later. I think my brain needs a break from how convoluted this case has become."

"You and me both," Thomas said. He resumed his work on the laptop and pulled up more files.

Bernadette left Thomas's room and tried to let all the talk of Valdis and Vasquez wash from her brain. She needed to concentrate. Her focus needed to be on the last words of Javier. There was something she was missing. If she gave herself time, she'd find it.

39

BERNADETTE STEPPED out of Thomas's room and saw Travis in the hallway. She walked up to him and folded into his arms with a hug. She looked up at him, "How are you holding up?"

He kissed her on the forehead. "I'm doing okay. The money is ready to be transferred. The Saint Lucian police will be ready to trace the kidnappers phone call. I'm just hoping by tomorrow I'll be hugging my parents."

"I hope you are, too. I'd love to hug your mom and dad and get to meet that crazy uncle of yours," Bernadette said.

"You'd like Uncle Max, he gets hard to understand sometimes when he's drunk, but other times he's okay."

"We still need to explore if there's a connection between your uncle and Valdis."

"You still think there's a link with my uncle and this guy who disappeared off the cruise ship?"

"I like to explore all options." Bernadette said. "I'll meet you later if you like." She gave him another hug and kissed him on the lips.

Bernadette opened the door to her room and instantly regretted that kiss. She needed to get control of her emotions. She was attracted to Travis—this was not the time to act on it. But in times of extreme stress like this, she couldn't stop herself.

Melinda was sitting on the bed. She had a diary open on her lap; she closed it when Bernadette entered the room.

"Don't let me stop you from writing. I'm going to check my emails if that's okay with you."

Melinda relaxed her shoulders and opened the diary again, "Thanks, I'm just putting the events down. I hope I can write a joyful entry in here tomorrow."

"I've got a feeling you will," Bernadette said with a forced smile.

Bernadette waited until Melinda returned to her writing. She turned to the laptop and let her mind focus on the last words of Javier. He'd said something about the Soufriere Hills and that the Coopers were safe in Patrick. The words were strange, but a dying man can say almost anything.

She opened Melinda's laptop and looked over her shoulder to see her friend deep in her notes. With one flick of the keys, she clicked onto the Google website and brought up Montserrat. There were news items that came up about the evacuation of the island, she ignored them as she went to the map.

Her interest was on the south side of the island, and where Valdis might have had a hotel. The site came up; she hit the plus button to magnify the map and—a chill went down her spine.

"Oh my God, there's a Soufriere volcano in Montserrat," Bernadette yelled over her shoulder to Melinda.

"Of course, there is," Melinda said as she raised her head from her diary. "The Caribbean Islands that were once French call their volcanoes Soufriere, it means sulphur mine. And they mined their sulphur there—didn't you know that? What's that got to do with the emails you're looking at?"

Bernadette nodded her head, "Yes, I know the French name for a sulphur mine, but they call the one in Montserrat Soufriere Hills... and I just wanted to check on that first before I looked at my emails."

Melinda smiled, "That's nice, I'm glad."

Bernadette looked back at the map. She traced the roads and

rivers from the center of the Soufriere Hills towards the coast. She looked for clues like she would when tracking game in a hunt. As her fingers traced over the screen, she found the answer—It was too obvious at first and then it made all the sense in the world.

"Holy crap! I found them—I discovered where your family is," Bernadette screamed. She jumped from her chair and ran out of the room.

40

BERNADETTE RAN from the room to Travis's door and pounded on it. "Travis, are you there?"

Travis came out of the room with a piece of paper in his hand. "What is it?"

"I've found them—I mean, I know where they are—it solves the riddle of what Javier told me," Bernadette blurted out, then took a breath.

Travis closed his eyes and opened them again, "You'd better come in and explain yourself."

Bernadette walked into the room and sat on the chair. Travis sat beside her while she took a few breaths. "Javier said the hostages were under the Hills of Soufriere and safe in Patrick. I assumed that meant they were with a person named Patrick. It's an actual place in Montserrat—Patrick is a district. That's where Valdis Kalnins built a hotel."

"Is that the man who is missing off the cruise ship?"

"Yes, and he was originally from Latvia. Don't you follow all the connections? Your Uncle Max was from Latvia. They must have met somewhere in Latvia or Canada. If we hire a plane and fly to Montserrat, we'll find your parents."

Travis leaned back in his chair and stared at Bernadette. "I appreciate you want to find my parents as much as I do, but this note from the kidnappers arrived moments ago. It includes a picture of my parents and Max. They left it outside the police station."

"They sent a picture?" Bernadette asked as Travis handed the note to her.

She took the paper and looked at it. Luke and Frida were sitting on a bed with Max in a chair by their side. They looked grim. There was no way to get a smile out of that photo. Both Luke and Max hadn't shaved in several days and Frida looked like she'd slept in her clothes. But they were alive. The photo had a date stamp of that morning.

"The first picture of them—they seem exhausted," Bernadette said as she held the photo. She read the body of the letter and looked up at Travis. "They say they'll release your family tomorrow after five o'clock. But they don't say where."

"I spoke with Vernon Charles on the phone after the police delivered this to me. He feels the entire thing about Soufriere was a ruse by Javier. It was to misdirect us. He's convinced we stay the course, pay the ransom, and wait for the kidnappers to comply with their end of the bargain."

Bernadette swallowed hard, her next words would be hard to express. "Travis, I don't trust them. Both Thomas and I think this is about the fifty million being held in escrow. One minute after five tomorrow, that money goes into the Caribbean Dreams account. Don't you get what's happening?"

"Why would they bother to kidnap my parents and my uncle? They could wait until this Friday and take off with the money. Your scenario doesn't add up, Bernadette," Travis said.

"There's something more to it. Why not let me check it out? I could go to Montserrat—if my intuition is right, I'll find your parents. If I'm wrong, you wait for the kidnappers to release them."

Travis exhaled, his eyes narrowed as he looked at Bernadette, "I'm tired of hearing this, we've been through this several times. Tomorrow we do the exchange. I need you to stay away from

Montserrat or any other place you think the kidnappers have my family." He stood up and took the paper from Bernadette. "Now, I have phone calls to my bank and lawyers..."

"—And you need me and my crazy ideas to leave—is that what you're getting at?" Bernadette asked as she stood. They were inches from each other. She could feel his body heat, but she was so pissed at him there was no attraction. In one motion, she turned and headed for the door, slamming it behind her as she left.

Walking down the hall, she noticed Thomas looking out his door. "What's going on?"

Bernadette stopped. "Nothing is going on, I found the key to the riddle I got from Javier. They are under the Soufriere Hill Volcano in Montserrat, in a district called Patrick. I explained it all to Travis, and he still won't accept it."

"He's lost in the moment between denial and reality," Thomas said. "Let's head down to the lobby lounge."

They found a table away from the other guests and ordered coffee. Bernadette went over her findings in Montserrat.

Thomas stirred his coffee and listened to Bernadette. He looked up at with a smile, "I wondered about Montserrat, myself. I did some research on the island as I thought it might be a place to hide the hostages."

Bernadette leaned forward. "There's no way the police or Travis will act on this. We need to get a plane for Montserrat."

"Unfortunately, we cannot do that," Thomas said.

"Why—who's going to stop us?"

"There're no commercial flights to Montserrat because of the volcano eruptions. The only way to get on the island is by boat. We'd have to fly to Antigua," Thomas said with a slight grin.

"You've already checked this out, haven't you?"

Thomas turned his head to one side, "Let's say I made some quick inquiries after you left my room. Now that you've made all the connections—we need to search the island for the hostages."

"But what about Travis—he'll fire you?" Bernadette protested.

"I've been as good as fired when Travis stopped listening to my advice on the hostage negotiations. He's made me into a babysitter—I suggest we go on the hunt—you up for it?"

"You'd have to tie me up to hold me back," Bernadette said.

Ezra arrived with Ramirez at his side. Ramirez looked tired and walked with a limp. Ezra sat him down in a chair and took the one beside him.

"You don't look too good," Bernadette said.

Ramirez put his hand to the back of his head, "Someone got me pretty good. I can't wait to find the person to return the favor."

Bernadette was beside him, she put her hand on his shoulder. "Concussions are nothing to be messed with. Maybe you need to take a break."

"I've had concussions before—any break in the case?" Ramirez asked.

"We've an idea where they're hiding the hostages. I can get us in by plane to Antigua with a quick boat to Montserrat. I'll need some wheels when we get there," Thomas said.

"Ezra can probably secure some wheels there—I can get us some protection when we arrive. I'm not going anywhere on this job without a piece," Ramirez said.

"Whoa, I'm booking you on a plane back to Miami and into a diagnostic clinic at my agency's expense," Thomas said. "You've done enough."

Ramirez shook his head, "No, I haven't done enough, someone got the drop on me. They're trying to make fools of us. If you've got intel that gives us even a chance of saving these people, I say it's a go."

Thomas leaned forward, "What kind of protection are we talking?"

Ramirez put his hand to the back of his head and winced slightly, "Ezra and I will head back to some of those rum shacks we saw in Gros Islet. There's always someone there who will sell some small firearms. We take them with us and dump them in the ocean on the way back."

"How are you in any shape to travel?" Bernadette asked.

"I'm a US Army Ranger, I served in Panama and the Gulf War

where I had several concussions. There's tinnitus in my ears that sounds like bells. I told my wife God gave me chimes to tell me I'm one of the anointed ones."

"She didn't buy into that bullshit... did she?" Bernadette asked.

"She's a Latino Catholic..."

Bernadette shook her head, "... I get it, I'm Irish and Native Cree Catholic, our weirdness transcends the imagination."

"If you're done discussing your strange ways, perhaps we'll get down to business," Thomas said. "Ezra, find us some transport in Montserrat. Ramirez, hold off on the weapons for now. I'll confirm our flights and a boat to Antigua. Keep everything to yourselves—I'll let everyone know in a few hours what we have."

41

FRIDA COOPER LAY on the bed beside Luke. The big event was over. Their jailers had marched in, told them to pose for a picture, and then left. That was it. For a moment, Max was in the room facing the little Spaniard and the strange man Max said he knew from Latvia.

Everything would be over tomorrow, the kidnappers promised. Frida did not doubt his words. She saw his massive hands flex several times as he spoke. It was a nervous tick. The little Spaniard she'd nicknamed Tony snapped their photo while the dark-looking man paced back and forth. Each time Tony took a picture, he looked at it and told him to take another. After several, he grunted his approval, and they left the room.

They had no time to speak with Max. He whispered, "I'm sorry," as the Spaniard pushed him out of the room. Max said he'd asked the kidnappers to take his life for Frida and Luke's. Frida hugged him and told him that was a gracious gesture, but she didn't think it would work.

Frida made peace with herself and accepted that tomorrow would be their last day on this earth. She wasn't the most religious of people, but she'd decided that if this was the way she had to die, there was one request she'd make. She'd ask them to shoot them in the heart and bury them in a shallow grave with instructions of where to find them.

As she lay there with Luke softly snoring beside her, she imagined a lovely funeral at their church with matching coffins for Luke and her. Max would probably be separate as his family in Latvia might have a say in it. She couldn't assume he'd want to be buried with them.

But there would be lots of flowers, a nice choir, and those little sandwiches with tea afterward. She let these thoughts spin round her head, then realized she was descending into madness. She sighed as the image of the coffins left the church in the funeral cars.

"Frida, don't get caught up in this. Kick that little turd in the nuts before he shoots you," she said out loud.

Luke woke with a start, "Did you say something?"

"No, dear, you were snoring—go back to sleep."

42

BERNADETTE AVOIDED TRAVIS THAT EVENING. She swam in the pool and came back to the room as Melinda was leaving for dinner with Travis. She begged off with claims of catching up on emails.

When Melinda left, Bernadette slipped back into Thomas's room to see what they'd come up with. Thomas was beaming when she came in.

"I've found a plane to take us to Antigua. It's a Beechcraft King Air, with an airspeed of three hundred miles per hour and seating for nine passengers. It will get there in less than an hour. Ezra contacted his old British Army group who are stationed on Montserrat."

"Does that mean they'll let us land there?" Bernadette asked.

Thomas shook his head, "No, unfortunately, the airport is closed to anyone but British Army and evacuation flights. Remember, they're still getting people off the island because of the active volcano. An army unit will meet with us in Sugar Bay on the south side of the island. From there we'll search the area called St. Patrick's."

"Is Ramirez going to bring weapons?" Bernadette asked.

Thomas winked at her, "I convinced him we didn't need them. The British Army will have all the firepower we need. And I told him that us carrying guns might jeopardize your chances with your police force in Canada. He agreed to back off on the idea."

"I'm so glad he went along with that. Guns in the hands of too many people make me jumpy—especially when the guy with the gun has a score to settle," Bernadette said.

"Good point," Thomas said. "I've also persuaded Ramirez to stay at the hotel tomorrow with the Coopers."

"He's okay with that?"

"He realized his bump on the head took more out of him than he thought. I'll have him on a plane to America as soon as this is over and get a full MRI to make certain he's okay."

"And of course, he won't go until this mission is over?"

"Of course not. There's way too much Army Ranger in him," Thomas said with a smile. He picked up a piece of paper, "the flight leaves tomorrow at 0600 hours, lands in Antigua at 0655. I've arranged a boat too Montserrat at 0745 to meet Ezra's British Army pals."

"What's our cover story for Travis and Melinda?" Bernadette asked.

"I'll tell them, Ezra, and you will be in different locations on the island. That way we can be there the moment the hostages appear."

"You think he'll buy that? Travis has already forbidden me anywhere near where I can get in the way," Bernadette said.

"I'll tell him I've cleared it with Charles," Thomas said.

"And you've actually done that?"

"Well, not really. I'll be leaving Charles a message late tonight that we'll help as much as we can. It will be very vague and hard to discern what I meant by it," Thomas said.

"You're very good at this. Did you learn this in your detective work?"

"No, in my years of working in the military police. Asking for permission often took hours—assuming permission took seconds. I'm sure you'll learn this in the police force, and it will make your life so much easier."

Bernadette entered her room and logged back into Melinda's

computer. Pulling up a website on Montserrat, she progressed through the complete history of the island. It listed the little island of ten miles long and seven miles wide as a British Overseas Territory.

As she scrolled down the island, she witnessed the devastation the volcano had caused since it erupted in 1995. Residents had fled to the north of the little island, which was called the 'exclusion zone.' The buildings lay covered in ash and a thick layer of mud from the pyroclastic flow, that was more worrisome than the eruption. The flow barreled down the slope of the volcano and engulfed all living things in a mass of smoke and heat that would suffocate them in seconds.

She heard Melinda's voice outside in the hallway. Bernadette closed the laptop and threw off her top and pulled off her shorts. As the door opened, she jumped into bed and pulled the covers over herself. She peeked out at Melinda with an exaggerated sleepy eye.

"Did I wake you?" Melinda asked.

Bernadette rubbed her eyes, "I was kind of tossing and turning myself to sleep. How are you and Travis holding up?"

Melinda's shoulders sagged. "We're trying to be strong for each other. We know if we can make it through tomorrow it's going to be fine." She paused for a moment and undressed. "I have a feeling everything will work out. Travis is doing everything he can to appease the kidnappers and the police are totally here for us. I just know it's going to come together."

Bernadette watched Melinda go into the bathroom and listened as she kept her monologue going. At this moment, she felt it imperative to let her ramble. None of it made sense now, but it's what Melinda needed to do.

She came out of the bathroom wearing silk boxers and a top in a floral print. It amazed Bernadette at how well Melinda dressed for bed.

"I keep wondering how my parents and my uncle are holding up, but I know my dad's such a total survivor and my mother... well, you know there's no stopping her. And, of course, my Uncle Max, he'll have them all in stitches with jokes..." Melinda said. She paused for a long moment and looked at Bernadette. "You need to tell me it's going to be okay..." She was holding back tears.

Bernadette leaped out of her bed and engulfed Melinda in a hug. "Of course, they'll be fine. I'll be hanging with Ezra and Thomas—and I'll be there the moment they're released. At that very moment, we'll call in the hug brigade and welcome them back."

Melinda burst into tears, "You're the best liar on the planet—but I love you for that."

Bernadette hugged her hard. "Yes, I tell marvelous stories, but I'm good with happy endings. Now get some sleep."

MELINDA SNUFFLED and wept for over an hour with Bernadette beside her. She had to wait until Melinda fell asleep and snored soundly to return to her own bed. Lying there and listening to Melinda's snores, she reviewed the events of the next day.

What if she was wrong? Had she really thought it through? Maybe all of this was a diversion? If Vernon Charles was right, Javier had told her a lie with his last breath.

Bernadette's mother had always told her to believe her first instincts, and now, as the night progressed into the early morning, she doubted everything she'd ever thought or learned. Her bedside clock showed forty-thirty. She got out of bed and treaded softly into the bathroom.

She slipped on her black bikini swimwear, not her first choice, but she hadn't had time to wash her underwear and her sports bra had bloodstains. Then she pulled on her t-shirt and a pair of shorts and put on her running shoes. The dust from the lava fields in Montserrat would probably trash her clothes, but she didn't care. With a deep breath, she crept out of the room and closed the door behind her.

This time, she truly hoped she'd return with the Cooper family and no regrets or disappointment. Melinda and Travis had enough of those. It was time to turn this situation around.

43

BERNADETTE MET THOMAS, Ezra, and Ramirez in the lobby. The hotel was in semi-darkness. A night clerk was at the front desk. Two police officers stood on the road outside the hotel, smoking cigarettes and talking.

Thomas looked at Bernadette, "You'll need some better clothes than that for the lava fields."

"No problem, boss. I asked the Brits to get her some gear. They'll have some for me as well," Ezra said.

"Well done, Ezra, your British connections came through," Thomas said as he placed a hand on his shoulder.

"I pulled those blokes' arses out of some tough shit back in the day. They told me they'd get us a few pints if we find the hostages. But they've got a betting pool at five to one odds we find nothing. I think that's a bit cheeky."

Bernadette dug her hand into her pocket and pulled out two one-hundred-dollar bills. "Put me down to win. I like our odds."

Thomas pulled out his wallet and took out the same amount and so did Ramirez. "We're in. You think your Brits are up for this?"

Ezra smiled. "They'll think we're easy marks." He turned to Bernadette as he extracted his own money out, "Well, me lady, we're all in as they say in poker—so here's to finding our people all safe and sound."

"There's one more wrinkle in this," Thomas said. "I can't go with you."

"What? You're the brains behind this, boss," Ezra protested.

"No, I'm not—Bernadette is. I must stay here to keep Travis from going off the deep end as we near the end of our timeline for today. I have a feeling that things will get unpleasant as the zero-hour approaches and our hostages haven't arrived. And remember, I'll need to cover for your whereabouts should Travis or Charles enquire about you," Thomas said.

Thomas took Bernadette aside, "Look, Bernadette, I know I may have called this hostage thing a game, but now it's real. I want you to stay safe, keep well behind Ezra and his British Army friends. I don't know what you'll find over there—but the hostage-takers are serious about getting the money. They'll kill you if they get the chance. You got that?"

Bernadette hugged Thomas, "I got that."

They piled into the SUV and headed to the little airport in the town. The strip was parallel to the cruise ships and smaller turbo-propped planes ferried passengers to various Caribbean Islands.

A thin ribbon of light broke through the darkness as they approached the airport. Bernadette checked her watch, it was five-fifteen, sunrise would be at five-thirty. The tiredness she felt disappeared, and the excitement of the hunt for the hostages replaced it.

They drove past the major terminal to a charter hangar. A man in a white uniform greeted them. Ezra stopped the vehicle and opened the doors. He pulled out a duffel bag and handed it to the man.

The hangar door opened, and a tractor pulled the plane out. Bernadette turned to Thomas, "That's a pretty big aircraft for just Ezra and me and the Coopers to return in."

Thomas was about to answer when an ambulance drove up. Two paramedics got out and began unloading stretchers. "I thought our hostages might need some help when you find them. These paramedics can't travel to Montserrat with you—their company wouldn't allow it. They'll remain with the plane until you return to Antigua."

"You thought of everything," Bernadette said.

"Let's hope so. If you come back empty-handed, I'll have an enormous expense. If you find them, I'll be handing the bill to Travis Cooper, which I'm sure he'll have no problem with. But I know you'll find them," Thomas said.

"You have that much faith in my instincts?" Bernadette asked.

Thomas placed both his hands on Bernadette's shoulders. "Young lady, if I could hire people like you with your talent and instincts, I'd be the number one detective agency in the world."

Bernadette hugged Thomas, "Thanks, I'm glad you have faith in me." She turned to Ezra, "Are we ready to board?"

"Yes, we are," Ezra said. He looked up at the sky overhead. "There's some weather coming in from the east. I'm hoping it moves north before it hits Antigua or Montserrat."

"What kind of weather?" Bernadette asked.

Ezra ran his hand over his face as droplets of rain fell, "Right now it's a category two hurricane. We'll see how it develops as we go."

They strapped into their seats. The two paramedics, a large man with a bald head in his forties and a woman in her mid-twenties, took seats in the back to secure their equipment. The plane took off with a roar of the twin engines, climbing into the morning sun. Bernadette looked below to see the crystal-clear ocean near the beach. The waters near the shore were a blue-green. There were coral reefs with a spatter of white waves breaking over them. Further out, the water darkened into a deep blue.

She let her gaze move to the east. An enormous wall of clouds was forming. There was a tower on top that looked like a massive castle. This was the hurricane Ezra mentioned.

Bernadette turned to Ezra. "How long until this hurricane hits us?"

"If we're lucky, it will turn before it does. But no matter which way it goes, it's going to glance us. Let's pray it gives us just a light touch," Ezra said. He looked away and closed his eyes.

44

Travis Cooper woke with nausea in his stomach. He drank some water, dressed, and headed for the hotel lobby. It was past seven, the smell of breakfast wafted in the air. A few guests lined up in front of the omelet station in the restaurant. The aroma of eggs hit his stomach like a hammer—he did a quick exit to the lobby toilets and made it just in time to throw up. He washed his face, combed his hair, and made his way into the lobby. Thomas was standing there.

"You, okay?" Thomas asked. "You look pale."

Travis ran his hand over his forehead. "Perhaps I picked up a cold."

"A case of the nerves. Don't worry, I've always had a nervous stomach in my cases. This one is no different. The key thing is to keep moving forward, is everything in place with your bank?" Thomas asked.

Thomas blew out a breath. "Yes, the entire ten million is ready to be transferred to the number they sent me last night."

"Do you mind if I see the instructions? I want to make sure everything is in order. I've done many of these, and one number out of place can make everything go off the rails as they say."

"Of course," Travis said. He took a paper out of his pocket and handed it to Thomas. "My bankers assured me this account will receive my deposit. We don't know where the money will end up, they could transfer it to several banks in a matter of minutes."

Thomas stared hard at the paper. He committed the bank and transit numbers to memory and handed the paper back. "It seems in order. Now, I suggest you get something into your stomach, even if it's a piece of unbuttered toast. This day will stretch until forever, or it will seem that way."

"I suppose you're right. I'll ask for some tea and toast and try to relax," Travis said. "Will you join me?"

"In a few minutes. I left something in my room. I'll meet you back here," Thomas said as he hurried away.

He turned quickly and made it back to his room. He opened his laptop and punched in the numbers he'd memorized into an email. The Coopers needed an added insurance policy. He was about to hand them one. It wasn't what they'd asked for, but Thomas's motto was to over-deliver in his services. His computer hacker had found the fifty million dollars in the bank in Barbados. The kidnappers would receive an error message from their bank when they tried to move it. And they'd get the same message when they tried to access the money from Travis Cooper. This would hold the kidnappers off until their own computer people sorted it out and buy the hostages more time. He hit send on the email and headed back to the dining room.

Thomas returned to the lobby to see Melinda sitting with Travis. She looked up; her eyes were pools of liquid. She'd been in tears. He sat down beside her and placed his hand on hers.

"You must hold yourself together, my dear. This will end well today—I feel good about it," Thomas said.

"Really? Because I got the same awful stomach as Travis. I understand you recommend dry toast and tea, Thomas."

"An old soldier's trick I learned in my army years. Keep the oil out of the stomach so there's nothing it can use for propellant," Thomas said with a wink.

Melinda sipped her tea, "Thanks for that. I just wish Bernadette was here. Do you know when she left? I didn't hear her leave the room this morning."

"Quite early. I believe Ezra dropped her in Gros Islet at half-past six and he drove to Soufriere. I had cell phone calls from them a half-hour ago," Thomas said.

"Would I be able to call her this morning? It would be nice to hear her voice," Melinda said.

Thomas shook his head, "So sorry, we need complete communication silence today. We don't want to interfere with the police in the region. I promised Vernon Charles we'd keep a low profile. But should Bernadette get any news, she'll call you immediately."

"Thanks, Thomas, it's so good she's out there with the police. I'm glad she's come onside to stop chasing every strange lead that pops into her head," Melinda said.

"Of course. I'm happy she's on our side as well," Thomas said. He glanced at his watch; they should land about now. The wind blew the palm trees outside. Napkins flew off the tables. A server rushed over to pick them up and close a window.

45

THE PILOT FOUGHT the controls to level the plane on landing. The aircraft hit the runway with a thump to drop safely out of the wind. They deplaned and met a large man who took them to a jeep.

"My name is Matthew," the man said. He was a middle-aged black man; his head was covered in a red bandanna that emitted dreadlocks at various angles. He wore a Bob Marley t-shirt and ragged denim shorts. His large feet were shod in well-worn sandals. "The wind was coming in hard where you landed, but we're heading to the leeward side of the island. The trip to Montserrat won't be idyllic, but if you hold tight, there's no need to swim."

He turned in his seat and threw out a big smile. Bernadette wasn't sure how much of his speech was a joke or bravado. When they reached the pier, she saw the waves—he wasn't joking. The waves broke over the pier and rushed towards the shore, crashing onto the beach. The wind was full of ocean spray.

Matthew led them down to the boat. It was a thirty-foot aluminum open fishing boat with a simple cab-over wheelhouse in the stern. Three rows of seats with cushions occupied the center and back of the boat, with a cargo hatch in the bow.

"She's not much to look at, but this is the most seaworthy boat this size you will find on this island. This single hull will bounce over the waves and not much can tip her. It might be rough on the way over—mind your bottoms," Matthew said with a smile.

Ezra stowed their gear in the bow and secured the hatch. He came back to sit beside Bernadette. "These boats are fine. We use them all the time in my village in Belize. But it's a bumpy ride. I find it best to ride the waves out by holding onto the handhold in front and using my knees as a shock absorber."

Bernadette leaned forward and grabbed onto the row of seats in front. Matthew hit the throttle on the two big twin Mercury outboards. The boat growled. A man on the dock threw the mooring rope inside and the boat moved into the bay.

The light blue water turned dark, and the wave turned from a pleasant white to an angry froth with large swells in between. The boat shot over the enormous waves, then dove into the troughs. Matthew feathered the controls to ride the crests. Sometimes he hit it perfectly, other times the boat hit the bottom of the trough with a resounding slam.

The slam reverberated through Bernadette. Her very core shook, her knees buckled as she tried to keep her butt off the seat in fear the downward force of the boat might shorten her spine.

The trip seemed like hours. Her arms were tiring from holding herself up and her legs had turned to jelly. Ezra stood beside her. He was doing the best he could and gave her a weak smile as their bodies were being pummeled by the waves.

When land came into sight, Bernadette was ready to jump overboard and swim the rest of the way. They rounded a point and came into a bay with tranquil waters. She slipped onto the bench and placed her head in her hands.

"You, okay?" Ezra asked.

Bernadette lifted her head, "Yeah, I'm fine, my legs feel like they've been on a mountain climb." She looked at the beach and saw four figures in army uniforms. "Are those your British Army buddies?"

"I hope so. If it's a patrol from the regular island expedition force, we'll be taken into custody and charged with unauthorized entry into a restricted area. This part of the island has been off-limits for several years."

"Good to know," Bernadette said in a sarcastic tone.

The boat slowed down and made its way towards the soldiers. When they got closer, they waved and smiled at Ezra.

A tall soldier with a red forage cap yelled to Ezra, "Hey mate, good to see you again. We thought you were too busy catching fish and drinking rum to do anything worthwhile."

Ezra laughed, "Ah, you know me, always looking for a bit of trouble to keep me hand in."

The boat hit the shore, the four men grabbed a rope Ezra threw to them and pulled it up onto the beach with each wave that hit it from the stern.

Ezra jumped on shore, and the two men slapped each other on the backs. Ezra turned to Bernadette as she jumped down. "This is Sergeant Braydon Blake. We did a couple of tours together overseas. Blakesy, this is Bernadette."

Blake winked at Bernadette, "I'm the reason he's in one piece. This wanker had the tendency to step on nasty things."

Ezra nodded in agreement. "Yeah, but it was the trouble me mouth got me in. Blakesy here kept me from sounding off to me higher-ups and put on charges."

"Nice to meet you, Sergeant Blake, and thanks for helping us out on this," Bernadette said, shaking his hand. She looked at Ezra with a raised eyebrow. "I'm curious to know what your nickname for Ezra is."

"You don't want to know that," Ezra said with his hand raised. "It's not fit for civilian ears."

The rest of the men laughed and picked up their packs. Sergeant Blake pulled some clothes and a pair of boots with socks out of his and handed them to Bernadette.

"Ezra told us you'd need some kit. This might fit you and be better than those resort togs you have on. There's lava rock and dust. All falls are nasty to the knees and dust will climb into every part of your body you don't cover up. We've also brought you both some protective knee pads and gloves."

"Thanks for the tip and the clothes," Bernadette said. She took the army issue pants and shirt and looked at the men. "I'll put them on now if you don't mind."

"About face, men," Sergeant Blake commanded. "And if one of you holds up your knife for a mirror, I'll kick your ass all the way back to the barracks."

"It's okay, Sergeant," Bernadette said, "I'm wearing a bikini swimsuit under my clothes."

Blake leaned forward. "We won't tell them that, will we? Keeps their little minds active," he said with a wink.

They turned slowly to face the land. Bernadette stripped off her t-shirt and wiggled out of her shorts. She got dressed in the army fatigues and pulled on the socks and boots. The shirt was loose; she tied it up at the waist and the pants were far more form-fitting than she'd have liked.

"Okay, you can turn around now," Bernadette said.

The men turned as one. One man whistled, another muttered, "I think we should welcome this lass into the platoon. A nice replacement for the Sarg."

"All right, you gormless pillocks. Enough out of you. Remember your manners if you have them. Now, everyone off the beach and let's get to it," Sergeant Blake commanded.

Bernadette turned to stow her discarded clothes into the bow of the boat. Matthew was standing in the bow and took them from her.

He shrugged when their eyes met. "I heard all eyes inland. I did as I was told. Thanks for the show. Nice bikini."

Bernadette blushed; the black bikini was more revealing than the yellow one. She turned back to the sergeant and Ezra. "We'd better get moving like you said, Sergeant. The clock is ticking on our hostages. I have a feeling the kidnappers will try to leave before the appointed deadline."

Sergeant Blake led them off the beach. They climbed a steep cliff and came to an overgrown road. Three British Army Land Rovers occupied the road with a soldier standing beside it.

"We brought a medic with us in case you need assistance," Sergeant Blake said. He pointed at the volcano that was billowing smoke into the swirling wind. "We can't bring a heli in here. The ash in the air destroys their intake system. The only way in or out of here is by land or by the sea route you took."

"That's good to know, Sergeant. That means the kidnappers have the same way to get out of here," Bernadette said. "Did you let Matthew know he might have company on the beach, Ezra?"

"I told Matthew to stay off the beach. He has a cell with my number. If he sees another boat arrive, he's to call me," Ezra said.

Sergeant Blake shook his head, "Our satellite phones and two-way radios are the only things that work on this side of the island. The cell tower blew away years ago in an eruption. I'll have one of my men run a radio to your man."

Ezra nodded at Blake. "Thanks for catching that. I didn't check coverage before we left."

Blake smiled, "No worries, Ezra, you've been too busy fishing and drinking rum, you've lost your soldiering instincts."

They climbed into the Land Rovers and headed inland. Bernadette looked at her watch. It was past nine. She wondered how long the kidnappers would keep the hostages alive. A large plume of smoke drifted from the volcano and the wind whipped at the stunted palm trees. The entire sky turned dark as the dust hid the sun.

46

FRIDA COOPER OPENED HER EYES, she noticed a shaft of light coming from the door. She got out of bed and made sure she didn't wake up Luke. They'd laid awake through most of the night wondering what their fate would be in the morning.

The door was ajar. She pushed it open and stood looking down the long hallway. The lights were on. But they always were. They never turned them off at night—the rhythm of their captivity had been when they received tea, bread, and jam for breakfast they realized it was morning. Four hours later, the Spaniard brought in beans, rice, and tortillas and five hours later, he brought in beans, rice, and fish or chicken. They'd turn off the light in the room some hours after dinner and called it a night.

There was no sound coming from down the hall. Usually, the Spaniard shuffled back and forth between the rooms or when the old man, that Max called Valdis, muttered orders to him. The air handling system blew tepid air from the vents in the ceiling. Frida kept walking.

She wasn't nervous about being caught out of her room. What would they do to her? Force her back in the room? Kill her? She felt in her bones they planned to do that anyway—she kept moving.

She stopped by Max's door, his loud snores were comforting to hear. He was still alive—for now. She smiled at that and moved on. When she got to the end of the hallway, she noticed an open doorway to the right; she crept towards it.

There were voices. It was the Spaniard and Valdis. She couldn't stop her feet, they wanted to get her ears and eyes closer. She merely followed them.

Stopping outside the door, there were two men with their backs to her. On the floor lay three long black plastic bags.

"I tell you. I don't want to be the one to kill them," the Spaniard said.

"What does it matter what you want? I'll give you a million reasons why you must. They cannot live to speak of who we are. You know this, they know this. They are prepared to die, I see it in the woman's eyes. You do them a favor. If we lock them in here, they will die a slow death. A shot to the head will be more humane," Valdis said.

The Spaniard turned to him, "Then you do it if it's so humane."

"Me? I'm the mastermind of this. Where would you be without my instructions? You would still work the bar on a third-rate cruise ship in the Mediterranean and hustling old women out of their money by sleeping with them."

The Spaniard sighed and turned away, "Okay, I will do it. But only at the last moment when the money arrives."

Valdis slapped the Spaniard on the back. "That is excellent. But I have news for you. The moment may arrive sooner than expected. I have contacted someone who might get us the deposits before five p.m."

"How is that possible?"

"Ah, the wonders of the internet. My contact will release the fifty million in deposits at noon today. Once we have it, we dispose of the hostages and make our way off this wretched piece of real estate. I'll be glad to leave this place, it was a poor investment to begin with. It is only suitable for the graves of some rich people we've swindled."

"But how can you get the deposits before the bank allows?"

"Simple, the bank is bogus. I set them up to make transactions like these. Once I give them the word, and a one-million-dollar fee, they will send the fifty million to our private account in Dubai. You and I will be on our way to an island full of liquor and women and all of this will be behind us."

Frida's stomach turned to ice. Her legs felt like stone as she propelled herself back to the room. They had only hours left to live. Did it matter? Yes, it did. It was their lives. She'd make them pay if they wanted to take them.

She entered the room, Luke rolled over in bed. "Where have you been?"

Frida closed the door. "They left the door open. I checked if Max was okay. He was snoring in his room."

Luke sat up in bed, "Do nothing to get us killed before they release us."

"I promise, I'll do nothing of the sort," Frida said, as she walked into the tiny toilet. She pulled out the small toothbrush the Spaniard had given her. Two days ago, she'd sharpened the end on the concrete walls. She'd seen it done in a prison movie. The prisoners called these things a 'shiv.' The point was now sharp. She would not tell Luke about it. Weapons made him nervous.She ran the point over her finger and imagined it going into the Spaniard's neck.

47

BERNADETTE SAT in the front passenger seat as Sergeant Blake drove the Land Rover away from the beach. The landscape changed from the lush green of the ocean side to one of ash and barren land. Homes they passed were empty with the doors hung open as if they'd just let everyone out.

"How long has this area been off-limits?" Bernadette asked.

Sergeant Blake shifted the gears and turned to her, "It's been five years. They stationed me here this spring and we've had fewer eruptions, but no one knows when the next one will be. They're building a new town in a place called Little Bay. Once their principal town of Plymouth got destroyed, they resigned themselves to rebuild."

"Paradise destroyed by a volcano. I'll bet that was a surprise," Bernadette said.

"The original settlers thought they'd found a second Ireland, without the secular fighting and the cold weather. There were about four thousand residents, but the tourism was on the rise. This place had one of the best music recording studios outside of New York or London, rather a shame it was ruined."

"Yes, it is a shame, but it's also the perfect hiding place for our kidnappers. Did you see any signs of other vehicles on your way here?" Bernadette asked.

"No, but we left our barracks early this morning—we didn't exactly inform our army commander we were heading here to meet you," the sergeant said with a grin.

"What happens when we find the hostages and the kidnappers—how will you report it?"

"If we find your people, there'll be medals. If not, we'll be in a great pile of shite!" Blake said.

"Well, I hope you get your medal," Bernadette said. "How far are we to the district of Patrick?"

"It's just up ahead in the higher elevation. The lava that flowed off the volcano followed the rivers on both sides of the district. The hot ash from the pyroclastic flow destroyed most of the buildings, and only a few survived. We're sent out to do a reconnaissance of the area whenever the volcano eases up. A bunch of volcanologists hitch a lift with us, and we take them around to measure things."

"What does the hotel look like? Is it in good shape?" Bernadette asked.

Sergeant Blake had a confused look. "What hotel? There's no hotel in Saint Patrick. I've been through there on several tours. I've never seen one."

"But there has to be. That's what Valdis Kalnins built before 1995. They forced him to evacuate and leave the hotel," Bernadette said.

"Sorry about that, but you're on a bit of a fool's errand. There's nothing but empty houses in this area and a couple of churches," the sergeant said.

Bernadette sat back in her seat and looked out the window, "Then we'll have to do a house-to-house search."

"Fine with me. I could use some exercise. I'll stop at the edge of the district, and we'll check every house."

The convoy came to a halt in front of a line of houses. Sergeant Blake got out of the Land Rover and signaled to the rest of the men. They formed in front of him. He gave the command to search the houses.

Bernadette and Ezra joined the men. They walked through the gray and black ash. A few birds flew overhead. Not an insect buzzed, or a dog barked. They felt like someone had dropped them onto the moon. From one desolate home to the next, they checked the residences, looked for trap doors, and examined the surrounding area. Each house was marked with a large X to show it had been cleared.

Bernadette paused and wiped her face with a forage cap the Sergeant had given her. A layer of black and gray ash covered her and sweat ran down every part of her body. Taking a gulp of water from a bottle, she looked back down the street and then at her watch.

They'd been at it for three hours. They'd covered only half the district. It was close to noon. At the core of her gut, she knew the kidnappers would not leave the transaction until five o'clock. She didn't know why she knew it. She just did. It was as if at the very moment she saw a picture of Valdis and read about his past—she sensed he'd never keep his promise on anything.

Her grandfather told her that when some people fall into a pattern, they never change. Valdis was one of those with his addiction to scams—his method of operation was to cheat. He'd orchestrated his own death to exit the cruise ship. He was here. She felt in every fiber of her bones. And so were the Coopers.

Ezra came beside her. "How are you doing?"

Bernadette ran a bandanna over her neck, "I'm doing fine, how about you?"

"Good, you still feel that we're on the right track?"

"Totally, let's get moving," Bernadette said. She pushed open another door, walked through the little home, and placed an X mark on the door. They had to be here. She hoped they'd make it in time.

48

ASSISTANT SUPERINTENDENT VERNON CHARLES looked at his wristwatch and out the window of police headquarters in Castries. The day was advancing at a rapid pace, with no developments. He'd kept a contingent of officers combing through the town of Soufriere in case the dying words of Javier had some truth to them. They'd found nothing after they'd searched every house and basement. He had a sinking feeling as he looked at his wristwatch again. The second hand swept around the face and another minute advanced— the time was now four o'clock.

In one hour from now, there should be something from the kidnappers. Travis Cooper was at the hotel waiting by his phone. A team of officers was with him with radios to relay information to officers all over the island.

Sergeant Alphonse came into his office and saluted; Charles motioned for him to take a seat. "Have you had any news from the districts?"

"Nothing yet," Alphonse said, as he took a handkerchief out and wiped his forehead. "This is strange. We are a tiny island, you'd think by now someone would have seen something."

Charles looked at his wristwatch again. "They could be underground somewhere. The slaves hid from the French and the English in the hills. Who knows where they will show up? We will find the answer in an hour."

VALDIS STARED at his email in disbelief. He'd asked his contact to access the fifty million early and deposit it in his secret account. He saw the transaction happen at noon—his joy turned to anguish when an error message appeared.

The red error message was still there—it flashed at him and threw him into a rage. He'd wanted to smash his laptop into pieces—he pounded his fists on the desk. After several more emails to his contact, he had no answer. The worst-case scenario was the entire transaction protocol had become corrupted. That meant they'd have to authenticate all the security measures to reactive the account.

His contact was working on it. Valdis felt his window was closing. How was he going to proceed? Could he get the Coopers to release the ten million? He needed to get moving on this. The ten million was a diversion, but what if the fifty became stuck in transit?

He yelled to the Spaniard, "You need to take another picture of the Coopers. I want it sent to the police station. Tell them I want the money early or I'll kill them."

"But you're going to kill them, anyway." the Spaniard protested.

"Yes—yes, we know that—but they don't know that. We need to turn up the heat. If we wait too long, it makes it impossible to get off this island. We need to be off here before the sun sets. I do not want to be taking a boat in darkness," Valdis said.

"Okay, I'll take another picture and send it, but you must hide your email address when you send it, otherwise they'll discover where we are."

"I will send it via our satellite phone."

"Okay," the Spaniard said. He took out his pocket camera and marched down the hallway. The Coopers had become harder to deal with since this morning. The woman, Frida, had a look in her eyes that he didn't like.

49

Frida heard loud voices at the far end of the hallway. She turned to Luke; it was time to tell him the truth.

"There's something you need to know," Frida said quietly, with Luke beside her.

"That you're still madly in love with me and want to have sex with me this very minute?" Luke asked with a grin.

"No, thanks, we'll do that if we live—it's that I plan to kill the little Spanish guy when he comes back in the room."

Luke shook his head, "How the hell do you intend to do that? The guy came in here with a gun at breakfast and again at lunchtime. Have you become faster than a speeding bullet? I didn't notice a red cape under your shirt."

Frida pulled the sharpened toothbrush from under the mattress. "I made a shiv. I'm going to stick this in his heart."

Luke dropped his head in despair. "My lovely girl, to stick that little pointy thing in his heart, you'd have to get through his rib cage. That thing would stick in his chest and make him angry. Which would make him unload all of his bullets into your sweet body."

"What do you suggest?"

"Well, as a surgeon, I'd say the easiest target is the right or left common carotid artery in the neck. However, it's still not a fatal blow. It takes time to bleed out. But it has a better access with that plastic sticker of yours. But why do you want to kill him? He's going to let us out of here soon."

"I overheard them this morning. They discussed how they'd kill us. They have no intention of setting us free," Frida said.

"When were you going to tell me this?"

"After I stabbed him and took his gun."

Footsteps sounded down the hall.

"Give me the sticker. That thing is best used in the hands of a surgeon," Luke said.

The Spaniard opened the door slowly. He held his gun in one hand and the camera in the other. Frida was sitting on the bed. She looked up at him. There was hatred in her eyes.

"Where is your husband?"

Frida looked at the toilet. "He's in there, he'll be out in a minute."

The Spaniard pushed the door open further and stepped in.

Luke rushed him from behind. He pulled his head back with one hand and put the shiv to his throat. "Drop the gun."

Frida jumped from the bed. She took the gun from his hands and leveled it at him. "I will shoot you," she said as she raised the gun to his head.

"We're going for a walk," Luke commanded.

They pushed the Spaniard ahead of them. Luke held onto his shirt collar and Frida held the gun at his back. They stopped in front of Max's room. Frida opened the door, "Max, come with us, we're getting out of here."

Max jumped out of his bed. He straightened his hair and adjusted his pants, "Are they releasing us? Are Travis and Melinda here?"

"No, Max, we've taken control," Luke said. "We're breaking free. Frida overheard they'd intended to kill us."

Max looked at the Spaniard. "I knew it, you will reside in hell for what you did to us. Can we shoot him now?"

"No, we're taking him to his boss. Then we'll find our way out of here," Frida said.

"His boss is right here," Valdis said. He stood in the hallway with a gun.

"Drop your gun or I'll shoot him," Frida said.

Valdis aimed his gun at the Spaniard's leg and fired. "There I did it for you."

The Spaniard screamed in pain and dropped to the ground.

Frida aimed the gun at Valdis, she stood there, her arm was shaking.

"There are no bullets in the gun. Do you think I'd be foolish enough to allow him a loaded weapon? His name is Pedro, he made cocktails on the lido deck on the cruise ship we served on. He hasn't the guts to kill anyone."

Frida pulled the trigger on the gun. It clicked. She pulled it again several times. The empty clicks resounded in the hallway.

"Now, get back in your room."

"Why should we, you're going to kill us, anyway?" Luke asked.

"If I get the money from your son, I will leave you here and inform the soldiers where to find you. This I promise you," Valdis said.

Luke turned towards Frida, "Come, my dear, let's go back into our room, we'll take Max with us."

Valdis waved his gun at Luke, "Take Pedro with you. I'll give you a medical kit to stop him from bleeding to death. I'll pick him up later."

Valdis shut their door and locked it. He returned a few minutes later and threw in a medical kit.

Luke moved Pedro to the bed and cut open his pant leg. He checked out the wound; the bullet had exited the leg and torn part of his calf muscle open. He'd probably need extensive surgery, but for the moment, he needed to stop the bleeding. He wondered if any of this would matter in an hour from now.

Pedro watched Luke clean his wound and bandage his leg. Frida gave him some water. He took a breath and looked at them. "I thank you for taking care of me. I swear to you on my mother's grave I would never have shot you. I am not that kind of man."

Frida arched an eyebrow, "I heard you tell your boss you would put a bullet in our heads. Were you lying to him, or are you lying to me now?"

Pedro sighed. "I would have done it out of mercy for you. I fear Valdis will leave us all here to die once he has his money. This basement has gone unnoticed for years. If he turns off the air systems, we will suffocate in here. I believe he intends for me to die with you."

50

Bernadette took a drink of water and tried not to let a sense of despair wash over her. After a search of every home and building in Saint Patrick, they'd found nothing—not a single car track or signs of foot traffic in or out of the area. How could she have been so wrong?

Ezra walked over to her with one of the British soldiers named Mare. They stood in the blazing sun, watching the rest of the group recharge near the vehicles. The day was getting late.

"I called Thomas using Blake's sat phone. They've no word from the kidnappers," Ezra said.

Bernadette looked at her watch, "They should have made a move by now, we're past four o'clock."

Ezra kneeled beside Bernadette, "Do you think we've hit a wall, then?"

"I can't figure this out. Valdis built a hotel here—the place would be a perfect place to hide the hostages," Bernadette said.

"You mean the hotel site that burned down three years ago?" Mare asked.

Bernadette's head rocketed up. "What are you talking about?"

"There's a site that once had a hotel, but burned to the ground in the eruption. The only thing left is a basement that's overgrown with vegetation," Mare said.

"How far away?" Bernadette asked.

"We passed the site on our way here. The remains sit on the ridge overlooking the ocean. I thought we were looking in houses."

"We need to see that site—now," Bernadette commanded. She ran to Blake, "One of your men informed me he knows of the remains of a hotel on the outskirts of town."

"I'll be damned," Blake said. "I didn't know that—let's go." He turned to the men, "Back in the vehicles—we're on the move."

The Land Rovers sped back to the site, they saw only vegetation with rubble. Bernadette jumped out and ran to the area. She stared hard at the rubble. As she walked over the area, she found a door on the ground.

Sergeant Blake came to her side. He reached down and tried to help her. "This door won't budge, the latch is inside."

"You have anything to pry?" Bernadette asked.

"I'll get my lads to try," Blake said. He got on a radio and had four men with pry bars and hammers work at the door.

After twenty minutes one man looked up, " No use, Sergeant, this door is a solid metal with no way to leverage an opening."

"How about if we used dynamite?" Bernadette asked.

Blake shook his head, "I don't have any dynamite, and they built the door in solid concrete. We'd only make one hell of an explosion above ground with hand grenades."

"We have to find another way in," Bernadette said. "Basements have to get air."

"Good thinking," Blake said, as he turned to his men. "Look for any vents or structures in the vegetation."

The men fanned out over the landscape. A man yelled out several minutes later. "Hey Sarge, I found something."

Bernadette ran to a cluster of palm trees. A ventilator shaft with a slight curve appeared when she moved the leaves. She put her face to the opening of the shaft. "I'm getting the smell of food—there're humans down below."

"We got some smoke grenades, and flash-bangs we could drop in —get them to come out," one soldier said.

"Too risky," Blake said. "We don't know where this air shaft leads, we might drop one on top of the hostages. First thing we do is check the depth of this thing." He turned to a soldier, "Get some rope and a weight."

The soldier ran back to the Land Rovers and returned with a long rope and tire iron. He handed the rope to Blake after tying several knots to secure the iron.

Bernadette put her hand to her forehead, "Ah... Sergeant, if you drop this iron down the shaft, we'll make one hell of a racket. You think maybe something softer...?"

Blake looked at the iron, "Oh, too right." He looked at the soldier, "Take off your boot and be quick about it."

The soldier removed his boot and hobbled over to hand it to Blake. The Sergeant looked at the soldier with a glare that declared the dissatisfaction of the tire iron and having the error revealed by a young lady.

The soldier jumped on one foot to the air shaft and attached his boot to the rope. He threaded the rope down the shaft down until he felt it stop. "I estimate about two meters in depth," the soldier said.

"Right then, I need a volunteer for a recon," Blake said.

"I'll go down," Bernadette said.

"We can't ask you to do that," Ezra said.

Bernadette looked around at the burly group of men. "Who else do you think will fit into that shaft? We need to find out if the hostages are in there."

Sergeant Blake shrugged. "I guess you've got the job, but I'll want you to take a weapon, I won't send you in without one. And you'll need a radio. We'll tie a rope around you to pull you out at the first sign of trouble."

"And promise not to use the gun, or your employment with the police force is done for," Ezra said.

Bernadette turned back to the shaft. "Anything else?"

"Be careful..."

51

BERNADETTE STOOD in front of the air shaft while Sergeant Blake found her a handgun with a lanyard she could hang from a strap around her neck. A holster wouldn't work. There was barely enough room in the first curve of the shaft to get her hips in. After much discussion, they realized a radio couldn't go with her as well. They'd drop it down the shaft by a rope. But she could fit a small flashlight on the gun.

For a moment, she stood there—almost lost in a trance. She was about to go underground. The dreams of the man with the evil enormous face had been below ground. At this moment she hated that her dreams sometimes foretold the future. With a deep cleansing breath, she cleared her mind and stepped towards the shaft.

She took the gun, a British Army issue Glock 17, checked the chamber, and hung it around her neck. Two soldiers picked her up and put her feet first in the shaft. Her feet went in, then her legs. As her body followed, her shirt became caught in the metal shaft.

"Wait, it's not working, my shirt is getting caught," Bernadette said.

The soldiers pulled her back out of the shaft. And placed her upright on the ground.

"That's it then. I'll call our base to get some tools to blast the door open. It might take some time, as I'll have some explaining to do to my commanding officer," Sergeant Blake said.

"No, wait. Let me try again." Bernadette pulled off her shirt and dropped it on the ground. She stood there in her bikini top, "Okay, put me back in."

The two soldiers looked at Bernadette and then at the Sergeant. They had stunned looks on their faces.

"You heard the lady pick her up and put her in the shaft—and mind where your hands wander," Blake said with a scowl.

"Aye Sergeant," the men said as they picked Bernadette up, now dressed in only her military pants, bikini top, and military boots. They doubted they'd be able to explain this to their wives or girlfriends back home.

Bernadette slipped into the shaft without a problem. "Excellent, I'm in."

She shimmied through the first part of the curve and found the shaft dropped to a horizontal shaft below. The soldiers lowered her slowly to its base. Her boots bounced on the tin airduct. She pulled on the rope to let them know she was down.

Bernadette stood to one side and waited for the radio to be lowered. She shone her flashlight upward to watch the small radio come down the shaft. It bounced onto the sides, then fell out of its carrier and came hurtling towards her. It missed her head as it hit the ground.

She picked it up and hit the on switch—there was no signal. If she tugged on the rope, they'd bring her up immediately and do this over again. That wasn't an option. Her instincts told her they were running out of time. She got on her hands and knees and crawled. The vent was full of volcanic dust.

Bernadette switched on the light and crawled along the corridor for over one hundred meters until she saw lights up ahead. She breathed softly and advanced—she looked down to see rooms below. The first ones were empty. A few cots and tables occupied them.

She pulled off a screen to investigate; the room had a metal door.

Not wanting to drop into the room and find herself locked in, she moved on.

In the third room, she looked down to see the heads of four people. It took her a moment to recognize the Coopers. She pulled off the screen and stuck her head inside the room.

"Anyone here call a taxi?" she asked.

Frida's head shot up to the ceiling. "Oh my God, Bernadette. I knew you'd come."

Bernadette pulled the screen aside and let herself down to the floor. "Sorry, I'm late. I got some bad directions, you can take it out of my tip."

She looked a sight, covered in ash and wearing a black bikini top with army pants and boots.

Frida rushed to her and hugged her. "Oh my, what a sight you are. Where's your shirt?"

"I wouldn't fit in the air shaft, I must eat too much—now, what's the situation?"

"THERE'S A MAN NAMED VALDIS. We think he set this whole thing up," Luke said. He turned to Pedro, "This is his partner, Pedro. Seems they've had a falling out."

"Anyone else besides these two?"

"Not that we know of. Did you bring Travis and Melinda with you?" Frida asked.

Bernadette shook her head, "Long story on that. The British Army of Montserrat is above us. But we need to open the hatch. It's blocked."

Luke looked stunned, "Monserrat! How the hell—?"

"Again, long story. Does Valdis have a gun?"

"Yes, he's already shot Pedro here with it."

Bernadette looked at Pedro, "Well, I guess we won't be using him as cover." She turned back to Luke and Frida, "How far away is Valdis?"

"He's down the end of the hall, it's about one hundred meters.

He's locked us in here. There's no one else in this place that we've seen," Frida said. "Can you get us out before he comes back to kill us?" Her lips trembled slightly as she finished her words.

Bernadette put her hand on Frida to calm her. "We have to get Valdis to open the door." She looked up at the ceiling and down at Pedro. "Are the sprinkler systems still working?"

Pedro shrugged his shoulders, "I think so. Valdis is afraid of fire. He talks about it all the time, so maybe it is working."

"Don't you need a match or a lighter?" Luke asked.

"You could shoot it," Max suggested. He looked at Frida to see if she agreed with his suggestion.

Bernadette gazed up at the four sprinkler heads on the ceiling. "I can see they have the latest glass bulb activators. The heat breaks the bulbs at over one hundred fifty degrees Fahrenheit. A bullet might ricochet in the room. But I have a better idea."

Bernadette grabbed the bed from the wall and tore off the mattress. She took her gun off the lanyard and pounded on the slats of the frame. One came off in her hand.

Bernadette motioned to Luke, "I need you to hoist me on your shoulders."

Max pushed Luke aside. "For this, you need a big fat man like me. My brother-in-law has no meat on him. You will crush his little body to the ground." He bent down and patted his back for Bernadette to jump on.

Bernadette climbed on his shoulders, and he hoisted her towards the ceiling. "Okay, move more to the right." Max wobbled slightly and moved her closer to the sprinkler head.

Bernadette placed the wooden slat in the head's opening and rammed it into the glass. The slat rammed into the sprinkler head. "Damn it—I bent it, move me over to the one on the left, Max."

Max was sweating. He lumbered over like an ox under a yoke and positioned Bernadette under the other head. His eyes turned upwards, "Be more careful. I cannot be forever under your weight."

Bernadette looked down, then back to the sprinkler head. The wire cage around it was just big enough for the head of the slat. This time, she pushed the slat up against the glass vial and rammed it home with the back of her hand.

The glass broke.

Frida and Luke put their hands over their heads to cover themselves from the impending water. Nothing happened.

"Valdis must have turned the water off to this room," Bernadette said. "You can put me down, Max."

Max dropped to his knees and Bernadette got off his shoulders. She looked back at the vent she'd come out of and down at Pedro, "How close is the boiler room from here?"

Pedro looked up at her and exhaled, "It is just past the office of Valdis. All the controls are in there."

"I'll get there and pull the master switch to set off the fire alarm system. I'm hoping with the distraction I'll be able to take his weapon."

"Be careful, Bernadette. Valdis is dangerous," Frida said.

Bernadette put the gun around her neck, "So am I." She turned to Luke and Max, "I'll need both of you to put me back in the vent."

Max groaned and dropped to the ground; Luke got beside him. Bernadette placed one knee on each of their shoulders. They hoisted her up. She grabbed onto the vent and did a pull-up to get herself back into it. Her arms ached as she inched her way back into the crawl space.

She took a moment to catch her breath. She heard the door to the room open—she placed the screen back over the vent and held her breath.

52

VALDIS WALKED INTO THE ROOM. "I heard another voice in here. Who are you talking to?" He held the gun in front of him, waving it back and forth between Luke and Frida.

Bernadette saw Valdis in the doorway. If he looked up at the vent, he'd catch her. She pulled herself away from the screen and laid face down. His was the strange and ominous face she'd seen in her dreams. The previous pictures she'd seen of Valdis were from years ago—his face looked like a mask of evil. A feeling of dread came over her. She slowed her breathing and waited.

"I was praying—that was my voice of prayer," Frida said. She looked at Pedro. His mouth moved as if to say something; then he closed it and looked at the floor.

Valdis looked back and forth at them, "Is this true what she says, Pedro?"

"Yes, she prays in a strange voice. I will ask her to keep quiet..." Pedro said.

"Good," Valdis said. He slammed the door and locked it.

Frida whispered to Pedro, "Why did you keep our secret?"

Pedro shook his head. "My chances are better with you and the pretty lady who dropped from the ceiling."

Bernadette moved as quietly as she could. The sheet metal gave with her weight and sprung back again. She needed to move by placing her hands and knees as softly as possible to make the metal spring back without a sound.

Her entire body perspired as she moved. Stopping at each vent, she looked down to check her progress. Finally, she reached the office of Valdis. He was busy with a printer and a fax machine.

She watched as he hit the send button. As the fax machine pushed the picture through, she moved on. Valdis was staring hard at the machine as it processed the picture of the Cooper captives.

Five minutes later, the hum of the boiler room grew louder. She moved towards it and looked down. It was a long drop to the cement floor. Uncovering the screen, she wedged herself out of the vent, then hung onto the opening and dropped.

She hit the concrete floor and fell to the left. Her face met with a pipe. Her hand showed blood when she ran it over her cheek. A quick examination of the wound showed it wasn't serious.

She listened for any sound of footsteps from Valdis. There were none. She began a search for the sprinkler system standpipe.

A large pipe with a red lever named "Main Sprinkler" was beside a backup generator and a large propane tank. She was just about to press the lever to open the water when she noticed something else.

A square package was attached to the propane tank. Bernadette kneeled beside it. She shook her head. "The bastard has rigged this place with explosives."

Studying the package, she found four sticks of explosives with a transmitter. She had no idea how to disarm, but realized it could be set off if she messed with the device.

She sat back on her heels. "This will change everything. Valdis doesn't have to shoot anyone. He can remotely activate the bomb... but he has to get out of here first," Bernadette said to herself.

"I'm glad you think so," Valdis said from the door of the boiler room. "I knew I heard someone come in here—drop your weapon or I'll shoot you."

Bernadette froze for a second. She raised her hands. Her gun was hanging from her neck. "I'll have to reach around my neck for my gun."

"Go ahead—I'm pleased you dropped by in such a delightful outfit. Take your time."

She raised the lanyard off her neck slowly to ensure she didn't get shot. As the gun came to her knees, she dived under the propane tank.

"You will only make this more difficult. You have no way of escape. I will close this door and leave you in here. When I activate the explosives, you'll die," Valdis said.

Bernadette squeezed under the tank where he wouldn't shoot at her. If he punctured the tank, he'd blow himself up as well. She aimed the gun at his leg and squeezed the trigger.

Valdis screamed in agony. "You bitch, you devil. I will kill you. I will destroy you." He dropped to the floor holding his leg.

Bernadette rolled from under the tank and raced towards Valdis. She kicked the gun from his hand. "Game over, Valdis."

A door opened down the hallway. Bernadette expected to see Luke and Frida walking towards her. Her eyes turned to saucers as Winston and Pierre walked through a door from the outside.

Winston pointed his weapon at Bernadette, "Drop your weapon."

Bernadette raised her gun, fired two shots, and rolled to the right.

She found herself behind a wall. She looked around the corner. Winston and Pierre were not to be seen.

"Winston, Pierre—drop your weapons. The British military will be here in a moment," Bernadette said.

Winston laughed. "No, my lady, the army is above us. We came in the secret door from the beach. We saw your friend on the beach, he is no problem now. You will give us Valdis and we will let you live until we get away. That is all we promise."

Bernadette reached over to Valdis. She grabbed the cell phone out of his hand. "I don't think you can activate the explosives without this cell phone—am I right?"

Winston paused for a moment.

"Then we must kill you, my dear. That is the only solution," a very French voice said.

"Ah, Pierre, you've made an appearance. The Saint Lucia police know all about you. I told them you left the boat in mid-ocean. I'm sure they'll believe me now."

Pierre laughed. "You must live to tell stories. You will not make it more than a few minutes."

Bernadette did a quick calculation of where Pierre was. She jumped from cover and fired two quick shots. His screams registered her accuracy.

"Merde!" Pierre yelled.

"Yes, I understand that's French for shit," Bernadette said. "I figure I got you once in the arm and once in the hand. Both of you have the firearms training of a two-year-old. The next shot I do—and that will be yours, Winston—will be a headshot. You want to play?"

"You bitch," Winston yelled. He fired several shots. Most were wide off the wall Bernadette was behind. Only one almost found her.

"Very good, Winston," Bernadette said as calmly as she could. "Why not fire your entire magazine. I've got lots of bullets. I only need one for your forehead. Drop your weapon or I'll take your head off."

They were silent.

Bernadette sat there and sweated. Handguns were only accurate up to within fifty meters. Hitting Pierre had been lucky. If these two outflanked her, she'd run out of bullets. A door opened—she held her breath in hopes it wasn't reinforcements for Pierre and Winston.

An English voice yelled, "This is the British Army—drop your weapons—on your knees."

Bernadette was never happier at the sound of the voice of Sergeant Blake. She peeked around the corner to watch his platoon advance with their weapons on Winston and Pierre. She stepped out from behind the wall.

"You, okay?" Ezra asked.

Bernadette walked towards Ezra. Her legs trembled slightly. She breathed deeply and let the anxiety of the gunfight pass.

"Yeah, I'm fine. Did these guys do something to Matthew? They claimed he was no longer a problem."

Ezra shook his head. "They surprised Matthew. He was sleeping in a hammock. They shot at him, but he got away and hid up in the hills. He called to warn us. We followed the sound of the ATV they took from the beach to here. If these guys thought they were making a secret rescue of Valdis, they were mistaken."

"I'm glad he's safe. Now, let's get the Coopers," Bernadette said. She led Ezra down the hallway. They opened several doors until they found the Coopers, Max and Pedro.

They ushered them out the back entrance to the waiting Land Rover. Sergeant Blake was there, holding Bernadette's shirt. She took it, put it on, and gave the sergeant back the gun.

Sergeant Blake took the weapon and looked at the captives. "I'll take these chaps into custody, then I'll turn them over to the police in Saint Lucia. My report will say that you helped us locate these men, and you took no part in their capture. There were some shots fired by myself and my men. I'll turn this weapon in as the one involved in the shooting. Are you fine with that?"

"I'm totally fine with that. Will Valdis and his men corroborate your story?"

Blake looked at Valdis, Winston, and Pierre. "You think they'll want everyone to know they got bested by a girl in a bikini?"

Bernadette laughed. "I hope you're right. I doubt my RCMP superiors would allow me into the force if I was involved in an active shooting."

"Too right. Now get out of here. The sun will set in an hour. You want to be off the water before it gets dark," Sergeant Blake said.

The army dropped them back at the beach. Matthew was there to greet them. Bernadette changed back into her clothes and got into the boat with the rest of them. The boat ride back was as smooth as glass. Frida and Luke Cooper hugged each other, and Max sat off to the side in contemplation.

They arrived back in Saint Lucia as the moon shone over the sea.

Travis and Melinda were waiting on the tarmac with Vernon Charles and Thomas. Bernadette took a deep breath. She had a lot of explaining to do.

53

BERNADETTE GOT out of the plane with the Coopers, Max, and Ezra and stood to the side as all the Coopers reunited. There were tears and shouts of joy.

Vernon Charles approached Bernadette, with Thomas by his side. "I am happy you found our hostages. But you might have informed us what you were planning."

Bernadette shrugged. "You're right, Assistant Superintendent. I should have. I'll make sure that I follow proper protocol from this day forward."

Charles laughed. "Yes, I doubt that will be in your stars. But you will make an excellent police officer. I will write a glowing commendation to the RCMP."

Bernadette shook his hand. "Thank you, that is much appreciated." She looked at Travis, he was walking towards her.

He wrapped her in a warm hug. "Bernadette, you lied to me and did everything I asked you not to do and brought my family back. I don't understand how you can be so obstinate and amazing at the same time."

"Well, sorry—not sorry, I guess, is the phrase," Bernadette said. "I had to follow my gut. Telling you what I was doing would complicate matters. I hope you see that now."

Travis kissed her on the lips. "Yes, I see that now. And I realize how much I love you."

Bernadette hugged him and broke away. She walked over and hugged Melinda and the Coopers and joined them as they rode back to the hotel.

THE COOPERS GAVE a statement to the police and a brief interview with the reporters and retired to their room. Bernadette showered, changed, and booked a flight for Sunday.

She'd avoided Travis. She told him she had emails to catch up on and arrangements to make for her return to Canada. Part of that was true. A call to Aunt Mary would get her another suitcase full of proper clothes when she changed planes in Edmonton for Regina and her last destination. Her beach clothes would be of no use on the Canadian prairies with the approaching winter.

At eight o'clock, she finished her emails, and planning. She threw on a dress and opened the door to the corridor. There was no one there. Softly closing the door, she walked down the hall.

Travis's door opened. He stepped out into the hall. "Bernadette. I've been looking for you." He came to her and opened his arms.

Bernadette put up her hands and stopped his hug. "Travis. We need to talk."

He stood there. A stunned look on his face. "But I thought we have a mutual attraction. I've been crazy about you since that evening on the lake."

Bernadette glanced at the floor, sighed, and looked at Travis. "We had a sexual attraction. And yes, I'd like to ride you like a stallion at the rodeo. But that will destroy our relationship. You and I are two different people. I'm going to enter the RCMP. They move us around every two to three years all over Canada. You're a big-shot computer geek with a fancy home in Vancouver. You can't live my life and I will not live yours."

Travis set his lips in a hard line and shook his head. "I could work remotely. I'd change for you."

Bernadette moved into his arms. "No, you can't, and you won't. If they put me in the far northern territories, you wouldn't last a month. We both realize it."

"I hate it when you're right. But you are... what if we just had sex together.... for something to remember each other by?" Travis asked with a smile.

Bernadette kissed Travis on the lips. "I'd ruin you for other women. But there is something you can do for me."

"Please—name it—it's yours," Travis said as he caught his breath from her kiss.

"You can put up the money to help the woman charged with murdering her husband that I met in jail."

"Done. Is that all? And you sure sex is off the table?"

Bernadette punched Travis on the arm. "Yes, it's off the table. You can buy dinner. Now let's go celebrate."

54

FRIDA AND LUKE COOPER spent most of Saturday by the pool with Melinda and Travis. Bernadette stayed with them for awhile, and went to her room to pack. There was no more to say to Travis, or Melinda.

They'd thanked her numerous times, but to her, everything she'd done for them was a thank-you for how they'd helped her to get where she was at this point.

She packed her small bag that night with a feeling of satisfaction. The next six months were in her stars according to her Cree Grandmother. There were just twenty-one hours of flying time to get there.

The next morning, Thomas Davina drove Bernadette to the airport. "There's a report you'll want to see," Thomas said as they got into the SUV.

"What is it?" Bernadette asked.

Thomas handed Bernadette a large brown envelope. "It's the preliminary report from the Montserrat Police. It seems your little friend Pedro couldn't speak up fast enough. Charles asked me to give it to you."

Bernadette opened the envelope and read it. "I can't believe it."

Thomas laughed, "Why? Because it's exactly what you thought it was? Valdis was in league with a Miami money laundering cartel. He planned to double-cross them all along. Luke Cooper was going to blow the whistle on his scam, so he kidnapped him as a diversion. All so he could steal fifty million in deposits. You were even right about the murder of Vasquez."

Bernadette read the report again and smiled. "I see that Sergeant Blake kept me out of it. And Charles lists you as the one who helped in solving the case. I'm noted as a concerned and helpful aide in the events. I love that. And I see Charles didn't mention when Valdis used his satellite phone to send his fax they knew his location."

"Yes, they did, but Charles realized the intervention of the British Army may have saved the hostages from Valdis doing something irrational with the explosives."

Bernadette put the file back in the envelope, "this all seems so surreal now."

"You don't care they didn't mention you were the key to solving this case and find the Coopers?"

Bernadette turned to Thomas, "Not one bit. When I'm a police officer and working my butt off to make detective, I'll care, but for now, I'd rather keep a low profile."

Thomas shook his head and smiled. It was obvious to Bernadette he thought she was wasting her life pursuing her dream of the Royal Canadian Mounted Police. There was no use in discussing it anymore.

He dropped her in front of the airport terminal, and Bernadette took her bag out. She winked at Thomas. "Perhaps our paths will cross again one day."

"That would be my pleasure. But if you change your mind at police training.... you have my number," Thomas said.

Bernadette took her bag, smiled, and walked into the terminal

BERNADETTE'S FLIGHT took her directly to Toronto, then a flight to Edmonton, and a backtrack to Regina. It was a crazy way to return, but it assured her of getting her clothes for her six-month training at the RCMP academy.

She thought about her days ahead. There were now reservations. Thomas Davina had offered her double the salary of an RCMP Constable and to locate anywhere she wanted. She could have lived in Vancouver with Travis. Part of her wondered why she didn't accept it. But her heart was set on the force. She had to give it her best effort. This had been what she'd dreamed about for years. Now it was to become a reality.

By the time she deplaned in Edmonton, she'd been traveling for fifteen hours with the layover in Toronto. She had a one-hour stop in Edmonton. It meant a quick run out of the departure lounge into the main terminal. Grab her bag from her Aunt Mary, put the bag onto the plane at check-in, and race back through security to her plane. It sounded good in theory.

She grabbed her carry-on bag from the overhead and shuffled out of the airplane at the usual snail's pace speed of the passengers. She ran past the other travelers to the exit. Aunt Mary was there with her bag.

Aunt Mary hugged her hard. "I'm so glad you're back safe. You didn't cause any problems with your police academy, I take it?"

Bernadette grinned, "It's all good. I'll send you an email when I get to Regina with the details."

"Good, now get on the plane. You don't have a lot of time."

Bernadette hugged her aunt and took her bag. She got back into the line-up for baggage, then the lineup for security, and made it to her plane just as they were about to close the doors. She collapsed into her seat with a sigh of relief.

The captain came over the intercom, "Good morning, we should be on our way shortly, we just have to check on a warning light that's come on with our landing gear. We'll let you know our progress in the next few minutes. Sorry for the delay."

The plane was two hours late when it arrived in Regina. Bernadette collected her bag and ran to the cab stand. She gave the address of the RCMP Depot and sat in the back, trying to control her anxiety. She had only fifteen minutes left to report in. Failure to report for training on time got her scrubbed from the roster.

"The RCMP Depot as fast as possible," Bernadette pleaded to the cab driver.

"Don't worry, it's only minutes from the airport," the driver said.

The cab pulled up in front of the RCMP training facility ten minutes later. She threw money at the cab driver, told him to keep the change, and grabbed her bag. A female RCMP constable stood at the gate. "You've got five minutes—haul ass, girl. Leave your bag with me."

Bernadette ran for all she was worth. She saw the parade ground ahead of her. The new recruits were there. The commander was giving his speech.

"Welcome to RCMP depot. You will be ours for six months. You will not rest from the moment your feet hit the ground to the time your head hits the pillow. Your asses belong to us. You got that?"

A chorus of "Yes, sir" rang out from the recruits.

A constable took out a clipboard and began roll call. He came to Bernadette's name.

"Bernadette Callahan."

"Aye, present."

～

Do you want to know what happens next in Bernadette Callahan's journey into the life of an RCMP officer? In the next book, it's 15 years later. She's faced with a strange series of murders in both Canada and Alaska that her superiors want solved quickly. Her instincts tell her there's something more. Click this link to download Polar Bear Dawn to start the next story in the series!

～

A FREE SHORT story awaits you! Bernadette Callahan never expected a car chase to lead her into a manhunt in an abandoned mine. Can she find her way out and find the criminal before it's too late? Click here to claim your copy of Treading Darkness today to find out what happens next.

～

NEXT IN THE SERIES

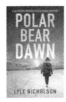

Detective Callahan knows she's right. But her superiors are intent on silencing her before she can prove murders in Canada and Alaska are connected. Will she stand her ground or be fired from the force?

As the media and police fight over the optics of the murders, Callahan's instincts tell her there's something more involved. The detective she reaches out to in Alaska is being pressured to wrap up his case in a tidy murder/suicide. She feels pressure from their bosses to come to conclusions that aren't right. Will she bend under the orders of her superiors, or follow her convictions?

Callahan discovers a series of unlikely suspects. A Chemistry Professor with a grudge against big oil, a Mexican low life gangster and Wall Street Executives. How are they connected?

Something is about to happen to oil supplies in the Arctic. Callahan can sense it—can she convince others to act?

In this first in series novel, Detective Callahan puts everything on the line. If she fails, it could end her career in the police force.

Download this book now to start your journey!

⌇

DEAR READER

I wrote this book as a sequel to Black Wolf Rising. In that book, I introduced the young Bernadette at sixteen years old in pivotal point in her life.

In the Hostage Game, I took Bernadette to Saint Lucia, an island I've visited twice in my travels. I wanted to put her instincts to the test, and meet up with Travis to see if there was still a love interest there.

If you enjoyed the book, perhaps you'd like others to know about it as well. By clicking here you'll be taken to the review page to let others in on Bernadette Callahan's adventures.

～

ACKNOWLEDGMENTS

I'd like to thank my good friend, Jeff Bush for the insightful first reads of my book and his artful humor.

And Patrick Bishop and John Appleton for being my Beta Readers. This book was edited by Peg Billingsley of Fairbanks, Alaska. I appreciated not only her edits but her comments and guidance.

I always give thanks to my wife, Tessa. She's always my first reader and sounding board throughout every book and all my years of writing.

∼

ABOUT THE AUTHOR

Lyle Nicholson is the author of nine novels, two novellas and a short story, as well as a contributor of freelance articles to several newspapers and magazines in Canada.

In his former life, he was a bad actor in a Johnny Cash movie, Gospel Road, a disobedient monk in a monastery and a failure in working for others.

He would start his own successful sales agency and retire to write full time in 2011. The many characters and stories that have resided inside his head for years are glad he did.

He lives in Kelowna, British Columbia, Canada with his lovely wife of many years where he indulges in his passion for writing, cooking and fine wines.

If you'd like to contact Lyle Nicholson, please do at lylehn@ shaw.ca

ALSO BY LYLE NICHOLSON

Book 1 Polar Bear Dawn

Book 2 Pipeline Killers

Book 3 Climate Killers

Book 4 Caught in the Crossfire

Book 5 Deadly Ancestors

Book 6 When the Devil Bird Cries

Prequel, Black Wolf Rising

Prequel, The Hostage Game

Short Story, Treading Darkness

Stand Alone Fiction

Dolphin Dreams, (Romantic Fantasy)

Misdiagnosis Murder (Cozy Mystery)

Non Fiction

Half Brother Blues (A memoir)

Made in the USA
Las Vegas, NV
07 April 2023

70336855R00144